MURDER IN ST. GILES

CAPTAIN LACEY REGENCY MYSTERIES, BOOK 13

ASHLEY GARDNER

JA / AG PUBLISHING

CHAPTER 1

London, 1819

I entered the house on South Audley Street one early April morning to hear my wife shouting.

I paused in disquiet. My wife—Donata, the former Lady Breckenridge—shouted at no one but me. Indeed, she enjoyed our occasional spirited quarrels, her voice rising in volume to match mine.

With all other mortals, she was as cool as a winter icicle. Any who displeased her were shown the door by Barnstable, her equally cool butler.

That her voice rang down from the upper floors, this early in the day—I was returning from my morning ride—worried me greatly.

"Who the devil is here?" I asked Barnstable, who'd come off the stairs as a footman took my hat. My concern was mirrored in Barnstable's brown eyes.

"Her cousins, sir," Barnstable said. "That is, Mr. St. John, a cousin of the late Lord Breckenridge, and Mr. Phillips, the cousin of her ladyship. They arrived shortly after you departed. They came unannounced," he finished in a chilly tone.

Timed well, then. They'd meant to corner Donata alone.

I tossed my coat over the footman's arm as I moved to the stairs. "A pity I decided to return early," I said, and I saw a gleam of satisfaction in Barnstable's eyes.

He stepped aside as I made my way up the staircase to the first floor of our elegant home. Though I was technically the man of the house, as had been Lord Breckenridge before me, this abode showed Donata's touch, her hand, her personality. Its male inhabitants only lived here.

I heard my wife's voice coming from a reception room tucked behind the stairs, a chamber in which guests waited before being shown into the grand drawing room in the front of the house. Her reception room was more comfortable than most, with soft chairs, pleasant paintings of flowers, and a few books left about for her waiting callers.

However, Donata coming to the reception room to see these cousins instead of having Barnstable or a footman show them into the drawing room spoke loudly of her disapprobation. She likely hadn't felt she could turn away her kin, but she could make certain they knew they weren't welcome.

I opened the door without knocking—I lived here after all— in time to hear Donata say, "If either of you touch him, I will shoot you."

"Now," came a voice that chilled me. "Don't be unreasonable, woman. You know his father wanted this."

"Then he'd have said so in his will. I read every word of that document, and it mentioned nothing of giving him to *you*."

"Donata." The thinner voice of the pair spoke placatingly. "St. John is only looking after your happiness."

"Happiness?" Donata spat the word. "You do not have any—"

I cut through her fury by putting myself between her and the two men facing her. I gave them my best regimental captain glare.

"Explain, sirs, why you have forced your way into our house and are badgering my wife."

The reedy-voiced gentleman was Edwin Phillips, Donata's cousin, son of her father's sister. He had dark hair receding far up his forehead, though he was only thirty, and watchful blue eyes in a narrow face. He'd wanted to marry Donata and hated me for cutting him out. Not that she'd had any intention of accepting him.

The second man was unknown to me, and it was *his* voice that had unnerved me so. The sound of it was very close to that of the late Lord Breckenridge, Donata's unlamented husband.

The man resembled Breckenridge as well, large and thick of body but tall, and only some of that thickness was fat. He had a broad face, sharp nose, and flat brown eyes. Like Breckenridge, he had little hair on top of his head but a thickness of it in the back. He sported full sideburns that had been trimmed to halt just shy of his jaw.

I hadn't met this man in the year I'd been married to Donata, and she rarely spoke of the Breckenridge side of the family. She'd told me about the two gentlemen she called Romulus and Remus, who were first cousins to her son, Peter, but I had seen them at a distance, and this gentleman was neither of those.

The Breckenridge cousin turned a cold eye to me. "This is not your business, sir."

He expected me to grovel before my betters, I could see. I rarely groveled, however, and I did not consider the cousin of a peer to be my better.

"Mrs. Lacey is my wife, and therefore it is my business," I stated.

Donata stepped beside me. She did not look at me, but I sensed her gratitude that I hadn't simply closed the door and left her to it, nor immediately knocked the two men to the carpet.

"Cousin Edwin and Cousin Stanton believe that Peter will be better off living in Somerset with the St. John family," she said coldly. "I am certain that would only be a short stay before Stanton moves into the Breckenridge estate to ensure that all is well for Peter to take over at his majority." Her voice cut like a whiplash, but the dark curls that trickled to her shoulders trembled.

A chill cut through my anger. This man, Stanton St. John, was several places removed from inheriting the viscountcy, but life was uncertain, and Romulus and Remus, the two rakehell cousins between him and Peter, could any time expire from disease, dissipation, drink, or wrecking their phaetons racing to Brighton.

Peter, Donata's son from her first marriage, was seven years old. While Peter was robust, many children did not live to see adulthood, a fact that had Donata keeping Peter close to home or well guarded by her parents in Oxfordshire.

I could see in Stanton's eyes the frustration about the gap between him and the Breckenridge fortune and title—a gap filled by two fops and a little boy. But if Peter were to fall from a horse while galloping across the Breckenridge lands ... Well then, one less person in his way.

I let my gaze harden. Stanton stared right back at me, knowing I understood him. But I also caught a hint of smugness, a look that said I would not have the last word in this debate.

"This house is Mrs. Lacey's to use for her lifetime," I said. "According to the settlements made by her husband."

"Yes," Stanton admitted reluctantly. His eyes darted to the fine paintings on the walls and the silver objet d'art, his look covetous.

"As mistress of the house, she can admit or deny whomever

she wishes," I went on. "As her husband, I can also say who enters and whom the butler should eject. In other words, gentlemen, you may take your leave. Now, if you please."

I noted no argument from the woman standing next to me. Her jaw was rigid, her dark blue eyes tight.

She made a stiff nod to her cousins. "Good day, gentlemen."

"Now, Donata," her cousin Edwin began. "He means only the best for young Peter."

"Good *day*," Donata repeated, a bit more firmly. "Barnstable will show you out."

With that, she turned her back on them and glided from the room. The door opened for her, one of her footmen always ready. My wife never touched a door handle in her own house if she did not wish it.

Donata walked with her head high, her step even and dignified. The discreet footman shut the door but not all the way—the latch did not catch.

This left me alone with Donata's male relatives, neither of whom liked me. Edwin had made it immediately clear how put out he was because Donata had chosen to marry me. He'd imagined himself as stepfather to a viscount and son-in-law to an earl.

Though I'd never met Stanton St. John, his dislike for me wafted from him like cloying perfume. While I had no legal power over Peter, I did have influence, and I now considered myself his father. I could see in the back of Stanton's dark eyes how much that rankled.

"Captain Lacey," Edwin said. "Surely you can understand that Mr. St. John is correct. The place for Peter is with his family."

"I must wonder how you stand to gain from this," I returned bluntly. "If Peter lives with Mr. St. John, surely that puts him out of your reach."

Edwin's cheeks went scarlet. I wondered whether Stanton

had offered him money or perhaps access to Peter if he helped with his petition. Their idea, I supposed, was that Peter would grow dependent upon his two cousins and be manipulated into granting them favors—gifts, position, power—in gratitude.

I read this in Edwin's flush, though Stanton looked flinty. I had to wonder how quickly Stanton would cut Edwin out of the bargain.

I leaned on my walking stick. "I have a rather large valet who aspires to be a pugilist," I said. "And another man who styles himself as my guard, who actually was a pugilist. I can call them to help me show you the door if you wish. One is young and vigorous, the other quite a skilled fighter. Within this house, they answer only to me."

Edwin looked worried, but Stanton's scowl deepened. "Keep your dogs contained," he said. "It will make no difference whether I am admitted to the house or not, Captain. Lady Breckenridge will receive letters about the matter, as I am certain she realizes. Good morning."

I stepped aside as he strode to the door, which silently swung wide for him. Bartholomew, the tall, well-muscled young man I'd threatened him with, was on the other side.

Bartholomew glanced at me, his eagerness unmistakable— he had pitched unwanted visitors to the pavement before. I gave my head the slightest shake, and Bartholomew withdrew, looking disappointed.

Edwin hastened after Stanton. I followed him, Bartholomew silently falling into step behind me.

When Stanton reached the bottom of the stairs, a footman handed him his coat, another positioning himself with Edwin's. Barnstable, stationed at the front door, gave them his butler's bow.

"Good day, gentlemen," he said.

A carriage had already halted at the doorstep. Stanton

climbed into it, barely waiting for Edwin to more clumsily ascend before the coach jerked forward.

Barnstable closed the front door. He looked up at me standing on the first landing, inquiring without words if he could assist.

I shook my head, told Bartholomew to go about his business, and turned to seek Donata.

Before I could set foot on the next flight of stairs, a commotion sounded beneath me. I heard the imploring voice of a footman, shocked into dropping his trained tones—"'Ere. You ain't allowed …"

A large man pushed his way past the servants trying to stop him emerging from the backstairs. He was Brewster, the former pugilist and thief who acted as my bodyguard, the second man I'd threatened Stanton with.

Brewster sent a grim look up to me. "You need to come, guv. My missus sent me to fetch you."

CHAPTER 2

"Is Mrs. Brewster all right?" I asked in alarm. I'd met Em Brewster several times now—she and Brewster lived in St. Giles, a corner of London rife with violence.

Brewster crushed his hat in his big hands, the only movement in his otherwise still body. His eyes betrayed his agitation, his face tight.

"Nothing wrong with her," Brewster said. "Bloke's been killed."

The answer both brought me relief and more worry. Men were killed in London every day, unfortunately—in accidents, while fighting—but there must be a reason Mrs. Brewster had sent her husband across London to summon me about this one.

"Damnation." I glanced up the stairs where Donata had fled. "Can you wait a moment?"

Brewster shook his head. "No, guv. I can't."

The blunt statement made me wonder still more, but I was not heartless enough to race away from Donata when the welfare of her son was at stake.

"Return to Mrs. Brewster," I said firmly. "I will be there as soon as I am able."

Before Brewster could object, I continued up the stairs.

I found Donata in her boudoir, at her window. Its pale draperies admitted light to touch the gold and white carpet, marble mantelpiece, brocade sofa and chaise, and paintings in gilded frames.

This feminine retreat had recently been invaded by masculinity in the form of my newspapers and a decanter of brandy, which reposed on a demi-lune table beneath a painting of a lavish country house, complete with horses.

Donata stood with her back to me, but I knew by the way she held herself that she'd heard me enter and close the door. Before I could think of words to ease her, she swung around, her eyes glittering with tears.

"They can do it, Gabriel. They can take Peter from me."

"No," I said at once.

Donata did not rush into my arms and beg for me to make everything better. She was not that sort of woman. She remained by the window, her face as pale as the curtains.

"Of course they can," she said in a brittle voice. "A woman is not related to her own son, did you not know? I am only the vessel for the man's seed. I believe that to be absolute nonsense, but it is the law."

"Lord Breckenridge named you guardian, did he not?" I pointed out. "The wording of his will should prevail."

Donata nodded glumly. "As awful as he was, even Breckenridge was wise enough not to trust his own family. Stanton is a greedy, foul man, and I never let Peter anywhere near him."

"Then there will be nothing he can do. Breckenridge stated his wishes, and that is final."

"Do not try to comfort me, Gabriel. You know Stanton could find an excellent solicitor—could use Breckenridge's *own* solicitor—to find chinks in the will and overturn my guardianship. Perhaps he could not have when I was simply ·Breckenridge's widow, but now that I've wed a nobody who married me to get his hands on the family silver, my judgment cannot be trusted."

I did not grow offended—Donata only repeated the well-known gossip that circulated about me.

I apparently had charmed my way into Donata's bedchamber so that I could take my ease, spend all her money, and influence her son into giving me a sinecure when he was older so I could continue my profligate life.

"You also have solicitors," I said. "Some of the best in England, who will countermand anything Stanton can suggest. Take comfort in that, if you will not from me."

Donata remained rigid. "And perhaps these excellent men of the law will advise me to do what Stanton wants. After all, a boy should be raised by gentlemen, not soft women. Peter's first cousins are far too reckless, of course, but second cousin Stanton is older and more dependable. My solicitors did not think me wise to marry you, Gabriel—I had to persuade them I wouldn't do anything so foolish as give you all my income before they'd grudgingly set up an allowance for you."

The extent of the money that trickled to me for clothing and sundries made me a bit nonplussed, but I made myself feel better by being frugal with it.

I went to her but did not reach for her. "Sending Peter off with a man who so obviously wishes to control the viscountcy will not please your solicitors either, I think. I will not let it happen, Donata. Peter will remain with you—with us—and out of reach of your repugnant cousins."

"I am pleased with your optimism," she bit out. "Forgive me if I do not share it." She jerked her attention behind me, her brows lowering to a scowl. "Yes, Bartholomew, what is it?"

Bartholomew, who had quietly opened the door, remained there, his tall body stiff in his dark suit. Donata was usually calm and polite with her servants, and Bartholomew blinked a moment at her waspish tone.

"Begging your pardon, my lady," he said. "Captain. Mr. Brewster has planted himself at the foot of the stairs and refuses to move."

Donata's mouth pinched. "Has he come to fetch the captain for another mission Mr. Denis won't soil his hands with?"

I answered. "Brewster's wife wishes to speak with me. Trouble in St. Giles."

"Is there?" Donata blinked back tears, reaching for her usual coolness. "Hardly surprising. You'd better go, Gabriel. Mrs. Brewster would not summon you for a trifle." She pinned me with a sharp look. "But you will tell me every word of what you find when you return, no matter how sordid the tale."

"Of course." I gave her a bow. "I hope it is a trifle, and Brewster is making much of nothing."

I spoke lightly, but I knew Brewster would not have rushed to me, tense and drawn, if the matter could be easily resolved.

Donata rose on tiptoe and kissed my cheek, her lips cold. "Godspeed," she whispered.

I turned from her to follow Bartholomew, whose youthful stride already had him at the stairs.

At the door, I swung back. "Why did you marry me, by the bye?" I asked Donata. "If I am a nobody after the family silver?"

Donata, a vision in ivory and blue, looked straight at me. "To save you the embarrassment of a love affair, of course."

WE HIRED A HACKNEY TO GO TO ST. GILES. THE COACH TOOK US from Mayfair and its tall houses with carefully cleaned brickwork, to rookeries whose tumbledown houses stood upright only because they leaned into one another.

The hackney driver let us down at Tottenham Court Road and Great Russell Street, then chirruped to his horses, which clopped away quickly. We proceeded into the rookery on foot.

Chimneys, nearly hidden by belching smoke, perched precariously on rooftops. I tripped over loose stones, lifting my feet to keep from treading in noisome mud. My stick found a hole that stank of a sewer, and I had to yank it free, catching myself before I fell into a larger hole, which was little more than an open cesspit.

Brewster walked ahead of me at a brisk pace, paying no attention to my struggles. The last time I had come into the area, a few months ago, I'd been beaten for my pains. I noted men hovering in the shadows, and I made certain to keep myself not far from Brewster's heels. I may have been a seasoned fighter, but the robbers here attacked in packs.

We moved through narrow lanes and around a dog that raised a listless head as I passed.

In a crooked street that dead-ended at a narrow house of three stories, an entire street's worth of washing fluttering above us, Brewster halted.

"In here, guv."

"Here" was a black doorway leading into the even darker interior of the house at the end. The smell that emerged was a mixture of urine, rotting vegetables, and a sickly odor of decay.

Brewster unlocked the door with a key, then he shoved it open, reached for a lantern inside, and lit it. Feeble candlelight flickered through the holes in the lantern and fell upon the body of a man lying on his back, arms outstretched.

"I dragged him here," Brewster said. "Didn't like to leave him in the street to be picked over."

The man lay as though Brewster had dropped him and ran for me without bothering to straighten his limbs. He was large, his torso square and covered by a patched brown coat.

Gray and brown hair, thin, barely covered a bald patch on the top of his head, and his un-gloved hands were those of a laborer—coarse, broken-nailed, dirty.

He wore breeches rather than trousers, the fabric shiny and

worn. Coarse stockings covered his legs, and he wore square-toed shoes with holes in their soles.

"Who is he?" I asked. I doubted Brewster would have hidden the body of a stranger and raced across London to find me.

Brewster cleared his throat. "Jack Finch. Me wife's brother."

I halted in astonishment. The dead man was as unlike Mrs. Brewster as Mayfair was from St. Giles—or at least as St. Giles was from a tidy, respectable district. This man had seen hard labor and was built like a fighter, very unlike the small, birdlike, and painfully neat Emily Brewster.

"What happened to him?" I asked. "Why is he dead in a back street near your rooms?"

"He were beaten to death." Brewster lowered the lantern to fully illuminate his face.

The man's head was bloody, his nose squashed, one eye open and filmed with white, the other crushed back into his cheek-bone. His throat was covered with bruises, not from someone holding him and strangling him, but from repeated punches. I saw the outline of a fist on one side of his neck.

His chest also had been kicked, boot prints clear on the ragged remains of his bloody shirt.

"Robbers?"

Brewster shrugged. "Don't know. He had nothing to steal but his clothes."

He closed his mouth, nothing more forthcoming. Not where the man had been found, who Brewster suspected had done this, what he expected me to do. Brewster was reticent at the best of times, and now he descended into absolute silence.

"Your wife sent for me, you say?" I prompted.

Another nod. "'Course she did. He's her kin."

I waited, but Brewster clamped his lips tightly closed again. I let out a breath. "Then I suppose I had better speak to her."

I glanced about the room, which was small and bare. A door

on the other side led to a larger room, but one just as bare and quite cold. There was no sign of anyone living there.

Brewster straightened the dead man's arms and legs from their ungainly position and pulled his coat square. He gestured me out then locked the door behind us.

The dog we had passed in the last street stood outside, watching us warily. It was thin, its pale coat ragged, a sorry and pinched-looking specimen.

The dog went to the door we'd closed, put its nose to a crack, and sniffed hard. It gave us another wary glance over its shoulder and began a soft whine.

"Is the dog your brother-in-law's?" I asked.

Brewster shrugged. "Don't know. We hadn't seen the man in donkey's years."

The dog ceased its whining and sank down, hollow-eyed, grunting a little as it rested its weight on the door. I studied the animal, which might have golden hair under the filth, its drooping ears that of a hunting dog.

It was difficult to turn from the sad eyes, but I made myself do so, as Brewster was already striding off for the next street.

I did not ask why Brewster hadn't run for a magistrate. We both knew that the first instinct of a Runner would be to arrest Brewster, a known criminal, for the murder. Even a fair magistrate would question him closely.

I scanned Brewster's face for telltale signs that he'd fought Mr. Finch himself, but with gloves on his hands and his collar turned up, I could discern nothing. His face bore nor bruises, but Brewster was skilled at deflecting blows.

Brewster lived with his wife in a building as sagging as any in these streets, the staircase inside winding upward through smells and noise. Brewster's landing was swept clean, the floor scrubbed, Mrs. Brewster doing her best to make her corner of this world respectable.

The door flew open as we reached the top of the stairs. "You brought him?"

Mrs. Brewster was willowy compared to her husband and stood a good foot and a half shorter than he. Her graying brown hair straggled from its knot, and her brown eyes were red-rimmed.

She regarded me calmly, but her anxiousness was apparent. "Come in, Captain. I'll give you coffee, as I know you're partial to it."

I followed Brewster inside, but not before both of us had scraped our boots on a worn metal rod propped in the hallway. Brewster did this without resentment, as though it were a habit. It would never do to get the mud and muck of London on Mrs. Brewster's floors.

Mrs. Brewster had already hurried to the next room and soon returned with a tray holding cups and a pot of fragrant, steaming coffee.

She poured out, her lips pursed. I accepted my cup with thanks and took a sip. The coffee was nothing like the expensive brew Donata had specially blended for me, but it was drinkable.

"Tommy and I found him," Mrs. Brewster began. She poured coffee for her husband and set down the pot and sat back, hands on her knees. "A-lying in the street, he was. Tommy says for me to nip back here, and he'll hide him, and I told him he must find you. 'The captain will know what to do,' I says. What *do* we do, Captain? Jack wasn't a good man, by any means—he was cruel as a north wind—but he's my brother. Wouldn't be Christian to leave him to rot, would it?" I noted that she did not meet my eyes.

Brewster took a noisy sip of coffee. I looked to him, but he didn't speak.

"How did you find him?" I asked. "Where was he? Does he live around here?"

Mrs. Brewster hesitated. After a quick glance at Brewster,

she said, "Let's just say he was living elsewhere, at His Majesty's pleasure. I ain't seen him in years. Me and Tommy, we was walking home from having a bit of breakfast in the pub, and there he was, lying across the street in a lonely stretch. I knew it was me brother, though I ain't set eyes on him in a long time. He's a bit older than me, gone from our house before I was grown. But it were him. Our Jack. Tommy says he'll stash him somewhere safe, sends me home, and runs for you."

They'd agreed on the story to tell before they'd parted, I could see. I'd have to be patient to untangle the true one.

"He'd been convicted, you said." The man's bare hands had been hard from manual labor, which meant detention in the hulks or a prison and then transportation to work in the Antipodes. "For what crime? Did he escape, or had he finished his sentence?"

Brewster shook his head. "No one escapes, guv. They hunt you down like a dog. As for what crime, could have been anything with Jack Finch. Robbery, fighting, breaking up a pub, counterfeiting, receiving, blackmailing, even killing if he could get the verdict reduced to manslaughter."

"He were a bad 'un," Mrs. Brewster said with a decided nod. "Always, even as a youth. Beat us younger ones if we crossed him. I was that glad when he disappeared when he were sixteen and never came back. We heard of him over the years, but he didn't come home again, thank the Lord."

It would be easy enough to discover what Mr. Finch had been sentenced for, where he'd been sent, and for how long. The Old Bailey kept records of trials, and I could ask Sergeant Pomeroy or my magistrate friend Sir Montague Harris to look into it for me.

"Was Mr. Finch trying to find you, do you think?" I asked Mrs. Brewster.

Again she would not meet my gaze. "He never wanted much to do with me before. But it's no secret I married Tommy, so if he decided to speak to me, he'd only have to ask about to know where we're staying."

"So he could touch you for money?"

Mrs. Brewster considered then dipped her head in a nod. Her husband said nothing, only took another slurp of coffee. He'd removed his gloves, and I did see abrasions on his fingers, but he usually had cuts and bruises, as he sparred with his fellows to keep fit.

"Everyone knows Tommy's got a decent wage," Mrs. Brewster said.

Everyone knew Tommy Brewster worked for James Denis, she meant, who was a generous employer.

"Maybe he was coming to see *you*," I said to Brewster.

"Don't know what for," he rumbled.

"You work for a powerful man. I imagine gentlemen queue up to ask you for intercession with him, perhaps even an introduction to the powerful man himself."

Brewster grunted. "They'd be unlucky. Mr. Denis don't like gossip about 'im, nor do 'e like us bringing around every friend and 'quaintence askin' 'im for favors. 'E's not a cherry-table hinstitution." Whenever Brewster was irritated, his language slid back into his thick working-class cant.

"Regardless," I said. "Your brother-in-law might not know you wouldn't speak to Denis for him, and come to find you on the off chance. There had to be a reason he was in the street for you to trip over him."

"I didn't bring you here to talk about whys and wherefores," Brewster growled. "We just need to know what to do now. Have a quiet funeral? Where do we store the man until then? Will any decent vicar bury him? I don't like to bother His Nibs with this little problem, so we were thinking maybe you could give us some advice."

"Tommy," Mrs. Brewster admonished. "Don't be rude. The captain came all this way." She turned to me, eyes holding worry. "We really don't know what to do. Tommy was all for dumping him in the river, but as I say, he's me brother. Is he all right where he is until we bury him? The poor lad should have that at least."

I should be amused, I supposed, that they'd turned to *me* to ask how they could hide a dead body. I, a stickler for honor, could be trusted to keep something so shameful as a murder in the family quiet, couldn't I?

"He's the victim of a crime," I pointed out. "Do you not want to know who killed him? To find him some justice?"

Mrs. Brewster shook her head. "Our Jack were a bad man, Captain. Only a matter of time before someone did him over. It'll be someone he owed money, or else he robbed the wrong man or had his way with the wrong man's wife. His life, such as it was, is over. I only want him to rest in peace now."

"That may be," I said sternly. "But this is still a crime, Mrs. Brewster. It will have to be reported to a magistrate."

"And the moment you rush out of here to find a Runner," Brewster said over his cup of coffee. "Is the moment I thrash you, Captain. No magistrates, no Watch. Or I beats you for it."

CHAPTER 3

I regarded Brewster with some concern, not for his threats but for whatever reason he might be making them.

"Did you kill him?" I asked.

Brewster moved the coffee cup from his mouth, squarely meeting my gaze. "Don't believe I did."

Brewster had been in his lifetime a pugilist and a thief. Somewhere along the way, James Denis had hired him for both his muscles and his skill in thievery.

While he might not fight for a living any longer, Brewster was strong and dangerous. He could easily have beaten his wife's brother to death.

"If you give me your word," I said.

"You have it."

I did not know what worth Brewster put on his own promises, but I'd learned the man did have principles. He'd saved my life more than once, nearly at the cost of his own. Brewster was adept at a lie, but he was also loyal.

"Very well then," I said. "I will take it. But I still believe we should report the crime. Someone else may have run for a magistrate already, and it will not look well when it is discovered who the man is, or that you found him and hid him away instead of reporting the incident."

Brewster sniffed and wiped his nose. "This is St. Giles. Watch and patrollers don't care what goes on here. They're afraid to come in."

"That's as may be, Tommy, but I think the captain's right," Mrs. Brewster said. "Folk will wonder why I let my brother be bashed to death and didn't say nothing about it. They'll think it's because *you* did it. I don't need you banged up and taken away from me. Who'd lug the washing water up the stairs?"

She spoke lightly, but her eyes were too bright, and one hand balled in her lap.

"I'll speak to a magistrate who is just," I said, trying to sound reassuring.

Brewster's lips tightened. "Don't matter. Runners will come into it, won't they? If ye swear to tell them I weren't nowhere near St. Giles at the time in question, then I'll let ye talk to your magistrate friend."

"I have no idea where you were. When did it happen?"

"Found him this morning. So sometime in the night."

"And where *were* you?" I asked.

Brewster took yet another noisy sip of coffee and pinned me with a hard stare. "Tell them I was running an errand for His Nibs. Back here by two in the morning—clock struck that as I let myself in the door—then with me wife the rest of the night."

"She can vouch for you?"

Mrs. Brewster's hands tightened. "I were asleep. I can't say exactly when he came home."

"What was the errand?" I asked Brewster. "Where did it take you?"

"It's His Nibs's business—why don't you ask *him?*" He trailed off into a mutter. "Cor, with you two in the witness box, I'm done for."

"You expect me to invent an alibi for you, in other words," I said.

Brewster slammed down his cup. "All you need say is that I were following you about, keeping you out of trouble. Takes me away from home most nights. I know you can lie, Captain. I seen you do it, nice and smooth. Or at least hide the truth."

"The trouble with that," I said, "is there will be other witnesses to say you weren't with me. My wife, for instance. Bartholomew, Barnstable, and a host of servants. They'll know you were nowhere near. They keep an unnerving eye on me."

"Aye, and they'll lie themselves black in the face for you if her ladyship tells them to."

No doubt that was true, but would they do so for Brewster?

"I'd rather get to the truth," I said. "It's easier to argue when you have the truth on your side."

Brewster's scowl told me the truth hadn't served him well in the past. "I'd never have bothered to tell ya, if Em hadn't insisted. I should have gone to His Nibs."

"Why didn't you?" James Denis, whom Brewster usually referred to as *His Nibs*, as though he were superstitious about speaking his name, was a very resourceful man.

Brewster heaved a rattling sigh. "He don't want no trouble from us. Something like this happens, we take care of it, discreet-like. He don't want attention drawn. If ye can't be discreet, please go away."

"Tommy! He's tryin' to help."

I set aside the coffee and moved my stick to brace my weight, but I remained seated for the moment. "I'll do whatever I can to find the culprit and bring him in. I owe you that. But if I don't speak to a magistrate, and the crime is reported, as I say, it will lead back to you. Better that we come forward."

"*You* go forward," Brewster growled. "I ain't going near a magistrate's house."

I climbed to my feet. "I can speak to him alone. I will ask you two things—that you do not touch the body again, and that you return to my wife's house and see that her bloody cousins come nowhere near the place. The butler will turn them away, but he might need assistance."

"Huh. No families hate each other more than aristos,'" Brewster said darkly. "I'll look after her ladyship. You make sure *my* missus don't have to witness me hanging, that's all I ask."

~

BREWSTER WOULD NOT ALLOW ME TO WALK OUT OF ST. GILES alone. He slid on his coat and took up his squashed hat and led me with poor grace through the rookery back toward Broad Street. That road led to High Holborn, where I could find a hackney.

As we passed the lane where the body presumably still lay, the dog we'd left by the door came toward me. He sat down as I walked by, watching me in a desultory way, tail unmoving.

"Get on," Brewster said to the dog, but it utterly ignored him.

I stopped. "He seems strangely attached to this place."

"Mayhap. Never seen 'im before. Can't imagine Em's brother having a dog what liked 'im. She didn't tell you the 'alf of what I know about Finchie. World's better off with him gone."

"Then I wonder if the dog belongs to whoever struck him down. Was he told to wait and guard? Or is he distressed about the killing? Dogs seem to understand things."

"Do they?" Brewster growled. "Can't say as I've noticed."

I'd grown up in the country, where dogs were as much a part of the household as the people in it. Dogs had been part of army life as well, officers bringing their favorite animals with them along with their wives. Sometimes the dogs were better treated than their spouses.

When their masters didn't come back from battle, the dogs seemed to know that they were gone forever, sometimes even sensed beforehand that they'd not return. Dogs had uncanny instincts, in my observation.

This hound was grimy and no doubt covered with fleas and other vermin. Donata and her servants would not thank me for returning home infested.

"What could you tell us, eh?" I said to the dog.

Brewster's stance was impatient. "Thought you had a magistrate to see to."

"Could you look after him for me?" I asked on a sudden. "Give him a few scraps and keep him near. Don't let the Watch round him up."

Brewster scowled. "I told you, Watch don't come to St. Giles. I think you've gone soft in the head, but all right. But I'm not keeping 'im long."

"Long enough for me to journey to Whitechapel and back. I'll pay for his keep."

"You said ye wanted me to guard your missus."

"Wait until I return. I believe the cousins have finished with persuasion for the moment."

"You really *are* soft in the head, Captain. Don't know what His Nibs wants with ye. But I'll do it."

I knew that if the dog were left to go stray, it would be taken by the Watch or other parties who kept the population of London's dogs at bay. Stray dogs formed into packs that could become dangerous—it had happened.

I didn't want this dog to be drowned or shot simply because a man had the misfortune to die. And perhaps, if I found his master, I'd also find the person who'd killed Em Brewster's brother.

~

THE HACKNEY FOLLOWED HOLBORN AND THE LONG, CROWDED, dusty way to the City. I rode through Newgate Street to Cheapside, to the center of finance at the meeting of Cornhill with Threadneedle and Lombard Streets. Nearby was the great synagogue where I'd sat entranced by the service with my friend Mr. Molodzinski. I reflected that I ought to look up the man, whom I'd not seen since my return from Egypt.

I left the hackney in Whitechapel and entered the magistrate's house.

The success of Henry and John Fielding's Bow Street Runners had engendered more such men working out of magistrates' houses across the metropolis—Queen Street, Whitechapel, and others. The Bow Street men were regarded as the best of the crop, but the other Runners did plenty to pursue criminals and bring them to trial.

I asked to see Sir Montague Harris. I was told he had gone out but was expected back soon, if I wanted to wait.

The clerks there, knowing I was an acquaintance of Sir Montague, left me alone to sit in a corner out of the way. I studied a notice that a certain woman in a yellow apron had stolen all the clothes and money from three children that had strayed from their nannies. This thief seemed to like working in Hyde Park. Another notice was for a man wanted for questioning about the body of his brother, who'd washed up in the Thames, plus the search was on for a gentleman who'd vanished on the eve of his wedding.

"*He* might have, as my lads say, 'legged it,'" a jovial voice came to me. "Panicked at the last."

Sir Montague Harris radiated warmth from his rotund body, along with the scent of wool and pipe smoke. I came to my feet and looked down into his round, wise face as I stuck out my hand.

"How are you, my boy?" Sir Montague asked in his large voice. "Involved yourself in another crime, have you?"

A few heads turned our way, including those of pickpockets and street ladies who'd been hauled in by the foot patrol while

I'd waited, but once Sir Montague beamed and shook my hand, they ignored me.

"As a matter of fact ..." I began in a low voice.

"Excellent. Let us adjourn."

Sir Montague used both his walking stick and the staircase railing to haul himself upward, grunting as he went. We reached a stuffy upper floor and a room in the back with one window overlooking a grimy courtyard. Sir Montague seated himself in a sagging chair and waved me to the only other seat in the chamber.

"Before we begin with the sordid business of crime, tell me how your extraordinary wife is faring. And your children? All in good health?"

"All are well, thank you," I answered, warming. "My daughter Anne is ... quite robust." Her cries filled the night, the nurse distressed that she'd wake the master and mistress. I journeyed often to the nursery in the small hours to walk with Anne until she quieted again. "Peter is tired of lessons and longs to run about in the country, and my older daughter, Gabriella, is due to arrive on Saturday."

Sir Montague gave me his hearty laugh. "The pride bursting from you is good to see, my friend. I always knew you needed someone to look after you. Now, what is this crime you've come to consult me about?"

I tucked aside my eagerness to speak about my children and gave him a truncated version of the tale of the dead Mr. Finch, never mentioning Brewster or his wife.

Sir Montague watched me with a shrewd sparkle in his eyes. "St. Giles, eh? Dead bodies turn up there all the time. Beaten, stabbed, left in the street for the rats, pushed into cesspits. Why does this one merit your attention?"

The answer slid from me reluctantly. "Because I do not want the wrong man arrested."

"Ah, now we come to it." Sir Montague sat back, the chair

groaning. "A friend is involved. Do not worry, I will not ask you which friend, not at this point. I will guess not Mr. Grenville, as he can pay for fine gentlemen of law to keep him from trouble. Plus, I gather, he has not yet returned from Paris?"

"He has written that he will be home by summer." Lucius Grenville, one of the wealthiest and the most famous gentleman in London had vanished in February with his mistress to Paris and hadn't been seen in London since. Talked about at length, yes, with the conclusion that Grenville had become quite mad since he'd taken up with the actress Miss Simmons.

"Then we have no fear for Mr. Grenville, except perhaps in his domestic arrangements." Sir Montague's chuckle vibrated the room. "I will guess not Mr. Denis, as most crimes committed by him or for him are not so obvious, or even known of by the rest of the world until many years later. I will keep my speculations about why you did not consult him first to myself."

"Murder is against the law," I said in surprise. "Why would I not report it?"

"Why not, indeed? Well, Captain, I will send my most trusted Runner to have a look, though crimes in that area belong to Bow Street or Queen's Square. I will also not speculate as to why you did not want one of those Runners to rush to St. Giles."

Sir Montague had likely already tumbled to whom I was attempting to protect, but he was also kindhearted enough to let me go through the motions.

"The Runners who would come in response to my information are not the most discreet of men," I said.

Milton Pomeroy and Timothy Spendlove, both of Bow Street, would be more than happy to confine Brewster to Newgate until they could be convinced he had nothing to do with it—Pomeroy good-naturedly, Spendlove with grim satisfaction.

"You are quite right," Sir Montague said, eyes alight. "Neither

Spendlove nor Pomeroy will do. I'll send the best man for the task, Captain, I assure you. He will, no doubt, ask you many pointed questions, but he won't rush after the first man he sees, nor will he threaten you for information. He's a good lad. Not long in London from Aberdeen, but he's canny, quite canny."

I imagined a tall lanky Scotsman with an indecipherable accent, but if Sir Montague recommended him, I would reserve judgment.

Sir Montague and I exchanged a few more pleasantries, he commenting that his wife was already clamoring to leave London for their country home, where she spent the summers in the clean air while he remained sweltering in Whitechapel.

I replied that this summer my family planned to divide our time between Norfolk and the Breckenridge seat in Hampshire. This reminded me of Donata's troubles with her husband's family, and I moved impatiently.

Sir Montague at last rose to his feet and stepped down the hall, calling at a bellow for one of the underlings of the house to send for Mr. Quimby. After a time I heard his rumbling voice and answers in a lighter tone.

Presently, Sir Montague returned, shook my hand, and told me Mr. Quimby would await me below.

I walked downstairs to find a gentleman of small stature with dark brown hair and very blue eyes, in a black suit that was neat if not well made.

"Good morning, sir," he said, with only a hint of a Scottish accent. He bowed as I came off the last step. "I am Mr. Quimby. Lamont Quimby. Sir Montague tells me you have a dead body you'd like me to have a look at?"

CHAPTER 4

*M*r. Quimby travelled back through London with me. He was quiet, not offering conversation, as our hackney pressed through the busy city.

His accent, what there was of it, was northern Scots, speaking of rolling Highlands and blue waters I'd only seen in paintings. His appearance and name, however, did not bring to mind the wild Highlanders in plaids and claymores who'd followed Bonnie Prince Charlie to within a hundred miles or so of London seventy years ago.

Mr. Quimby was fairly young, perhaps just into his third decade, but he had a calmness about him that suggested age and wisdom. His hair and eyes, dark brown and blue, suggested a Celtic ancestry rather than Saxon or Viking. He held his hands carefully on his lap, his small fingers in leather gloves resting precisely in the same place on each knee.

We reached St. Giles, descending where Broad Street ended in the curve of St. Giles High Street before it became the northward Tottenham Court Road.

The church of the parish lay beside us, a square building of Portland stone with a fairly austere facade popular with architects of a hundred years ago. St. Giles was a very old parish, and this church was only the newest of many that had risen here.

I liked its simple face with arched windows of plain glass and a spire that rose to a graceful point a hundred feet above us. The modern gate to the churchyard, added at the turn of this century, was incongruous, a pseudo-Roman affair with a very busy scene of the Resurrection in its arch.

I led Mr. Quimby from here into the warren of streets where Brewster had left the body.

The day had commenced, which meant the lanes were full. St. Giles was a crowded place, where the poor who'd flooded to London from the country in hopes of a better life drifted when they needed to make ends meet. Lodgings were cheap, and cheaper still if one was prepared to live with a score or so others in only a few rooms.

A makeshift market had been set up in the middle of one street, with baskets of wilted beans and spring greens presided over by a woman whose face and hands were covered with sores. Dogs wandered about as did cats, who paid no attention to the rats skulking in the shadows.

Mr. Quimby took this in without a flinch or even a change of expression. The denizens gave him a sharp look, as they did me. They'd seen me before in the company of Brewster, and knew him for my protector, but they stared hard at Quimby.

The end of the lane Brewster had showed me was deserted, as though the residents of St. Giles had sensed where trouble was and avoided it.

I unlocked the door with the key Brewster had given me, and let Quimby into the tiny room. The noise of outdoors faded in this deserted place, and I lit the lantern Brewster had left behind.

Quimby leaned down, hands on knees, and studied the man, his nose almost on the body. He viewed Finch's battered face and his fingers now frozen into curled fists. Quimby bent nearly double, looking over the corpse from head to foot.

"Poor fellow," he said, straightening. "He fought hard, but the other—or others—beat him thoroughly."

"You think there was more than one?" I asked, startled.

"Difficult to say. But I'd guess so. He's a large man, looks capable of defending himself. This fist ..." Quimby balled his own hand and placed it against the marks on the neck. "This one is quite big. But this ..." He moved the man's shirt open to reveal a similar mark on his upper chest, almost covered in wiry black hair. "This fist was smaller, much smaller. I'd say even a woman's, if it hadn't delivered the blow with such force."

"A woman can strike hard if she is desperate," I said. "And some farm women are quite strong."

"Oh, yes, I am familiar with the strength of country lassies." A smile darted across Quimby's lips. "I grew up with ladies who thought nothing of scrapping, even with men, but they were not dainty and small, no."

"We are looking for a man with petite hands, then."

Quimby shrugged. "Possibly. I will rule out nothing yet."

Brewster's ham fists were candidates for the larger prints. My throat tightened.

Quimby examined the body closely once more, and I leaned with him, curious.

"His hands," Quimby said, turning one over. "What do you make of them?"

"He's worked hard with them. I'd thought he'd been transported, but I have been told that no one escapes and lives to tell the tale."

"Not necessarily. A man can make a friend of a guard or promise him a fortune if he gets free. Guards do not have the best life, watching over dangerous men, keeping them shut away. Compassion can enter into things as well—a guard hears a man missing his family, lonely, mayhap not as deadly a criminal as he was made out to be ..."

"The guard assists him," I finished.

"And he finds his way back to London. *His* hands and face are rather sunburned, as is his neck and chest. That tells me he's done labor in a sunny clime, shucking his shirt to keep cool."

Sent to the Antipodes, he meant. I knew of another man who'd been transported across the ocean to either New South Wales or the large island south of it, Van Diemen's Land. He'd managed to return without anyone being the wiser.

That man was a surgeon, who was now more or less in Denis's employ. He'd saved Brewster's life once upon a time, and made certain my wife and daughter lived through Donata's rather difficult labor this New Year's.

The surgeon had slim, competent hands, as thin and deft as a woman's.

I wondered very much if Jack Finch had met the surgeon on the far side of the world. The surgeon would be executed if it were discovered he'd returned from a penal colony.

Perhaps he'd spied Finch inquiring about Brewster among Denis's men, and feared Finch would betray him, even inadvertently. The surgeon could have followed Finch, watched Brewster drag him into this small house, and finished him off once Brewster was gone. He'd know exactly where to strike to kill, even with his bare hands.

I tried to keep my expression neutral as these pictures formed and dissolved, but Quimby watched me with interest in his eyes.

"You have a theory?"

I shook my head, discarding the idea. "I can think of nothing that fits."

The surgeon, if he'd wanted Finch dead, would have made a quick and efficient kill, and it was quite likely no one would have ever found the body.

Quimby waited for me to say more, but I pressed my mouth closed, and he returned to his scrutiny of Mr. Finch.

Presently, he rose again and flexed his shoulders as though easing out soreness. "He will have to be taken to the coroner for examination, and then the coroner will conduct a hearing. His family—if the poor bastard had any—must be told. But in finding the family, we might find the culprit. That is so often the case."

I had not known Quimby long, but I already discerned that he was no fool.

"What will you do now?" I asked, trying to appear ingenuous.

His brief smile flickered. "In the usual case, I would canvass neighbors and passers-by for witnesses. But in a place like St. Giles, I have no doubt that out of the thousands who roam these streets each night, exactly no one will have seen anything at all. Therefore ..." Quimby straightened his hat. "I will try to discover who he is, where he came from, and whether he had enemies, which seems likely. Those enemies I will question until I find one or two whose hands fit the prints on his body and who have no alibi for the crime. But you must know this, Captain. You have assisted the Runners before."

I gave him an acknowledging nod. "But the Runners I am acquainted with have their own methods. I wondered what yours were."

"Ah, I am familiar with Mr. Pomeroy and Mr. Spendlove." His eyes sparkled with mirth. "I am not gifted with their bulk, no, and so I must tread more carefully before I arrest a man—or woman. I must be certain of myself before I strike, and also take with me several stouthearted foot patrollers."

I believed him. If he tried to arrest Brewster, he would need a mob.

"I am afraid, though, that we will have to involve Bow Street, as they are the nearest house." Quimby shot me an apologetic look.

"Indeed," I said, as he seemed to wait for my answer.

Quimby led the way out and closed the door. He told me to lock it and then asked me for the key, which I gave him with reluctance. He did not ask me how I came by the key, which made me more nervous than relieved.

"I will fetch the coroner and have this fellow removed," Quimby said. "I will break the news to Bow Street myself after that."

He meant after the coroner shut away the corpse, out of the reaches of Spendlove and Pomeroy. They would not thank Quimby for elbowing in on the possible reward money Runners made when the criminals they caught were convicted.

Quimby pocketed the key and shook my hand. "Good day, Captain. I will find a hackney—will you have a carriage to take you home, or perhaps I can let you down at your destination?"

His expression held nothing but helpful inquisitiveness, but I already knew that this was a watchful man—Sir Montague would not have sent him if he hadn't possessed astuteness.

"Thank you, no," I said, settling my hat. "I will find a hackney or send for my wife's coachman."

"Just so. Well met, Captain. Have a care wandering these parts."

"I always do," I said.

He gave me another fleeting smile and walked away from me up the lane, his stride even and light. Not a man who drew attention to himself.

I waited until he'd turned the corner at the far end of the passage, and then waited longer to see if he'd return.

I ought to simply go home. Leave it for Sir Montague and Mr. Quimby to decide whom to seek for this crime, and be done with it. I had the pressing matter of Donata's bloody cousins to claim my attention.

But I wanted to speak to Brewster again, and warn him about what was happening.

When I left the passage, I saw no sign of Quimby. The crowds had thickened, the taverns and gin shops now open.

Young women in thin gowns strolled along the street, and several glanced hopefully at me. The game girls would know that I had more coins than most in St. Giles, and many of them were skilled pickpockets. I only tipped my hat as I moved quickly by, my walking stick ringing.

Quimby had truly gone. I had long ago developed an instinct of knowing when I was being watched, and I did not feel the sensation as I crossed lanes and made my way to Brewster's rooms.

I found the dog in the stairwell outside Brewster's door—I imagined his wife had forbidden him farther. He twitched his tail once when he saw me.

Brewster was inside, readying himself to go out. "His Nibs summoned me," he said as Mrs. Brewster bundled him into his coat. He took the low-crowned hat she dusted off and jammed it onto his head. "He'll have my hide if I leave you in St. Giles on your own, so you'd better come."

"Very well," I said without argument. I had hoped to ask more questions of Mrs. Brewster about her brother, but I'd have to save that for another time. I had questions for Mr. Denis as well. "I will pay for the hackney to take us there. But we have to bring the dog."

CHAPTER 5

*J*ames Denis was on the ground floor of his town house in Curzon Street, preparing to go out. Behind him, the painted white staircase with warm wooden railing twisted upward from the black-and-white tiled floor. Like the facade of St. Giles-in-the-Fields, this house was the embodiment of the subdued but elegant decor of the past century.

Denis's suit and light greatcoat, with kid gloves that clung to his hands, were another manifestation of restraint, though his clothes were of the latest fashion. But unlike the dandies who tried, and failed, to emulate Grenville, Denis did not draw attention to himself.

Four men stood in the ground-floor hall with him, waiting for their master with as much patience as the dog had waited for me. They were large men, former prize fighters, who surrounded Denis wherever he went. I found myself glancing at their fists to see if any matched the size of the print on Jack's neck.

Denis's eyes were blue like a chilly ocean no sun could warm. "I did not summon you, Captain." He took his hat from his butler, another former fighter, though smaller and older than the others.

"It was my own idea to visit," I returned. "Whims move me now and then."

"I have no time to speak to you. I have an appointment elsewhere."

"As I see." I gave him a conceding bow. "I will return later."

Denis had little patience with me at the best of times, and he disliked my habit of turning up whenever I wanted to ask him a question. In his view, the arrangement was that I came only when he called.

He had, in the past, simply walked out past me or had his butler keep me waiting a good long time, but today he sent me a nod, handed another lackey his hat, and walked into the reception room.

I followed him, and Brewster came behind. I was not certain whether Brewster entered to protect me or Denis.

Denis began speaking before I could, but he addressed Brewster. "You acted rashly, sending for the captain before speaking to me, but it cannot be helped. It is in the hands of the magistrates now."

I did not marvel that Denis knew exactly what had happened to Brewster's brother-in-law, or that I'd gone to look into the matter and had already involved Sir Montague.

"Begging your pardon, sir," Brewster said. "But I never sent for Captain Lacey. The wife did."

"I see." Denis's cold look told us he did *not* see. If Brewster had sought Denis's advice right away, his disapproval said, Finch's body would have vanished and no murder would have been reported.

I tried a smile. "So speaks a man who has never been married."

Something flickered in Denis's eyes before the cold flowed down again. "What did you wish to ask me, Captain?"

"Whether I can talk with your pugilists. Not to accuse them," I added hastily. "But to ask them about fighting. And fighters."

"No." The one word was harsh, chill, and final. "Good afternoon, Captain. Brewster, remain."

Now two pairs of eyes rested on me, Denis's blue and Brewster's brown. Both men expected me to obey.

I would accomplish nothing by arguing, and I knew it. I gave them both a rigid bow, departed the room, and put on my hat as I stepped out of the house.

Clouds had moved in from the east, a stiff wind blowing from the Thames. A few drops of rain pattered down as I reached the hackney.

I was not discouraged by Denis's answer. I had other means with which to make my inquiries. Also I needed to see to the dog.

Neither Brewster nor the hackney driver had been happy with me lifting the old fellow in, but I could not expect him to follow the coach all the way across London, and the driver had no intention of letting the dog up on the box with him.

The dog thumped his tail several times as I climbed back inside, his ears lowering in the canine expression of relief.

"Poor old lad," I said to him. I did not stroke or pat him, because, as I suspected, he was all over fleas, which was why Brewster had been unhappy to ride with him.

"Me wife will put me out if I bring fleas into the house," he'd growled.

Vermin must be a common problem in the slums, but Mrs. Brewster, I had noted, was fastidious. I'd callously suggested Brewster have a bath before he went home, which had only earned me a glower and a few foul words.

The coach rumbled up the crowded avenue of South Audley Street, but I bade the coachman pass the house where I now lived and pull up in the mews behind it. There I gave him the last of the money in my pocket and lifted the dog down.

Donata's coachman, Hagen, rested on a box outside the stables that held Donata's coaching horses and the hunters Peter and I rode. The groom with him puffed on a long-stemmed pipe and looked on with interest as I lugged the large yellow dog out of the hackney coach.

"John, lad," I said to one of the stable boys who'd popped out for a look. "Can you give him a bath? Must have him immaculate before he meets his ladyship."

~

BECAUSE MY WIFE, AS MUCH AS BREWSTER'S, WOULD OBJECT TO fleas on her person, I went straight upstairs and immersed myself in hot water I had Bartholomew fetch. I also told him to not only clean my clothes but to hold them in smoke. Bartholomew withdrew with them after looking at me askance.

I scrubbed all over, soaking my head in the water before it cooled. I finished, emerged, and redressed in clean clothes.

I did not have a chance to tell Donata all that had happened because, I learned as I left my chamber, she had gone out on her round of calls.

I had no appointments for the rest of the day that I knew of, and so I went upstairs to the nursery. Peter was deep into lessons with Mr. Roth, his tutor, in the schoolroom.

I did not interrupt them, only listened for a time as Mr. Roth told Peter about Athenian democracy and voting in the agora. Peter's eyes had glazed, and I felt a twinge of sympathy. I'd found ancient politics tedious as a lad—ancient battles had been much more to my liking.

At Michaelmas term, in November, Peter would begin at Harrow. I would be unhappy to see him leave, but had reasoned that he would return home for the vacations between terms. Harrow, after all, was only a bit north and west of London.

However, in the light of Stanton St. John stomping in to

demand Peter be given to him to raise, I was now uneasy about sending the lad to school. I feared Cousin Stanton might swoop in and steal Peter away while a host of weedy tutors did nothing to stop him.

We must certainly curtail Stanton. My ideas were no doubt more violent than Donata's, but I would not dismiss violence entirely. Peter was in my care now, and I refused to let uncertainties of the law endanger him.

I left Peter and Mr. Roth to Athenian debates and continued upstairs to the nursery.

My daughter Anne had grown considerably since her birth in January, and now she was chubby, pink, and sturdy. When her blue eyes fixed upon me, she made a high-pitched, wordless baby sound, and began to kick her legs so that she nearly fell from the chair in which she'd been planted.

The nurse dove for her, but I caught up my daughter and raised her high.

Anne squealed, her mouth open in a wide smile. I swung her up again and then settled her in the crook of my arm.

The servants of the house were now well aware of how soppy I was about my children, but they still did not know what to make of me. Most gentlemen would ignore a girl child except for an inquiry from afar about her well-being. Later, the girl would require a dowry so she could be married off into another family who would take over the care of her. Female children were regarded as expensive and inconvenient.

I had no intention of ignoring Anne or regarding her as inconvenient. She was a light in my life, and moments spent with her dispelled any lingering melancholia of my dark days.

My other daughter, Gabriella, would be arriving in London on Saturday, four days hence, from France, to continue being showed off at balls and other social gatherings by Donata and Lady Aline Carrington. I would be a happy man when Gabriella was again under my roof, though the purpose in bringing her to

London was to find a match for her. I was not so sanguine
about that.

I left Anne to her routine and descended to the adult realms
of the house. There I found I had a visitor of my own.

"Good God," I called out as I hastened to the ground floor.
"Grenville!"

Lucius Grenville was in the act of dispensing his coat and
hat into the arms of a footman. He flashed a grin at me, his dark
eyes twinkling, pleased he'd surprised me.

"When did you return?" I shook his extended hand in a tight
grip. "We weren't expecting you for another few months."

"One grows weary even of Paris," Grenville said, affecting his
ennui. "Rather a smelly city, actually. Small wonder one stays
drowned in brandy."

"London too is odiferous," I pointed out. "Which is why we
remain drowned in port. Come in and share a bottle."

I wanted very much to ask him about Marianne, my former
upstairs neighbor and now his mistress, but I held my tongue.
Theirs was a turbulent companionship, and who knew what
had happened out of my sight?

I hadn't thought I'd see Grenville again until summer—if at
all. Grenville easily tired of a place and had enough money to
travel the world any time he wished.

We installed ourselves in the room that had become my
retreat, the library where I liked to lounge and read on a slow
winter evening. The late Lord Breckenridge and his father
before him had purchased large swaths of the library whole, and
I doubt Breckenridge had ever opened one of the books. Indeed,
I had to cut the pages of almost every tome I took down.

Grenville stretched out his well-shod feet, took a sip of port
Bartholomew, with a grin of welcome, handed him, and sighed
in contentment.

"You are well set up here, Lacey. I salute you." Grenville
lifted his glass as Bartholomew retreated.

"My wife indulges me," I said. "Truth to tell, she prefers me shut away in here and out from underfoot."

"As I am acquainted with Donata, I have no doubt this is true." Another sip, then Grenville's head went back as he savored the thick wine. "I know you are too polite to ask, Lacey, but yes, Marianne returned with me. She is unpacking at the Grosvenor Street house and is in raging good health."

I relaxed, that worry dispersed. "Did you find Paris so very dull?"

Grenville studied the liquid in his glass with a professional eye—he was a connoisseur of fine wine. "In private, no, I did not. In public." He grimaced and lifted his gaze to me. "We were demanded to admire this writer or that painter in a paean of praise, whether they deserved it or not. An Englishman, even one as famous as I, was to have no opinions."

"That must have plagued your vanity."

"It did indeed." Grenville chuckled. "I am used to my pronouncements looked upon as though they came from the angels. And speaking of such things, I had a fine visit with the unfortunate Mr. Brummell."

"Did you?" I was sorry not to have been there. A meeting between the former ruler of fashionable London and the current one would have been most interesting. "How does he fare?"

"As well as you would expect. He is still dependent on friends for assistance—Alvanley mostly. Brummell is as fastidious and fashionable as ever, or as much as he can be in his reduced circumstances. He has many new friends in Calais, where he now dwells, and continues to spend, imprudent fellow. Or perhaps not so imprudent—I settled several of his bills." Grenville looked chagrined and took another sip of port.

I hid my amusement. "I never met the fellow, but he must be quite beguiling if he could survive among you lot for so long."

"Oh, he has the gift for fascination," Grenville conceded. "More than I do—I have less patience and a quicker temper."

"You also have a fortune. People will forgive your pique. More difficult when you owe and cannot pay." Well I knew this truth.

"You are no doubt correct. Brummell held his head up throughout our visit—in which we enjoyed ourselves criticizing the whole of London society—but I pity him. So many were quick to abandon him when he fell from grace."

Such was the precariousness of our world. Brummell had been an outsider to the *ton* after all—a middle-class man making a name for himself based solely on his wits and ability to entrance. When he could not pay his debts of honor, he'd had no one to which he could turn.

The story made me realize, with a chill, how much power a man like Stanton St. John, from an old aristocratic family, possessed. He was not one to be trifled with.

"Now." Grenville set aside his port and came out of his lazy slouch. "Tell me what adventures *you* have been having. Leave nothing unsaid, my friend. I will find out if you do."

I took a sip of port. "This morning, I was shown a dead body in St. Giles—a man has been murdered." I let out a heavy breath, my enjoyment of Grenville's expression short-lived. "And I will tell you in deepest confidence that I am very much afraid Brewster had a hand in it."

CHAPTER 6

*B*rewster?" Grenville asked, sitting up straight in his chair. "Are you certain? I admit that I at first found Brewster unprepossessing, but he's proved his worth several times, especially in the wilds of Egypt."

"He is also large and strong, was a champion fighter, and had nothing good to say about his brother-in-law. He has been quite sharp-tongued today—it is not uncommon for him to be irritated with me, but usually he is more resigned."

Grenville remained flatteringly still while I told him all that had happened, and he grew more troubled as I spoke.

"Suppose this man Finch began threatening Mrs. Brewster," I finished. "She told me he was a bully when they were younger. Brewster would not stand for anyone endangering his wife."

Grenville shook his head. "But why would he lead you to his body, in that case? Why involve you at all?"

"Mrs. Brewster insisted. She believes I can help. Whether she thinks Brewster murdered him or not, she wants me to put it right. I saw that in her eyes." I sat back, unhappy. "There were marks of two different fists, so Brewster might not have acted alone. Even if he did not land the killing blow himself, he might know who did."

"You did not mention Brewster to the Runner, Quimby?"

I shook my head. "He knows only that a man has been killed in St. Giles. Possibly a convict returned from a penal colony."

"I see." Grenville rose to pour himself another glass of port. "What do you plan to do?"

"Try to discover the other man—or men—involved. Make certain Brewster is well out of it. I owe him that."

"Hmm." Grenville fell silent, neither condoning nor condemning my words.

At this point, I had no idea whether Brewster's heavy fist had marked Finch's neck or anywhere else on his body, only my suspicion.

"Very well, then," Grenville said brightly as he sat down and flourished his glass. "What do you wish *me* to do?"

~

I COULD NOT RUSH TO ST. GILES AT ONCE AND BEGIN TO question the residents, because it was a spring evening during the London Season, I was married to an earl's daughter, and my nights were full.

If we were not at Drury Lane watching the newest tragedy with Mr. Keane, or at an opera at Haymarket, we were at supper balls in houses crammed from top to bottom while we dined on too-cold soup and too-warm salads, or attending at-homes where we were served no food at all. We rounded out the nights at musicales where the comestibles were flutists or tenors or lady violinists.

I enjoyed the musicales most of all, partly because many of them took place in our South Audley Street home, but mostly because I was partial to music. Perhaps not having any talent for music whatsoever myself made me appreciate it in others.

Tonight we adjourned to the theatre in Covent Garden to listen to a lecture on the beasts of India, complete with drawings cleverly projected by a magic lantern onto the large wall, followed by a troupe of tumblers.

Donata, in our box with ten of her friends, was as cool and satirical as always, but I saw that her brittleness, which had all but disappeared in the last year, had returned.

I'd not had time to speak to her further about the matter of Peter. When Donata had returned from her calls this afternoon, she'd closeted herself with her maid and then departed to another engagement, arranging to meet me at Covent Garden afterward. We sometimes did this, as Donata had reams of invitations each day, and she did not expect me to escort her to every event she accepted.

At the interval, after the tumblers had exited the stage by means of handsprings, Donata remained conversing determinedly to her friends, they dissecting all who fell within the sights of their lorgnettes. I left them to it, making my way downstairs and outside to breathe in the cool of the night.

Ladies of the demimonde lingered under the portico, enticing gentlemen whose wives were even now in their boxes upstairs. I was a familiar sight to these ladies, as I'd lived nearby for years, and they knew me well enough to know I was not beguiled by their charms. I nodded at a few of the friendlier ladies, but they passed me to chase easier prey.

Brewster materialized from behind a pillar.

"Tread carefully," I said, keeping my voice light. "You might be taken for a ladybird."

He ignored my feeble humor. "*You* tread carefully. If you're harmed as you wander about, it's me what answers for it."

"Shall we adjourn to my old rooms, in that case?" I said. "I'll be safe enough once there, and it's a few short steps."

Brewster said nothing, only hunkered into his coat and followed me.

I thought it unwise to take Brewster down Bow Street, and he never felt comfortable on that lane, so we went west the short way to James Street, then south to Covent Garden itself, skirting the square and its night dwellers. Someone had started a bonfire on the cobblestones, and a group of acrobats—ones who'd never have the privilege of performing in the large theatre behind us—flipped and tumbled around the flames.

My rooms above the bake shop were cold and deserted. When I'd returned from Egypt, I'd allowed my cousin Marcus to stay here, but he'd gone to Norfolk at the New Year and not returned. Marcus was another matter I'd need to attend to this spring.

"What do you want to ask me, guv?" Brewster said as I struck a spark to the kindling my landlady, Mrs. Beltan, kept stocked for me in case I wanted to use the rooms. "You'd not bring me out of the way of your lady wife if you didn't plan to put me to the question."

I blew on a small flame until the kindling caught, and then I gently eased it with the poker over the stacked logs. "What I wish to ask first is why Denis sent for you today."

"Wanted me to find the surgeon," he answered readily.

I jumped, the poker clattering from my hand. "Why?"

"Mr. Denis don't waste his time telling me why. He only says *do this*, and I do it."

"But you're not a fool." I retrieved the poker, jabbed at the logs until they were burning nicely, and set the poker back in its holder. "It occurred to me that your brother-in-law returned from imprisonment across the ocean, and so did the surgeon. I imagine that Denis, like me, wonders if there's a connection."

Brewster's stoic expression didn't change. He folded his arms, leaning on the doorframe of the bedchamber. "He might."

"And did you find the surgeon?"

I moved to the wing chair and sat down heavily, stretching my leg with its old injury toward the fire.

"No." Brewster closed his mouth, and at first I thought the information would cease, but then he said, "Appears he's been gone to the Continent for the last several weeks."

Which let him out as Finch's murderer, unless he had surreptitiously returned.

I let out a breath. "You know I must ask you, point blank, whether you killed your wife's brother."

Brewster's face set. "You asked me that before."

"And you said you didn't *believe* you had. Is there a doubt?"

More silence, then Brewster opened his lips a crack. "I might a' done."

Damnation. I'd hoped he'd stare at me and wonder aloud what had given me that idea.

"You gave me your word," I growled. "On the strength of that, I brought in a Runner, for God's sake."

"I said I *might* a' done. I don't know if I killed him all the way. But I beat him when I found him in our flat this morning and trying to grab hold of Em, and I carried him away to where I took you. That's the only thing we lied about—we didn't find him in the street."

"Bloody hell, Brewster."

"Let me finish, guv. I decided to give Finch money to take himself out of the country and never come back. I left him where I showed you to fetch some coin, and when I reached the house again, he were stone dead. I locked the door and went home. Em and me, we talked things over, and Em convinced me to ask your advice. I'm sorry she did now."

I came out of the chair, my temper rising. "You ought to have told me from the start. I can't help you if I don't know *everything*."

"I promise you, guv, he were alive and breathing when I left him."

But a man could die of his wounds, and the person who inflicted the wounds could be found guilty of murder.

"Well, now that you've landed me in it, damn you, tell me all."

Brewster's eyes widened. "I didn't land you in anything, begging your pardon, Captain. You told a magistrate and showed the dead man to a Runner. You're out of it."

Meaning I could wash my hands of the affair and walk away. Let Mr. Quimby rush about St. Giles and learn nothing. I had not let on that the dead man's name was Jack Finch or told Quimby of his connection to Brewster and his wife. Finch had likely been gone from these shores for years. I could retire from the field, let Denis protect Brewster, and have done.

"Devil take it, Brewster, Quimby—the Runner—is very bright. He'll discover Finch's identity and that he was your relation. I can't let you be hung for this. Give me every detail."

Brewster shrugged. "I did. He turned up on our doorstep out of nowhere while I was off getting our breakfast. Don't know how Finchie knew where Em was, but she don't keep her whereabouts secret. He wanted money, and when Em didn't have it, he started to hit her. I came home right about then and tore into him. He were always a good fighter—used to be on the circuit. Took me a while to wear him out, as weary and broken as he seemed to be. Finally I got him knocked down, and like I say, I hauled him away. But I knew he'd never leave Em alone, so I went and fetched a packet of me own money to give to him." Brewster rubbed the end of his nose. "And when I came back, there he lay, dead and gone. Saved me a bit of coin, I have to tell you."

"Did anyone see you wandering about the streets with an unconscious man over your shoulder? Or rushing to fetch your cash? If you keep it in a bank, they'll have a record of you coming to withdraw it. So would a man of business."

Brewster gave me an incredulous look. "I don't keep me money in no bank, or with a fraud of a man who'd charge me for looking after it. I have me own ways, me own places."

"Even so, someone might have seen you go there."

He shook his head. "They did not. Trust me that I know how to keep me funds safe from all eyes, including a bank's—God help us."

"Then we are back to who might have seen you carry Finch through the streets of St. Giles."

"No one. I do know how to go about things, as you'd say, *covertly*." He stretched out each syllable.

I relaxed, but only a bit. "Then our best recourse is to find this other person who came upon Finch after you left him, and prove he committed the murder."

"'Fought that's what you were already doing."

I curled my hands. "Do you know what the word *obdurate* means, Brewster?"

"Happen I do."

"Good. Shall we move on to who you might think wanted to kill Finch? Or at least give him another beating? What does Mrs. Brewster think? Finch likely made enemies among pugilists and fellow convicts. What was he convicted for, by the bye?"

"Don't know. I imagine you could find out. There'll be records, like as not."

Blast the man. He was trying himself to wash his hands of the matter, but neither of us could.

Both Brewster and I today had received unwelcome visits from unwelcome members of our families. Brewster had dealt with his in a way I wished I could have dealt with mine.

"Do you mind if I speak more with Mrs. Brewster about Finch?" I asked.

"You can." Brewster gave me a ready nod. "She won't know more than me. She ain't seen him in years."

"Perhaps, but she might remember something that is relevant." And perhaps Mrs. Brewster would tell me something out of her husband's hearing that she did not wish him to know.

Brewster and I remained in uneasy silence for a few more moments, then I banked the fire and we departed.

When we arrived at Covent Garden I learned that Donata had already gone, having left with an acquaintance for another gathering. I was not alarmed, as she sometimes did this—she had far more stamina for gadding about all night than I did.

What alarmed me more was that though I bunked down in her soft, feminine bed to wait for her, she was not there when I woke in the morning.

At times Donata spent the night with her friends, particularly Lady Aline, if the hour grew late and she was too tired to ride home in the coldness of dawn. I'd also requested she do this after an altercation we'd had last year, so I could be assured she wasn't wandering about dark, deserted London streets, even attended by her coachman and maid.

But she always sent word when she'd stay the night out, and this time, she had not.

Most alarming of all, when I went upstairs to fetch Peter for our morning ride, I found him missing as well.

CHAPTER 7

"Devil take it, woman, are you saying you never noticed?"

I roared at the poor nurse who struggled to keep Anne quiet. My daughter objected to my loud voice and tried to drown me out with hers.

"Miss Anne was colicky all night, and I slept next to her cot," the nurse said, tears running down her plump face. "I looked in on his lordship, and he was sleeping right as rain before Miss Anne and I fell asleep." She openly sobbed as Anne continued to bawl.

I tried to calm myself and reason things out. Peter had been fast asleep when I'd looked in on him and Anne before retiring last night, so if Peter had been taken, it had been well into the small hours of the morning.

An abductor would have to get past the rather burly footman who stayed on the front door all night—or, if he entered via the scullery stairs, the servants in the kitchen, who rose very early to begin cooking and cleaning for the day.

The man would then have to pass the ever-vigilant Barnstable and the sturdy Bartholomew, if he even made it that far.

The nurse—or at least Anne—might have woken at any noise in Peter's bedchamber, and Peter himself, a strong little boy, would have struggled and called out. I myself, snoring in my lady's chamber, had heard nothing.

If Peter had been quieted with laudanum or opium, he might not have made a sound, but then there was the problem of getting him to take the stuff.

That would point to a person already inside the house slipping laudanum into his drink or food, and I doubted any of the servants here would assist in kidnapping Peter. Many of them had come from Donata's home in Oxfordshire, and they doted on her. Their loyalties were to Donata and her son, not the Breckenridge side of the family.

My suspicions fell on Peter's tutor, Cyril Roth, a clever young man for his dithering manner. If Mr. Roth had asked Peter to walk out of the house with him, Peter would see no reason to object. Mr. Roth sometimes took him to the British Museum or to view other collections of historical interest. Could Stanton have bribed Mr. Roth to bring Peter to him?

That theory evaporated when Mr. Roth arrived, his face draining of color the moment he heard that Peter was gone.

"Good Lord!" He stared at me, wisps of hair on top of his head trembling as he removed his hat. "Have you sent for the Runners? His lordship does like the horses—perhaps he slipped out to the mews? And he's heard you brought home a dog. He will dart out there on occasion, I am afraid, sir. His young lordship is quite crafty."

"We have already checked the stables," I snapped. It had been the first place I looked. "Are you certain you know nothing of this business?"

Mr. Roth looked so bewildered and taken aback that I was inclined to dismiss the notion he was complicit. I could always ask his landlady whether he'd been in all night, in case he was simply a brilliant actor.

Bartholomew had grabbed his hat, ready to race forth and tear up London looking for Peter. "Want me to send for a Runner, sir? Mr. Pomeroy would be very keen."

"No, I have a closer resource. Dash down the road to Mr. Denis. If he wants me obligated to him, he will certainly have my obligation for this service."

Brewster arrived as Bartholomew ducked out the front door. "What's the fuss, guv?"

"Peter has disappeared," I said, trying to keep my voice steady. "I am very much afraid Donata's cousins have abducted him."

"No they ain't."

I halted. So did Bartholomew, who'd run a few steps down the road. He whirled back. "What are you saying, man?" Bartholomew demanded. "Out with it."

Brewster gave us a stolid look. "Her ladyship sent for me last night, after I saw you home all right, Captain. She wanted me to hire a coach that would take her out of London, with guards for the same. She had me bring her here from Berkeley Square, then she let herself inside through the kitchens and came back out with his young lordship. Hired coach was waiting, and off she went."

I grabbed Brewster by the lapel of his coat and pulled him into the house. Brewster walked in readily enough, but he removed my grip with a very strong hand once we were inside.

"Before ye shout at me for not telling you," he said, "she paid me a fair amount to wait and bring you the news this morning. Ye rose earlier than I expected, is all."

"Damnation, Brewster!" My voice rang to the top of the house. "Did you not think I'd be off my head with worry? Why the devil didn't you come to me immediately? And why didn't you stop her?"

I saw a flash of fury in Brewster's eye, the brutal rage that must have awakened when he'd beaten his brother-in-law for threatening his wife. He remained calm, however, his patience grating on me.

"Her ladyship is well," he said firmly. "The blokes I sent with her won't let a hair on her or his little lordship's head be disarrayed. Any road, *she* paid me, guv. Not you."

"Bloody, bloody ..." I turned away and kicked the bottom step of the staircase multiple times before I swung back to him. "If she gave you a destination, you had damn well better tell me."

"She didn't," Brewster said without hesitation. "Like as not, she knew you'd try to pry it out of me."

"God, give me strength."

Donata was not a lady to wait and ask her male relations what to do. She made up her mind, and she acted.

I tried to calm myself and reason through what she must have decided.

If she feared for Peter, she would take him to the place where he would be the most protected—her father's house in Oxfordshire. Cousin Stanton would not prevail against Earl Pembroke, and even less so against the very formidable Lady Pembroke. Donata had acquired her icy stare and cool wit from her mother.

Stanton, however, had recruited Donata's cousin Edwin, the earl's nephew, most likely to intercede with her family. Not that I believed the ambitious Edwin would succeed, but would this dissuade my wife from taking Peter to her father's?

And why the devil hadn't she told me what she was about? My rage flared.

Because she believed I'd make a hash of it, I realized. Donata had known exactly how to slip into and out of her own house without any in it—including me—being the wiser.

The maids and footmen surrounded me now, anxious, all waiting to see what I'd do. Barnstable, noticing, at last slid into his butler's dignity and coldly informed them to go about their business.

Brewster remained planted in the hall as the servants reluctantly dispersed, a rough boulder in a place accustomed to marble statuary.

"Em says she'll speak to ye," he informed me. "That is, unless ye want to rove England looking for your wife."

I closed my mouth over more swearing. As much as I wanted to race after Donata, I knew it would do me no good. I'd lead Stanton straight to her, which was no doubt another reason she'd refused to tell Brewster her destination.

"Please give me your word that Mrs. Lacey and Peter are perfectly safe," I made myself say.

"I'd have gone with them meself," Brewster answered calmly. "But she instructed me to stay and look after you. *I* chose the blokes who went with her, no one else. Prize fighters they used to be, and now they're fists for hire, but once you buy them, they stay bought."

Excellent, I thought wryly. I assumed he'd recruited Denis's best men—I saw much of Denis's hand in this arrangement.

As angry as I was at Brewster for the moment, I knew he'd acted in Donata's and Peter's best interests—at least *he* believed so.

"If any harm comes to her ..." I began.

Brewster gave me an understanding nod. "You can take it out of me hide, guv. I'd deserve no less. But ye won't have to, I promise ye that."

❧

I FORCED MYSELF TO RETURN TO THE QUESTION OF WHAT HAD happened to Mr. Finch, hiring a hackney for our journey to St. Giles so I could speak to Mrs. Brewster. I did not want to use Hagen, Donata's coachman, who was incensed she hadn't woken him, because I did not want to take a fine coach with the viscount's emblem on its doors into the rookeries.

Rain had begun this morning, and St. Giles was a dank and muddy place.

In a warren off Charlotte Street, men were fighting. Not in violent rage, I saw as Brewster and I neared the crowd on foot. The men were sparring, stripped to the waist, bare skin ruddy in the cool rain.

The men and women who'd gathered encouraged them. They'd chosen a favorite, a man with a black beard, who seemed to be the darling of the crowd.

"Go to, Jem!" a man shouted. "Teach 'im a fing or two."

Jem's opponent was a young man, but I saw a wiry strength in him. He had sandy blond hair and light-colored eyes, and he circled Jem, fists raised, with a patient wariness.

They went around and around each other, watching for weakness or a predictability, any telltale sign that the other man was about to strike.

Jem was adept in footwork, shifting his weight one way then the other, difficult to follow. His younger opponent moved less but watched more.

They circled, the crowd encouraging. Jem feinted a punch left, but the young man didn't take the bait and blocked Jem's true right-fisted punch instead. The spectators cried their dismay.

A portly man in a long greatcoat, his tall hat too small for his head, stepped next to us. "A wager, Tommy? How much for Jem to fell him?"

"Two bob," Brewster returned.

The bookmaker looked displeased. "That all? What about you, Captain?"

That he knew who I was did not surprise me—everyone recognized Brewster and his injured cavalryman. The man gave me a look from glittering eyes that said he thought I'd be too prudish to wager on a backstreet match.

"I'll put my stake on the other fellow," I said, indicating the younger man with my walking stick. "What odds?"

"Seven to two against. I warn you, Captain, he's not had much experience."

I studied the young man's form. He didn't have the bulk that Jem did, but weight could be used against one in such a match. He was also careful, watching Jem quietly for an opening, but showed no trepidation about fighting a larger man.

"I'll place a cautious wager of tuppence," I said.

The bookmaker gave me a weary look but nodded. I was certain my fellow would win, but if I made a large bet on him, and he did win, these spectators would not be happy with me. The denizens of St. Giles could not afford to lose much, and I didn't need them tackling me for my winnings.

"The captain wagers tuppence on Mr. Oliver."

I heard laughter. The bookmaker scribbled on a scrap of paper with the stub of a charcoal pencil and handed me the slip.

The men continued to circle. The crowd had moved back to give them space, enjoying the best spectacle of the weekday morning.

Jem threw a punch straight at Mr. Oliver's jaw. It should have sent Oliver to his knees, but Oliver caught the arm coming at him and propelled Jem past him, then spun to knock Jem's feet out from under him.

Jem stumbled, but managed to remain standing. With a snarl of fury, he launched himself back into the fight.

A mistake, I knew. A pugilist should have determination but not anger. Anger made one careless, which was how I'd lost most of my matches when I'd sparred for amusement in my army days.

Jem lunged at Oliver, throwing punch after punch. Oliver blocked most and jabbed back. He couldn't withstand all of Jem's blows, however, and took a few on his shoulder, his jaw, his chest. I saw him move with each hit, lessening the impact by giving with the strike.

Noise surged as the crowd flowed forward, yelling for Jem. The bookmaker and men I took to be his bullies blocked them, giving the two pugilists the chance to finish the match.

Jem sent a massive punch at Oliver's face. Oliver deflected the fist and seized Jem's arm. He quickly stepped behind Jem's leg, bending the unfortunate Jem nearly double with a grappling hold.

The watchers roared their rage, but the bullies held them back. Oliver, with his arm locked around Jem's neck, punched and punched Jem's face. Jem struggled, trying to throw Oliver off, but Oliver stood solidly, planted on legs with plenty of muscle.

The match would only be over if one of the men surrendered or fell upon the ground and could not rise, even with the assistance of the crowd. Otherwise the fight could go on, with grappling holds, eye gouging, biting, or any other means with which a man could disable his opponent.

Jem was not about to surrender. His face was bloody, but his eyes blazed. His teeth came down on Oliver's arm, but Oliver held on, blood running freely on his pale skin.

The two men moved like one creature together, the crowd shifting around them.

Jem clawed at Oliver's arm and finally loosened it. His admirers yelled encouragement.

The next moment, Oliver seized Jem by his beard. Jem howled. Oliver took advantage of this distraction to drive his elbow into Jem's gut.

Jem flailed, struggling to keep to his feet, but he slid on a muddy patch and fell heavily to his knees.

Oliver was upon him, one arm around Jem's throat, a knee between his shoulder blades. They both went down, Oliver on top, while Jem flopped about like a bug. Oliver thunked Jem's head a few times into the pavement, and then Jem went limp, groaning.

Mr. Oliver scrambled to his feet and stood breathing heavily, hands on hips. The bookmaker, who apparently was also the referee, lifted one of Oliver's hands.

"Fight to Mr. Oliver!"

The victor did not gloat. He only nodded and took a linen shirt from one of the bullies, wiping blood from his face before slipping the shirt over his shoulders.

One large man started for Oliver, fists balled. "To hell with you!"

Brewster stepped in front of him. "Now, Mackie, 'e won fair. I was watching. It were an even fight."

Mackie halted, but his face reddened until it was purple. "He ain't one of us."

"Don't mean he don't know how to fight, ye daft beggar. Jem has bad days now and then. This might teach him to use a razor."

Mackie's eyes were round with fury, but he did step back from Brewster's placid stance. I recognized Mackie as one of the men who'd tried to pummel me earlier this year, not far from here. Brewster had run off the assailants.

"Ah, Captain," the bookmaker said next to me. "Your winnings." He slowly and deliberately dropped a few copper coins into my palm. "I believe that is a grand sum of —ninepence."

"Thank you," I said.

The bookmaker shook his head. "I imagine the gentlemen at White's are terrified to see you coming."

"They are indeed," I answered without a smile.

"Another match," Mackie called. "Mr. Oliver against Tommy."

The crowd, which had not disbursed, liked the idea. They

hefted Jem aside and sat him against a wall, where he was tended by two men who looked disappointed in him.

Brewster lifted his hands. "Naw, I leave that to the younger blokes these days."

Cries of, "Come on, Tommy!" "Teach 'im a lesson," and "You owe it to us," rumbled through the crowd.

The bookmaker placed a strong hand on my shoulder, and the bullies hemmed us in. Mackie wore a snarl, showing his blackened and crooked teeth.

Brewster gave the crowd an assessing glance, sighed, and slid off his coat. "Just know, Mackie, that if Mr. Oliver pummels me to death, it's you what has to answer to Em."

I was pleased to see a flicker of uneasiness in Mackie's eyes. "Ye better win then," he muttered.

CHAPTER 8

$\mathcal{A}$s Brewster stripped down, Mr. Oliver removed his
bloodstained shirt, shook it out calmly, and glanced
about for someplace to put it. I offered to hold it for him, and he
handed it to me with a look of gratitude.

The bookmaker hovered next to me. "Now then, Captain,
what's your wager? Are you going to back the interloper or stay
true to your friends?"

I looked to Brewster who peeled off his shirt. Brewster's
fighting days might have been long ago, but his arms were tight
with muscle, his stomach barely showing a paunch. He didn't
posture or stretch, only shook himself, folded his arms and
waited for the match to start.

Oliver moved to face him in the ring that formed around
them.

"What odds on Tommy?" I asked the bookmaker.

"Ooh," the man said softly, breath hot in my ear. "Let's say
four to one against?"

My brows rose. "You have that much faith in him, have you?"

The bookmaker shrugged. "It's me job to calculate odds,
not to have faith. He's twice the young man's age, wouldn't

you say? And I haven't seen your man fight, while I've watched Mr. Oliver take on far bigger toughs than him, and win."

I shrugged. "I must be loyal to my friends. A guinea on Brewster."

The bookmaker's smile flashed. "Done, sir."

I handed over a pound and a shilling and got another scrap of paper in return. I noted when I glanced at it, that it was a piece of a book, and I caught sight of a tattered, bound tome in the bookmaker's pocket. Paper was expensive, but a book could be bought third or fourth hand—or stolen. I wondered what writer of old had had his tome turned into betting slips.

A roar went up from the crowd. Brewster and Oliver circled each other in quick moves, fists at the ready. As before, Mr. Oliver's footwork was simple but careful, his shuffles to the side or backward steps precisely calculated.

The young man had trained under a professional, I could see. Did the bookmaker take him about, proclaiming he was inexperienced, to goad the toughs of each parish into betting against him? No doubt the toughs thought they'd take down the youthful Mr. Oliver in a trice.

Meanwhile, the bookmaker accepted plenty of bets and collected his money. A nice game.

Brewster was not as quick-moving as Oliver, but he placed his feet deliberately, his fists loose as he watched the other man.

Mr. Oliver struck first. He came in with a series of brisk swings which Brewster competently blocked, but in the end, Brewster had to give way, and they circled again.

Brewster's expression remained placid as he watched Oliver with a skilled eye. Oliver was as impassive as Brewster.

At times I accompanied Grenville to Jackson's boxing rooms in Bond Street, where "Gentleman" John Jackson, a former prize fighter famous for winning against the great Daniel Mendoza, taught the upper classes the art of pugilism for a fee. Our matches in Jackson's salon ended when an opponent touched the floor with his knee or hand.

The street matches were far less civilized. Sometimes a man died when his followers threw him back into the fight, no matter that he was clearly unfit to continue.

Jackson's style was similar to Brewster's—calm, watching, waiting for the best opportunity to strike. Oliver did the same. He never lost his composure.

Watching them was akin to observing two very cool-eyed bankers come together to discuss bond exchange rates. The crowd began to howl their displeasure.

Oliver attacked once more while Brewster defended, Brewster sidestepping to deflect blows.

I did not note the exact moment when Brewster ceased his defensive stance. One moment he was using arms and shoulders to keep Oliver from landing blows, the next, he had a strong leg locked around Oliver's, Oliver floundering while Brewster drove a rapid succession of punches into his face and chest.

The crowd's shouts echoed from the narrow canyon of the street.

Oliver managed to defend himself and regain his balance, but Brewster thrust a strong foot behind Oliver's boot. Oliver teetered but caught Brewster a good punch on the jaw.

Brewster's head rocked back, then he quickly recovered, shoved his shoulder and elbow into Oliver's side, and dropped the man onto his back. He stood astride him, resting one giant boot on Oliver's shoulder.

"Ye done, lad?" Brewster asked him.

I saw Oliver note the spectators closing around them, and he nodded.

I knew the young man could have fought on—he was barely winded. He was deciding that surrender was the better part of valor today.

Brewster removed his foot from Oliver's shoulder and gave

him a hand up. "Good fight, lad. Clean yourself up, and I'll stand you a pint."

Oliver, breathless, assented. I handed Oliver his shirt, which he again used as a towel.

"I will join you," I told them. "As soon as I collect my winnings."

I turned to the bookmaker, expecting him to snarl at having to pay out at four to one. That meant five guineas to me, a princely sum.

I found, to my annoyance, and to the fury of the rest of the pack who'd wagered on Brewster, that the bookmaker and his bullies had vanished.

~

WE ADJOURNED TO A PUB IN THE TOTTENHAM COURT ROAD, MR. Oliver with a coat he'd retrieved from a corner to hide his bloody and sweat-stained shirt.

Mr. Oliver's Christian name was Geoffrey, and he'd met the bookmaker, Mr. White, a few months ago, he said, agreeing to fight for a cut of the betting money.

"Not astonished he fled," Oliver remarked after taking a long draught of bitter, wincing as he moved his bruised face. "I've never lost, ye see." He had a London accent, but I wasn't familiar enough with every dialect in the metropolis to place it. "I suppose I'd better make myself scarce, in case your pals try to take their winnings from me."

"I'll keep 'em off ye," Brewster said. "You're a bonny fighter, no mistake. Course, the bookmaker might turn up in the river one morning if he's that much of a trickster. Dangerous game."

"I'd have refused the challenge if I'd known I was fighting Tommy *Brewster*," Oliver said, admiration in his voice. "Serves me right."

Brewster regarded him with modesty. "I haven't fought in years, lad. Why should you know me? Who trained you?"

"Mr. Hayden Shaddock," Oliver said.

"Really?" Brewster's eyes widened. "Old Shaddock." He took a thoughtful sip of ale. "Bugger me. I thought him long gone."

"He's seventy, I think." A smile crossed Oliver's bruised features. "And still knows his business."

"Thought I recognized some of his moves. The sidestep and off-center punch." Brewster demonstrated as best he could sitting down. "Good tactic. Bad for you, though—I saw it coming."

"Caught me unawares. Well fought, Mr. Brewster."

"Naw, call me Tommy. No one calls me mister, except for the captain's wife."

Oliver had been studying me when he wasn't ogling Brewster as I sat at the end of the table, letting the two professionals relive the fight.

"How did you know to wager on me, sir?" Oliver asked me. "Against Bearded Jem?"

I shrugged. "I could see you had form, nerve, and equanimity. Jem was overly confident and a hothead. Odds were good on you."

"Changed your mind on the next fight, though," Brewster said. "Why'd ye wager on *me*?"

"Because I know you to be an excellent pugilist," I answered. "With much experience. Youth is an advantage, but experience, in my ... experience ... usually trumps good but unseasoned training."

Oliver found my explanation reasonable. "Shaddock speaks highly of you, sir—er, Tommy. Was sad when you retired."

Brewster waved a negligent hand. "Grew weary of having me face scraped up all the time, and waking up sore. Needed a softer billet. The fighting ring loses its charm after a time."

Oliver nodded, not quite believing.

"How *is* old Shaddock?" Brewster asked him. "And why the devil has he let you wander the streets of London to take up with a disreputable bookmaker?"

"He's been poorly." Oliver looked uncomfortable and took another long swallow of ale. "Truth to tell, he turned us all out a few months ago. Said he was ill, but he's right as rain if you ask me. Scared of something, or someone. But he closed his school and shut up his house."

Brewster listened, troubled. "Maybe I ought to pay him a visit. Friendly like. I know powerful people now, lad. Might be able to help."

Oliver shrugged as though he didn't care one way or another, but I saw relief in his eyes.

"Well, I might have known," came a female voice full of irritation.

I rose to my feet, and Oliver, after a startled look at me, did as well. Brewster remained seated. "Em," he said in a faint voice. "Love."

Ladies didn't enter a taproom, but Mrs. Brewster let no such thing worry her. The others in the pub didn't pay her much mind, except to look amused, from which I concluded she must often storm in here after Brewster.

"Asked you to bring the captain 'round, didn't I?" she said to him. "I walk into the street to see if you're coming, and I'm told you got yourself into a brawling match and then went to a pub, sweet as you please."

"Least I could do," Brewster said without concern. "I knocked the poor lad on his arse, so I had to give him a drink. This is Mr. Oliver—me wife, Mrs. Brewster."

"Pleased to meet you, I'm sure," Mrs. Brewster said, barely giving him a glance. "Sit down, Captain. Waiting on you lot has left me dry, so I'll join you if you don't mind."

~

Mrs. Brewster had no intention of talking about her deceased brother with Mr. Oliver present. She bade the passing barmaid bring her a half pint of ale and sipped it while Brewster and Oliver continued to converse about their fight, pugilism in general, and about Mr. Shaddock in particular. Brewster was worried about him.

"Suppose I'll look him up," he said once our tankards and Mrs. Brewster's glass were drained. "He still in Wapping?"

"That's where I left him," Oliver said, and rose to depart.

I pressed some coins upon him before he went, because much of Oliver's money, except what he'd had in his pockets, had been held by Mr. White.

"You're a soft touch, Captain," Brewster said after Oliver set off and the three of us strolled back toward his rooms. "What's to say he won't meet up with White somewhere outside of London and split the takings?"

Nothing, I knew. But I wanted to give him the benefit of the doubt.

When we reached Brewster's lodgings, Mrs. Brewster asked her husband to fetch them dinner from the tavern at the end of the road. Brewster, to my surprise, walked away without a word.

"Now then, Captain," Mrs. Brewster said she settled me in the front room. "I have some coffee brewed. Give me a tick to warm it up."

I sat idly while she disappeared into her tiny kitchen. The chamber was furnished comfortably, without ostentation, but without meagerness. It was hardly derelict.

Mrs. Brewster brought in the coffee, and then sat down and regarded me closely while I sipped.

"I sent Tommy away because he don't like it when I talk about Jack," she said. "It were Jack's fault, ye see, that I took up with a blackguard that led me to living in a bawdy house. Me mum and dad weren't up to much, but they worked hard, poor souls. There were never enough money, and mum and dad were in the factories all the day long. Jack decided us little 'uns needed to earn our keep, so he sent us out thieving. We had to bring all we got to him, and he'd hoard the lot for himself. I met a man I thought would look after me, so I run off with him to get away from Jack." She spread her hands. "I discovered my mistake too late, but I made more coin working in the bawdy house than I would have at a factory, so it suited me."

I tried to give no reaction while she told me this tragic tale. She spoke matter-of-factly, as though she'd come to terms with her lot long ago.

"What about your sisters?" I asked when she'd finished. "Or brothers?"

"I only had the younger sister." Mrs. Brewster threaded her slim fingers together. "Jack was hard on her—we'd get a beating if we didn't bring home enough every night, but I tried to protect her from him and took her with me when I ran off with the blackguard. Not long after that, Jack vanished from our lives, and we didn't half breathe a sigh of relief. My sister, though, never really recovered from it. She got a factory job and married a man she met there, but she's always been sickly. Lost her children afore they were born."

She trailed off in sadness.

"I'm sorry," I said. "Does she live in London?"

Mrs. Brewster nodded. "I look after her still. She's not much use on her own. Her husband's gone now too."

I took a sip of coffee, uncertain how to respond. "You never saw Jack again after he left home?"

"Once or twice." Mrs. Brewster twisted her fingers more tightly. "He come to ask me for money—what else? Was in a nunnery then, and Ma Campbell's bullies ran 'im off. He threatened his revenge, but he left me alone."

"Is that why he came this time? Revenge?"

"I don't know." Mrs. Brewster wrinkled her brow. "He said I

owed him, and I needed to pay, and he smacked me good and hard across the face. But that's all he got out before Tommy run in and grabbed him. I started shrieking, I was that scared, and then I was afraid Tommy had killed him ..."

She broke off. "Captain, he never meant to. Jack was still breathing when Tommy carried him out down the back stairs. Ye have to find whoever finished the job. I can't live without me Tommy." Her eyes brimmed with tears.

"I will do my utmost," I vowed, trying to put comfort into my voice. "Did Jack say anything else? Perhaps mention a person he was meeting?"

"No, but ..." Mrs. Brewster sniffled. "He was saying the words—*You owe me, Emily, ye little tramp. Give me every penny you got*—but I had the oddest feeling he was thinking of something else the whole time. Like he'd rehearsed what to say. Distracted. Frightened. As though he were glancing over his shoulder."

"Frightened?" I asked. "That's interesting. Frightened of whom?"

"I couldn't say, because nothing ever scared our Jack. Folks were scared of *him*. But he had a wild look in his eyes, desperate." Mrs. Brewster shivered. "I don't like to think of a man who could terrify our Jack."

"The man who could terrify Jack might have killed him," I said.

I'd learned in my life that a bully who'd never been crossed possessed the confidence of an emperor or a rajah of India, until he met a bully even greater than himself. Finch must have encountered such a one.

I wondered if Finch had made this enemy before or after he'd been transported—if he'd been transported at all. I would have to look closely into the history of Mr. Finch.

I agreed with Mrs. Brewster that Tommy would have to be cleared, because I did not want to do without him either. Brewster had become a friend, and I would do no less for him than I would for Grenville or indeed, my own family.

~

BREWSTER RETURNED WITH A JOINT OF BEEF ON A COVERED PLATE. Mrs. Brewster carried it to the kitchen, but I declined her offer to share the meal with them, and took my leave.

Brewster walked out with me. "We ain't destitute, Captain. Ye don't need to fear taking food out of our mouths."

I knew Denis paid his men well. Brewster had also managed to return from our journey to Egypt with a few valuable pieces from our find.

"It was not from charity that I refused. It was the look on your face," I said. "You did not fancy dinner conversation with me. Also I am anxious to return home and see if there has been any word of my wife."

"She's perfectly safe," Brewster said, unoffended.

"I believe you. But I will feel better when I know exactly where she is and when she will return."

Brewster gave me a shrug. I knew that if *his* wife had pulled up and fled, he'd never take the word of one of Denis's thugs that she was fine and well. I could see, however, that Brewster was unmoved by my concern.

He put me into a hackney, and I returned to South Audley Street. There I went 'round to the mews to see what had become of the dog.

John the stable boy proudly led out a golden specimen whose clean fur had been brushed until it shone. The dog's long ears were perked, and his tail waved slowly but eagerly.

"You're a lovely lad," I said, giving his shoulder a sound pat. "You've done well with him, John."

John, whose hair was in far more disarray than the dog's, looked pleased. "Did you give him a name yet, sir?"

"Haven't thought of one. Have you?"

John nodded, his gaze on the dog. "I thought we could call him Oro. It's Spanish. Means gold. Course, coachman says it's daft to name a cur."

"He's not a cur." I patted the dog again, and his tail waved harder. "This is a fine dog from someone's hunting kennel, bred to fetch birds from the marshes. He is lost, or was stolen." I stroked the silky head. "Oro is a good name for him."

"Is he ours now?" John asked, eyes still averted. "Or will you find the gent what lost him?"

Oro seemed pleased to be with us, and I had the sudden desire to present him to Gabriella. She'd like him, I thought.

"Needle in a haystack," I said to John. "If I happen to hear that his owner is looking for him, well and good, but his home is here for now."

John grinned in relief and finally met my gaze. "Thank you, sir."

Oro was already a remarkable beast. He'd made me bring him home and now decide to keep him.

Darkness was falling by the time I left the mews. I washed in my chamber and went down to the dining room, where a single place had been set at the table.

I could only hope Donata and Peter had reached their destination or a safe place to put up for the night. And I hoped she'd break her stubborn silence and send word to me.

I did have a caller as I ate a light supper, my appetite diminished. But it was not Grenville, as I'd expected, but Marcus Lacey.

CHAPTER 9

I shook hands with a man who was close to my age, my height and build, and had the same dark hair and eyes.

While he didn't have my leathery skin earned by years of marching under sun, wind, and rain in all climates in the army, he retained the sunburn he'd acquired in Egypt.

"I thought you were in Norfolk," I said when the greetings were over.

Marcus took a seat at the dining table, and Bartholomew, looking interested, served him a cutlet and wine.

"I was."

"How are they there?" I asked cautiously.

"Wary." Marcus flashed a brief smile. "But growing used to me."

Marcus had been nonplussed at my acceptance of him as my cousin. Donata's man of business continued to check Marcus's bona fides, but so far, I was convinced he was indeed my first cousin on my father's side, and possibly the rightful heir to the Norfolk estate. Those in Norfolk, however, were understandably not as quick to embrace him

"I have had time to learn the house and ride over the farm," Marcus said as we ate. "The renovations your wife has begun are going smoothly."

I did not know the details of the restoration, leaving that to Donata's capable planning and the supervision of Terrence Quinn, an old friend who'd lost an arm in battle and now was my steward.

"Good," I said. "Mrs. Lacey and I will journey there this summer."

"Ah." Marcus finished his cutlet and idly traced designs through the mushroom sauce. "I came to London to speak to you, in truth ..."

Now we came to it.

"About the farm."

A gazed at him, perplexed. I wasn't certain exactly what I wished him to say, but a discussion of cropland was not it.

"What there is of the farm, you mean," I said, lifting my wine glass.

"The north field has been lying fallow, but it could bring in a decent yield," Marcus said. "That is, if we plant it soon—we've already left it a bit late. But it's been in clover for years, and the soil is rich, ready."

I'd had no idea what was in the north field, and I felt a twinge of guilt at my neglect. "What does Mr. Quinn say?"

"Mr. Quinn agrees with me." Marcus laid his fork across the porcelain plate. "So do we plant the field, or not? If the rains are right, we could have a nice crop of barley come harvest. If it's well done, it will bring a good price with the brewers."

I shrugged. "If Mr. Quinn says so, then have him go ahead. I know nothing of farming, I'm sorry to say." I'd spent my life in the army, which meant I'd trampled crops instead of growing them.

"Well, I do." Marcus shot me a look that held more fire. "I

farmed in the wilds of Canada, believe it or not. Challenging, but I did it. Wheat, and sweet corn for the cattle."

"I see," was all I could think of to say. If Marcus was who he claimed, then he had every right to do with the fields what he liked.

"Plant the barley, then," I said. "Terrance is no fool, and he's lived in the area most of his life. Take his advice on all things."

Marcus peered at me. "You decide things quickly, Captain."

"Best way. Saves weeks of pondering and worrying."

"And if you're wrong?"

I waved my hand. "Then I face the consequences. I do not seek to put the blame for my blunders on others."

"A risky way to live."

"That is true, but I do not seem to be able to change my habits."

"Ah," Marcus said, "that explains the fact that you chased and fought me instead of wisely retreating and letting others catch me."

"I must wonder why you, being a Lacey, expected anything less," I said.

Marcus lifted his glass to me. "Touché."

I lifted mine in response then set it down without drinking. "You are expecting me to believe that you made the journey to London from Norfolk solely to ask whether you should plant the north field. A letter would have sufficed."

"An excuse, as you've no doubt deduced." Marcus cast an eye to Bartholomew, who was doing his best to be the perfect, invisible valet.

I followed his gaze. "Bartholomew, you may go. I'll ring if I need you."

Bartholomew let none of his disappointment show as he bowed and glided from the room.

"You may speak freely," I said.

Bartholomew would no doubt be hovering near the door,

but I wanted him there in case Marcus did anything violent. Marcus might have grown impatient in the months of waiting to prove who he was.

No matter what happened in popular melodramas, just because a man turned up and claimed to be the rightful heir, the family didn't simply turn everything over to him without question. Proofs were in order, reliable witnesses sought.

"I wanted to see if we could be friends," Marcus startled me by saying. "I've gone a long while without much family." He spoke slowly, as though choosing his words. "Living with anger grates on a man."

"I well know this," I admitted.

Again we sat in silence, and finished our wine. I rose to lift the bottle and pour more for both of us.

"I apologized to Mr. Brewster for shooting him," Marcus said. "But I never did to you. Because of course, I was aiming for *you*."

"This is an apology?" I asked with a touch of amusement as I trickled red liquid into his glass.

"An attempt at one. You are a better man that I expected, given what I knew about your father. But you are not he, no matter what heinous crimes he committed."

"Fratricide, no less." I upended the bottle and set it on the table. "My father was a selfish, cruel man. He made my mother's life a misery. If it is true that he killed your father, he has no forgiveness from me. Condemn him all you like. I will join you."

Marcus gave me a slow nod. "I suspected you felt so. You have proved to be not like him, and speaking to the inhabitants of Parson's Point, I find that they agree. They much admire you and much loathed your father. I am asking your pardon for confusing the two of you in my mind."

"It is given," I said without heat as I sat down again. "We are friends then?"

Marcus opened his hand. "It is a beginning."

"It is indeed."

There did not seem to be much more to say. We continued to drink wine as we moved to less treacherous conversation—speaking of the repairs to the house and happenings in the village of Parson's Point.

After another half hour, Marcus departed. He refused my offer to put him up here or in my rooms in Grimpen Lane, claiming he'd found lodgings of his own. He had plenty of pride, I saw, like a true Lacey.

As soon as Marcus had gone, Bartholomew approached me with a note from Grenville. He'd invited Donata and me to dine with him and Marianne, four friends together.

"Send my regrets," I told Bartholomew. "We'll attend when her ladyship returns."

Bartholomew, who had begun his career as Grenville's footman, eyed me doubtfully. "Mr. Grenville won't be happy if you don't turn up."

"Mr. Grenville will have to accept it," I answered.

I did not wish to enjoy myself with Grenville while I worried about Donata. I alternately feared for her and raged at her.

To be fair, I'd deserted her at the theatre when I'd wanted to quiz Brewster. She might have looked for me to tell me her plans and carried on when she could not find me. I wondered if an incident after I'd gone had set her off, or if she'd planned to hide Peter as soon as Stanton appeared at the front door in South Audley Street.

I spent a restless night and woke with a headache. Rain was pouring down in the morning, not improving my mood.

Brewster appeared shortly after I finished breakfast.

"I want to discover why Finch came to London," I told him as Bartholomew slid my greatcoat onto my shoulders. "We'll start with wherever he took lodgings and trace him from there."

"Seems fair." Brewster looked on as Bartholomew tried to hand me an umbrella and I declined it. A hardened cavalryman did not fear a bit of rain. "I'll take you to Shaddock, my trainer," Brewster continued. "If you want to know about fighting and how Finch might have been killed, he can tell you."

"I would be happy to meet him." I'd planned to ask Brewster for an introduction to the man for that reason and also because I was interested in the trainer who'd produced a champion like Brewster.

"Begging your pardon, sir," Bartholomew began, a hopeful light in his eyes. "But Matthias and me, we can ask about for tales of this dead man. Find out who he talked to, maybe easier than you can."

He had a point—I had a reputation of working with Runners and magistrates, which might make those in St. Giles reluctant to speak to me, even with the threat of a hovering Brewster.

"St. Giles is a dangerous place," I said in warning.

Bartholomew's smile could be called placating. "I've lived in London all me life, Captain. I know blokes from all corners. Jeremy the footman comes from St. Giles. People will talk to family and their friends quicker than they'll talk to you."

"Lad's right," Brewster said. Rain dripped from his hat to spill on Donata's polished inlaid floor. "Even I'm an outsider in St. Giles, no matter how long I lived there. Em's the one what's known."

"Very well," I told Bartholomew. "But be careful. At any sign of trouble, be wise and flee."

"Depend on it," Bartholomew said gravely.

I slapped on my tall hat. "Keep no secrets from Grenville. Tell him what you're dragging your brother off to do. Also inform him that my cousin Marcus has returned. I'd like the three of us to dine soon, if I can discover where Marcus is billeted." He'd departed without disclosing that fact.

Bartholomew agreed and Brewster and I ascended into the coach Barnstable had hired for me for the day. I wanted Donata's landau to be at her disposal if she returned.

Brewster rode inside with me, sitting in the opposite corner and stretching out his big legs.

"I can find out where your Mr. Lacey is resting," he offered as we started.

"Don't trouble yourself." I glanced out the window as we turned to Mount Street, heading toward Berkeley Square. "He came to discuss improvements to the estate. It will keep."

"That's what he told you, is it?"

I became aware of Brewster's sharp scrutiny. "Yes. Why?"

Brewster's look turned pitying. "He didn't waltz all the way to London to ask you about what walls need shoring up or what fields need plowing. He came because His Nibs sent for him. For a job. Mr. Denis is the one who's putting him up. Oh, not in Curzon Street, but he'd have found Mr. Lacey some decent digs, mark my words."

CHAPTER 10

*B*rewster stopped my hotheaded rush to Denis to demand exactly what he wanted Marcus for. His Nibs' business, Brewster said, and Mr. Denis wouldn't thank me for interfering.

My business when it's my family, I thought but did not say.

I kept myself calm as we headed for St. Giles, though I fumed at both Denis and Marcus. Marcus had said he'd come asking forgiveness, but he hadn't bloody told me the truth about his trip, had he?

Once in St. Giles Brewster began asking in local lodgings whether Finch had stayed there. Bartholomew would be doing the same when he and Matthias could get away, but we might turn up something.

"Would he have even stayed in the area?" I asked after we'd had no luck in three houses that had signs reading "Lodgings for Travelers" in their windows. "If he'd wanted to lie low, would he not choose a district where he and his family were unknown?"

Brewster shrugged. "Finch weren't the brightest burning candle. He fixed on a purpose and didn't consider the danger."

I didn't entirely agree. If Finch was indeed a convict, he would try to hide himself. The penalty for a transported man returning before his sentence was up was death.

We checked more houses but only had shrugs and "mayhaps" from the landlords. Even the liberal sprinkling of coins brought forth no information.

"He could have put up with a 'cquaintance," Brewster said as we went along. "A lady, I mean. Or slept at a nunnery. The abbesses will let a man stay regular if they knows him and if he pays."

"Even an escaped criminal?"

"If he pays enough. Most houses have men meaner than Finch to keep gents tame."

I scanned the crowded street, the brick houses marching in a long, sagging line.

After London's massive fire a hundred and fifty years ago, houses were no longer built in the beautiful old half-timbered style that could still be seen in villages in East Anglia.

Much of St. Giles had been built up since the fire, but its houses were already falling down, making life inside precarious. The lanes south of Great Russell Street were narrow and filthy, the stench overpowering. St. Giles was where the last Great Plague of London had begun.

"Which are the nunneries?" I asked Brewster, looking down the lane. "They don't post signs."

"Throw a brick," Brewster grunted. "The ladies inside won't peach on their best-paying customers, mind. But Em can ask. She's mates with many of them still."

Before I could comment on this, the door of a house opened to disgorge Lamont Quimby, Runner for Sir Montague Harris.

He saw me and stopped short, then he smiled and tipped his hat. "Good morning, Captain. I see you have a similar idea. Discover who the dead gent resided with. Any luck?"

"No," I had to say.

Brewster faded a step behind me, grim and silent.

"Alas, nor I. A Runner is not welcome in these streets. But I have discovered a few things. Shall we find a public house or tavern that will give us coffee—or ale if your man prefers?"

My "man" said nothing. I acquiesced, and Mr. Quimby and I walked to High Holborn, Brewster lumbering behind.

I expected Brewster to vanish into the mist, but he was still with us when we entered a public house already doing a lively business. I asked for coffee and was given an indifferent brew, but I drank it, grateful for the bitter taste to jar my senses.

Quimby asked Brewster to join us at our table, and he did, to my surprise. Quimby took coffee as well, and Brewster had a mug of ale.

"The coroner examined the body yesterday," Mr. Quimby said after a fastidious sip. "You might be astonished to learn, as I was, that the cause of death was not the beating."

Brewster stopped in the act of taking his first drink. He coughed and set down his tankard. "It weren't?"

"No, sir." Quimby met Brewster's gaze. "Mr. Jack Finch was stabbed to death."

Our reactions must have been satisfying. Brewster's jaw went slack, and I felt my own mouth hanging open. The twinkle in Quimby's eyes betrayed his enjoyment.

"S'truth," Brewster said. He sat back with a thump and wiped a hand over his face.

"He *had* been beaten rather thoroughly," Quimby went on. "A lesser man might have died of those wounds, but this gent was tough enough to survive them."

"I saw no stab marks," I said, blinking. "No concentration of blood."

"Not revealed until the coroner did his examination. Had to wash away many layers of dirt to find the wound, and his clothes concealed it well. Upward thrust through the ribs. Very professional. Very little bleeding. A trained man who knew exactly where to strike to kill." Quimby darted Brewster an amused look. "That lets you out, Mr. Brewster."

Brewster's brows lowered. "How the devil do you figure that?"

Quimby took another calm sip of coffee. "You are well known to the magistrates, Mr. Brewster. You have, as we say, form. But yours is a reputation for thievery and bare-knuckle fighting and as a bone cracker. Not knifing and assassination. For the last ten years, you've been quiet and well behaved, no longer of interest to the Runners. Also very careful. They could never fit you up for anything."

"Well." Brewster let out a heavy breath.

"Your fists are your usual weapons," Quimby said. "And by the state of your hands, you've been using them."

Brewster's jaw tightened and he slid his hands to his lap. "Course I did. Yesterday. Fought a young bloke what wants to be a pugilist. Laid him out. He's not a bad lad, but he has more to learn."

"Indeed, the streets of St. Giles today are rife with tales of your prowess. You are well respected."

"Aye, well." Brewster lifted his ale with an air of relief.

I knew Quimby didn't believe for a moment that the abrasions on Brewster's knuckles came from the fight with young Mr. Oliver alone. But he said nothing.

"How did you discover the man's identity?" I asked, trying to sound offhand.

Quimby looked wise. "We're sent reports when prisoners escape. Takes a bit to get to us, but we have descriptions and drawings. One fit our dead man exactly—Mr. Jack Finch, sent down for robbery with violence five years past."

"I see," I made myself say.

"But you must have known his name," Quimby responded in his quiet way. "We looked for his family and found one Emily

Finch, who is listed in the church of St. Giles-in-the-Fields' register as having married one Thomas Brewster."

Brewster gave him a resigned nod.

"The mark of fists as large as yours on Mr. Finch were plain," Quimby went on. "But there were marks of a smaller hand, as you saw. Did you attack him alongside a second man, Mr. Brewster? And who was he?"

"S'truth," Brewster whispered again, sweat beading his brow.

"You do not have to answer," I said quickly.

"It don't matter." Brewster wrapped his reddened hands around his tankard. "He already knows, and I guess he'll get the evidence if he wants it. I did fight with the bloke. Finchie gave me a good run, but in the end, I had him on the floor. As I told the captain here, I stashed him in that house and went to fetch money to make him go away. When I returned, he were dead. I never saw a second man, never saw no knife. I didn't look. I knew Finch were dead, and I locked the door and left him there. That is God's honest truth."

His words rang with sincerity. The fear on his face spoke of it too.

"Thank you," Quimby said. "For now, I will take that as the sequence of events. Between the time you left him and your return, a second man turned up and stabbed Mr. Finch to death. Or perhaps two men—one to hold him if he tried to defend himself, and one to kill him. Now, I couldn't tell by the signs how many men stood in that room—there were far too many boot prints, trampled over each other and smeared. Also the paw prints of a dog outside the door. The place was a mess of mud, and it's been raining this week."

Quimby took another sip of coffee and fell silent.

"How long did it take you to fetch the money?" I asked Brewster.

Brewster studied a beam on the ceiling. "Reckon half an hour? Maybe three-quarters? I weren't looking at any clock."

"Plenty of time," Quimby said cheerfully. "Now, Mr. Brewster, tell me who could have wanted to kill Mr. Finch."

"Any cove what met him."

"I am gathering that. But what about his family? His enemies?"

Brewster shook his head and repeated what he'd told me—that Mrs. Brewster hadn't seen him in years and that she and her sister had been happy to see the back of him.

"And where is her sister?"

"In St. Giles," Brewster said. "Not far from our rooms. Em looks after her."

"Hmm," Quimby said. "Finch might have gone to see your wife's sister first."

"Mayhap," Brewster said. "But Em was head of the family, like. Everyone went to her."

"Even so. I would like to speak to her sister, when it is convenient."

Brewster sent him a dark glance. "She's not a well woman."

"I will not have to worry her long," Quimby said. "We can call upon your wife along the way. I have no intention of browbeating her, only asking a question or two."

Brewster scowled but nodded.

Quimby continued to enjoy his coffee, in no hurry to leave. "I am trying to discover not only Mr. Finch's history but to follow his path after he was condemned. He spent time in the hulks in Sheppey before being shipped to the penal colony in Van Diemen's Land. Sending for information from the Antipodes will take some time, but the guards at the hulks might be worth speaking to. There's a merchant captain who docks near there that we suspect makes arrangements to help prisoners leave their captivity in New South Wales when they're tired of it. I'll be heading to Sheppey in the morning."

Quimby spoke optimistically about what might be a damp

and joyless journey, but I saw why Sir Montague had given him this case. He was nothing if not dogged.

"Now then, Mr. Brewster." Mr. Quimby drained the last drops from his cup. "Shall we pay a visit to your sister-in-law?"

～

MRS. BREWSTER, AS EXPECTED, WAS LESS THAN HAPPY TO SEE HER husband bring home a Runner, and certainly did not want to lead him to her sister.

Quimby spoke quietly to Mrs. Brewster, at his most reassuring. "I wish only to ask a question or two. You may attend, as well as your husband and the captain."

Mrs. Brewster was not put at her ease, but seemed thankful that I was coming along. I suppose she believed I could keep Mr. Quimby curbed.

Martha Cowper, nee Finch, lived a few streets from the Brewsters, in a tiny room above a muddy courtyard. She received us in a room with comfortable if not elegant furnishings—I saw that Brewster's income must fund her as well.

Mrs. Cowper was as thin as her sister, but her slenderness was frail rather than wiry. She did not rise from her chair near the fire as Mrs. Brewster led us in, having first come up to warn the lady.

"He come here," Mrs. Cowper said to Quimby. Her eyes held defiance. "Jack were after money, as usual. He took all I had." She gestured to a box on the mantel. I moved to it and opened it, finding in it nothing but dust.

"I'm sorry for that," Quimby told her, his voice gentle. "Did you see anyone following him? Did he tell you he was worried about any particular person?"

Mrs. Cowper shook her head. Her hair was the same shade of brown as Emily Brewster's, but it was lank, pulled into a sloppy knot under her cap. "I can't rise from this chair to be looking much out the window," she said with a frown. "And he didn't say nothing to me. Only grabbed the money and was gone. Worth it to be rid of him."

She sank back and closed her eyes.

Mrs. Brewster shooed us out. She remained with her sister while we three gentlemen descended to the street.

"I doubt very much she skulked after Mr. Finch and stuck a knife into him," I told Quimby. "She is obviously ill."

Quimby nodded. "Yes, poor thing. I was not so much in search of a suspect, Captain, but interested in learning more about Finch. She did confirm that he was enough of a bully to rob from his ailing sister. Such a man will not endear himself to many."

"True enough," Brewster grunted.

"Well." Quimby adjusted his hat against the rain that had begun to come down again. "I'll do one more canvass of the area, then return home to prepare for my journey. If you discover Mr. Finch's lodgings or a person who saw him, you will send word to Sir Montague, will you not?"

I assured him I would. Not much point in refusing.

Once we parted from Quimby, Brewster said, "Let the Robin keep poking around St. Giles and get his beak broke. I'm off to find old Shaddock."

I agreed we could probably do no more here. Matthias and Bartholomew might have more luck.

A hackney took us from St. Giles to the river and east along this to Wapping. Nearby, at the office of the Thames River Police, my friend Peter Thompson looked into thefts and other crimes involving the huge merchantmen that docked along the Thames.

Bare masts rose black against the white-gray sky, gulls calling as they circled, looking for food among the flotsam.

Several streets from the river, Brewster bade our driver stop before a small house sandwiched between others exactly like it.

He pounded on the door, which was opened by a stout woman with allover gray hair and a hard expression.

That expression turned to amazement. "Good Lord, it's Tommy Brewster. What you want, after all these years?"

Brewster gave the woman a nod. "He in?"

Her hazel eyes widened. "That all you have to say? After all this time? Yes, he's in, all right. In the back, staring morosely at his garden. I'm Mrs. Shaddock, dear," she said, shifting her gaze to me. "Are you a fighter? That how you injured yourself?"

I removed my hat. "Captain Gabriel Lacey, at your service. The injury is from the Peninsular War."

Mrs. Shaddock's face softened. "Poor lamb. It's cruel the young men who came back without an arm or leg, or too sick to work. And the price of grain going up so high a body can't afford a piece of bread to feed himself. No wonder there's so many riots."

"Indeed," was all I could think of to say. The hardship of those who had little turned to frustration, which was eking out in unrest, stirred by men like Henry Hunt and others.

"Well, as I said, he's in the back," Mrs. Shaddock said. "Willing the Lord to slow down the rain so he can go out and get his hands all mucky. *Stick with fighting, love,* I tell him. *You're a much better pugilist than you are a gardener.* But a man must have his hobby."

She took my hat and greatcoat, shaking them off before she hung them beside the fire to dry.

I followed Brewster through a narrow passage to a room at the back that ran the width of the house.

Large windows gave onto a tiny walled garden softened with ivy and rows of green. A large patch of wet loam gathered rain in the middle. A number of birds from sparrows to wrens to robins were hopping about this patch, pecking the upturned earth.

"They're stealing all me seed," a small, elderly man spluttered, glaring out the window. He rapped on the glass. "Go on. Get out of it!"

A few of the birds fluttered away but returned to probing the dirt, the rain not bothering them one whit.

"Greedy little buggers." The man growled and turned from the window. "Oh, it's you, is it, Tommy?" His eyes held trepidation, though he attempted to hide it. "Mrs. Shaddock, bring in ale for our guests. Don't dawdle, my girl."

"I'm already bringing it." Mrs. Shaddock rustled in, bearing a tray, an earthen jug, and four tankards. "Keep your britches on, Mr. S. There now, Captain. You'll find it cool and refreshing."

She set down the tray and poured out ale for each of us and one for herself.

"It's a reunion," she said raising her glass. "With new friends. Here's to you, Tommy, and to Captain Lacey. What do you think, Mr. S? The captain here fought Boney the Bastard."

"Not personally," I said.

"Course not." Mrs. Shaddock flashed me a grin, letting a pretty young woman peek out from behind the gray hair and faded skin.

"Eh?" Shaddock peered at me.

What struck me was how small Mr. Shaddock was. His body was bent with age—I put him about seventy—but he had never been large.

I'd been picturing a giant of a man like Brewster himself, or powerful and sinewy like Jackson. But Shaddock was tiny. His wife topped him by a foot and was twice his girth.

Shaddock's hands bore scars that showed they'd been broken and healed, I guessed several times in his life. I found myself wanting to compare the small prints on Finch's neck to Shaddock's fists.

But Shaddock was elderly, and I doubted he would have had the strength to go against a big man like Finch. Even already half broken by Brewster, Finch could have fought back. And if

Finch had been unconscious when Shaddock found him, why bother punching him with such great force?

I *could* imagine Shaddock getting under Finch's reach and stabbing him. Shaddock's movements were quick and sure, not the slow shuffle of many men his age.

Shaddock lifted his glass to us. "Your health, Captain." After we drank, he said, "Why'd you look me up, Tommy? Thinking of returning to the game?" He did not look hopeful.

"Saw young Geoffrey Oliver in town," Brewster said. "Scrapped with him. He's got promise."

"Aye, a bonny fighter is Geoff." Shaddock looked wistful. "Were I a younger man, I'd take him and show him off all over. As it is, he's had to find his own way, poor lad."

"He was with a bookmaker, an unscrupulous one," I said. "Though I believe that partnership is now dissolved."

"Bastard ran off with the money, did he?" Shaddock returned his gaze to the window. "Like a magpie, he was. Wanted everything shiny for himself."

"You know him?" I asked.

Mrs. Shaddock answered for him. "Mr. White. Can't be his real name. He comes round wanting Mr. S. to train lads to stage their fights, choose who wins and loses, so Mr. White can make a packet. Says he'll share the punters' money with us—a tiny percentage, you understand. Lion's share goes to him for arranging it."

"One reason prize fighting was made illegal," Brewster put in.

The other was that the combatants sometimes died or were crippled for life, and also because young gentlemen ruined themselves completely with the wagering. Not that this had made the wagering cease.

"Beggars like White ruin the sport," Shaddock spluttered, then he brightened. "Why don't you take Oliver in hand,

Tommy? Show him off, let him come into his own as he deserves."

Brewster considered this for the span of a heartbeat. "Already have a job." He jerked his thumb at me. "Looking after this one."

Shaddock scowled. "Working for a criminal, you mean. You were one of me best, lad. What happened to ye?"

Brewster did not look abashed. "Mr. Denis gave me work when no one else would bother. If not for him, I'd a' seen the gallows a long time ago. Don't need the thieving when I have a nice lot of cash to take home to me wife. All I have to do now is keep the captain's bones whole—which ain't as easy as it sounds, believe me."

Shaddock pinned him with a severe gaze. "Thieving's what ruined you in the first place. Ye could have made us all a pile with me exhibiting you. You could have your own training school now or set up like Jackson to teach moves to the toffs. 'Gentleman,' my arse. He ain't no more a gentleman than me or you."

"That's as may be, but I have a wife to keep and no wish to grub for me living."

Shaddock deflated. "Aye, well, it's an old argument, and a reason we fell out in the first place. I'm happy ye came back to me. We're too old for all this now. Friends again?"

"'Course." Brewster's eyes flickered, as though he wanted to say more, but he shook the hand Shaddock offered him. "You might have had the right of it, but nothing for it."

"You were never a patient lad," Shaddock said. "Talented, but restless. Ah well, I have wisdom now, but you see me reduced to chasing the crafty birds out of my seeds. I'm trying to bring up some summer squash and runner beans so Mrs. S. don't have to run all the way to the market every day. She's a dab hand with the cooking, is Mrs. S."

Mrs. S. flushed. "Go on with ye now."

They were comfortable with each other, enviably so. I wondered whether Donata and I would ever be as they were.

The thought reminded me of Donata's flight, and my anger and fear came at me all over again.

"I wanted to meet you not only for Brewster's sake," I said, trying to keep to the matter at hand. "But to ask you a theoretical question. Could an untrained man—or woman—bring down a larger man? Enough to drive a knife into him?"

"Certainly he could, if that untrained man was wily enough," Shaddock answered. "You don't have to be large to win a fight, just strong, fast, and clever. It's how Danny Mendoza, a middleweight, won the championship for heavyweights. I had the devil of a time teaching Tommy not to rely on his size." He took a drink of ale. "Why? Who's had a knife driven into him?"

"Me wife's brother," Brewster said. "Jack Finch."

I had let my eye stray out the window to the space of garden. Shaddock's skill—despite Mrs. Shaddock's disparagement—showed in what looked like rows of lettuce or other greens, neatly hoed, next to the straight furrows of wet earth where the birds happily feasted.

I became aware of a heavy silence behind me. I turned to see both Shaddocks staring at Brewster. Shaddock's face was such a deep shade of gray I sprang forward to catch him and lower him into a chair.

Mrs. Shaddock rushed from the room, but she was back in an instant with a glass of brandy she shoved under her husband's nose.

Brewster remained firmly planted where he'd been, his eyes narrowing. "So, you knew Finchie, did ye? What was he to you that his passing gives ye such a jolt?"

CHAPTER 11

"ord help me. Jack Finch." Shaddock wheezed and took another gulp of brandy. "Dead and gone. Thank the Lord. An answer to a prayer, that."

"What you on about?" Brewster demanded. "Ye never told me ye knew 'im."

Mrs. Shaddock stood straight, anger in her eyes. "We didn't —not when you was around. Finchie came later. Threatening us. Wanting money. Blackmailing, cheating, thug he was. Dead, is he? Happy to hear it."

"Everyone knew Finch, Captain," Shaddock said, his voice faint. "He had bookmakers under his thumb, trainers and fighters terrified. For years, when he'd show up at a match, we knew there'd be trouble. Like Mr. White, he'd demand for us to throw fights, but with Mr. White it's a choice—he smiles and walks away if you won't. Finchie would have the lads waylaid and beaten until we learned our lesson. Or he'd have us start the fights in the streets and then demand we pay more not to have the law come down on us. You know only exhibition fighting is legal now, Captain, but we must make ends meet. Finchie gave the Watch and Runners backhanders to arrest those he accused and let others go. Shared the conviction money with them."

Shaddock shrank into himself, smaller than ever.

"If he was that awful, it's curious I'd never heard of the man," I mused. "I attend pugilist matches, but have never noticed him."

"You attend with gentlemen," Shaddock corrected me. "Your lot have matches with rules and referees. So very polite. It's different when you're taking your lads around trying to make a living. We hope they move up to the Fancy, where a gentleman might sponsor them, but mostly, it's matches wherever we can get away with them." He drew a thin breath. "In any case, Finchie up and disappeared about five year ago. We hoped that was the last we'd see of him. And now he's dead. Thanks be to God." It was a fervent prayer.

"Five years ago, I was being invalided out of the army," I said. "And apparently Finch was arrested and sent to the hulks to await transportation. Which also explains why I never heard about him. I wonder if he tried to blackmail the wrong man."

"A toff, maybe," Brewster suggested. "Or a Runner what didn't like being told what to do."

I could imagine Pomeroy cheerfully taking Finch's money for looking the other way, and then arresting Finch in the next breath. Spendlove would arrest Finch on the spot for simply offering him a bribe. Perhaps Spendlove got wind of Finch's corruption and swooped in for the kill.

"He's dead and gone now," Brewster said, reaching down to squeeze Shaddock's shoulder with a gentle hand. "Rest easy, old friend."

"Let's hope his secrets died with him." Shaddock gulped more brandy, and he wouldn't tell us what he meant.

∾

We left the Shaddocks—Mrs. Shaddock hovering over her shocked husband—and rolled back toward town.

"I'm off to Bow Street," I said to Brewster as the carriage rattled through Temple Bar to the Strand. "You might wish to absent yourself."

Brewster looked aggrieved and asked to be dropped at Covent Garden and the marketplace. Least he could do was bring poor Em the shopping, he said.

"Can you find out for me where my cousin Marcus is staying?" I asked him as he stepped down from the hackney. "Denis notwithstanding, I'd like to be able to put my hands on him if need be."

Brewster sent me a pained look but nodded. "I'll turn him up." He put a large hand on the open carriage door, ignoring the impatience of the coachman. "*You* stay whole and don't go wandering off on your own. Remember who gets trounced if you're hurt." He slammed the door and backed away. "Cor, I'm a bleeding nanny," I heard him mutter before the coach rumbled on.

The Bow Street magistrate's house, a tall edifice near the bulk of Covent Garden Theatre, was crowded, as usual, with the arrested men and women of the night waiting to see the magistrate.

Pomeroy was in—very much so. I saw as I ducked inside past thieves and game girls that he had two men by the backs of their necks and was hauling them toward the courtroom.

The doors of this chamber were open, the room within crammed with those standing before the magistrate and those watching or waiting their turn. The magistrate sat on his dais to hand out quick judgments—sentences for lesser crimes or remanding those committing the greater—robbery, murder—to Newgate to wait for trial.

"These two decided to beat down a young lady and have their way with her," Pomeroy roared to me as he passed. "On *my* patch. Said they thought she were a game girl. As though that would make a difference to me. They'll have the noose when I'm done with them."

The sorry specimens, still half drunk, looked pathetic and small in Pomeroy's large hands. I climbed the stairs to Pomeroy's room to wait until the magistrate decided the men's fates. Thankfully, I did not see Spendlove, and I hoped that Runner was far across the country pursuing villains.

Timothy Spendlove was determined to find a way to get his hooks into me, in order to use me to destroy Denis. These days, however, I believed he'd be happy to see me in the dock for my own sake. I'd outmaneuvered him so far, but Spendlove was a ruthless man.

Pomeroy returned in a surprisingly short time. "They're off to Newgate, the pair of them," he said in the hearty voice with which he'd dressed down soldiers during the Peninsular War. "Don't feel too sorry for them, Captain. You didn't see the girl they had at. She might live, or she might die, and might never walk again if she does live." He traded his jovial expression for one of frightening grimness. "They might not last until their trials. Even hardened murderers don't like them as hurt little girls. I leave the lads to their fate. Now then, Captain, what ye want?"

"Jack Finch."

"Oh, yes?" Pomeroy sat behind his desk with a thump. "I'll never forgive you for taking that murder to another magistrate's house, Captain. After all we've been through together. Should be *my* conviction, not Quimby's. The Governess we call him, because he's so prim and proper."

"He seems competent," I said.

"Oh, he is that," Pomeroy admitted grudgingly. "I complained to my magistrate, but he says let the Governess investigate. But I'm still hurt."

"I apologize, Sergeant, but if I'd come to you, I'd even now be trying to spring Brewster from Newgate. Mr. Quimby at least had the decency to ascertain Brewster didn't do it, instead of immediately arresting him."

"It's by no means certain he didn't do it." Pomeroy's cheerfulness returned. "I've read what Quimby so carefully wrote up about the crime. All he's decided is the man were killed by a knife, not the beating, which Mr. Brewster admits he did do. Don't mean Mr. Brewster didn't stick the knife into Finch when he came back, and then ran off and told you the man had been murdered. Mr. Brewster has a colorful past. And present."

I knew full well Pomeroy had a point. "Precisely why I did not seek you," I said.

Pomeroy folded his hands on his desk, the backs of them covered with pale hair. "I bang up those who *might* have done a crime because they so often *have* done it. Once they're in Newgate, I know they're safely stashed while I collect the evidence to convict. Don't have to worry about them running off out of the country. If I find as I investigate that they *didn't* do it, or I lay my hands on the right bloke, then I let the innocent man go." He gave me a comfortable nod.

"'Course, those I arrest are never entirely innocent," he continued. "I only lock up a bad man what's done *something*. If I can get them on the crime in question, well and good. If I can't find anyone else what done it or any reason they should be let off, well then, I know I ain't sending a good man to the gallows. They're paying for something else as bad they done in the past. I've never thrown a true innocent to the wolves."

Justice according to Milton Pomeroy. I could see his logic, and also his flaws, but decided not to argue.

"Do you know much about Finch?" I asked. "He apparently was terrorizing street fighters while you and I were battling in Portugal and Spain, and was convicted five years ago, according to Mr. Quimby."

"Oh, aye. I started asking about him as soon as I got word

you were interested in his death. Mr. Spendlove had been after him a long time, even before he became a Runner. Spendlove learned his trade chasing the man, you might say. Finch was a famous pugilist in his own time, a heavyweight and a champion. But a right bastard, by all accounts. Let him be dead, and give a medal to whoever killed him, is the consensus."

"I would," I said. "But I don't want Brewster to be sacrificed for the crime."

Pomeroy looked aggrieved. "You are softhearted for a hard criminal, Captain. Will get you killed one day. Spendlove finally got to Finch in the end. He were tried for robbery with violence —don't know whether that were the actual crime he were doing when Spendlove nicked him, but that's what he stood trial for. Judge couldn't be convinced to hang him, but Finch did get sent off to the hulks and then Van Diemen's Land to work himself to death." Pomeroy shuddered. "Hanging's quicker and kinder, if you ask me. Spendlove says judge was in Finch's pay, or at least in fear of him. He sentenced transportation to hard labor right quick, soon as the jury returned. Good riddance, sounds like."

"And yet, he turned up again," I said.

Pomeroy laced his hands behind his head. "Wager he extorted his way back, threatening and bullying. But now he's dead. Ah, well. Don't have to worry about him hurting anyone again."

"Do you have any idea who could have killed him?" I persisted. "Apart from Brewster, I mean."

"Who's to say? Bloke from the prison who escaped with him? His fellow passengers on his journey back? One of his victims in London? His sisters? His woman, if he had one?" Pomeroy studied the ceiling as he ran through the list. "I like the idea of his woman. Ladies can always be relied upon to go after a man they think has betrayed them. Or maybe a pugilist forced to throw a match because of him. Fighters don't like to pretend they ain't the best."

"A wide field then," I said glumly.

"Your Mr. Quimby will narrow that down." Pomeroy propped his feet on his desk, his muddy boots making short work of the papers there. "If I find anything, I might tell ya, or I might keep it to meself. If I discover the man what done it first, the reward is mine. If Governess Quimby finds him, then …" He spread his hands. "I will concede the contest. And you can stand me several pints to make it up to me."

~

THE HACKNEY HAD WAITED FOR ME AT THE CORNER, THE DRIVER passing the time with coachmen from other hired hacks. I asked him to take me to Berkeley Square.

I ought to have been relieved I was journeying to a more civilized part of town, but I'd learned in my brief years in London that Mayfair was only civilized in its veneer. The beautiful mansions that rose along Piccadilly and the streets leading to the stately squares held plenty of corruption and men capable of violence.

By the time I reached Lady Aline's in the middle of Berkeley Square, it was one in the afternoon.

The lady was awake, her maid told me, when I plied the door knocker, and she would inquire whether she would see me. But after I waited about a quarter of an hour in a reception room, sipping port Lady Aline kept stocked for gentlemen callers, the maid returned with a note for me.

I am hardly fit to be seen, dear boy. But if you call this evening, you can take me to the theatre. Turn up precisely at eight. A

At eight pm, dressed in my finest, I duly arrived and handed Lady Aline Carrington, a stout woman of fifty-five and proud of her spinster status, into Donata's landau. I took the seat across from her, facing rearward as was polite. Lady Aline's gowns were made to flatter her large figure, the sumptuous velvets and fluttering silk drawing the eye from her ample features, and tonight she was resplendent in silver and green.

This lady, left very wealthy by a wise father and given use of the Berkeley Square house by her brother, a marquis, had proposals every Season by smitten suitors, but she turned them all down.

"I am well provided for," Lady Aline would say. "And my brother is kind to me. Why do I need the bother of a husband?"

"You'll be wanting to know about Donata," Aline said as we rolled off toward Covent Garden, the feathers in her headdress waving. "Well, I shall tell you all, but after we arrive."

She turned to gossip about the *ton*, and I had to retain my composure and let her chatter.

It took some time to make our way through Piccadilly and Leicester Square to Long Acre and then to the theatre, and I chafed at every delay. Once we arrived, I handed Lady Aline out of the coach, and we ascended through the crowd to Donata's box.

We found it already occupied by Lucius Grenville, and with him, Marianne Simmons, resplendent in the best Parisian finery.

"Ah, you've brought him." Grenville rose to greet us, flushed with eagerness as he shook my hand. "Forgive the underhanded method, but you are confounded difficult to run to ground." He slid his arm around Marianne, who'd risen beside him, and every lorgnette in the theatre flashed our way. "Do tell me everything, and I'll reveal what I have found out myself."

CHAPTER 12

I hid my impatience as I escorted Lady Aline to her seat in the box as the act onstage—a man and woman singing popular songs—finished and retired to applause.

Marianne was looking particularly well. Her gown of russet silk was nowhere near matronly, but neither was Lady Aline's deep green velvet.

It was not the clothes that changed Marianne, I decided, studying her, it was her countenance. *Raging good health,* Grenville had said. Marianne's face bore a soft flush, and the lines about her eyes had relaxed.

Dared I believe that Marianne Simmons, former actress of the Drury Lane company and impoverished fellow inmate of my old lodgings, looked happy?

The main entertainment, an opera, began. It was *Marriage of Figaro,* a lively piece I enjoyed. I preferred comic operas to tragic ones, as I had seen far too much of life to want to sit through the more morose operas and plays. Those had been written for kings and queens who'd known only softness. But no sooner had the overture faded than Lady Aline planted a large elbow in my ribs.

"The Prince Regent is here," she said, peering at a box above the stage. "Look how he glares at you, Grenville. Jealousy, no more. Ungrateful wretch—after all you and Captain Lacey did for him. He's with the awful Lady Conyngham. Trumped up commoner, can't speak below a screech. The man can barely move—I can't think what they can possibly get up to."

Grenville's lorgnette came up, but he pointedly did not train it on the Regent. While on the stage, Suzanna tried on her bridal gear and Figaro measured his chamber for his wedding bed, Grenville and Lady Aline dissected the audience. Marianne ignored them and watched the action on the stage with a critical eye.

"Had a chat today with Pierce Egan," Grenville said presently, as he lowered the glass. "You remember him, Lacey—met him at Astley Close during the regimental affair."

Of course, I remembered. I'd met Donata for the first time at the house of Lord Fortescue in Kent. I'd liked Mr. Egan, who'd come to write about the exhibition fight of a Mr. Sharpe, famous pugilist of the day.

I'd knocked Donata's husband on his backside at that match. A thoroughly satisfying afternoon.

"Indeed," was my only reply.

"Egan has stories about Jack Finch in his pugilist days," Grenville continued. "Finch was brutal, he said. Men had to be carried away, half dead, when he finished with him."

I nodded. "From what I have learned of Finch, I am hardly astonished."

"Indeed, Egan was quite disgusted with him, and he admires almost every fighting man. But he did tell me a story which I thought might interest you."

The audience burst into laughter at various characters onstage hiding behind pieces of furniture. I glanced at the antics but Grenville had caught my attention. "Go on."

"Egan was invited to a house in Kent last autumn—a gentleman's estate on the coast. While there, a pugilist match was got up among the convicts from hulks at Sheppey."

"Good Lord." Laughter surged below when the count, with a loud bellow, leapt out from hiding. "This gentleman took Mr. Egan to the hulks?"

There was a naval shipyard on the Isle of Sheppey, at the mouth of the Thames. I could not imagine the officers in charge letting in a party of pleasure-seeking gentry to gape at the convicts. Such things were done in prisons on land—in fact, in some places, gentlemen paid to watch women stripped to the waist and caned—but hulks were full of hard villains, and few wanted to risk their escape.

"Not at all," Grenville said. "The prisoners were brought to the gentleman's house for the fight and then went right back— overseen by the hulks' governor or some of the guards—Egan didn't know which. In the garden of this gentleman's home, they did battle with each other for the entertainment of the gentlemen and ladies. For the wagering on as well. Lengthy bouts, with one poor fellow nearly dying. He was whisked away and out of sight before Egan could speak to him. Egan said that when these fighters were led away, all had had at least one bone broken, and they were so bruised and battered he could scarce tell one from the other."

I listened in growing disquiet, and Marianne spoke before I could.

"Like trained dogs," she said, her lip curling. "That's the gentry for you."

Lady Aline fanned herself, her repugnance evident. "You'd be horrified at what some folks get up to, my dear. All in the name of enjoyment."

"Exactly," Grenville said. "Cock fighting—that's how Egan put it. Some of the prisoners were all for it, but he could see that others had been dragged into the fights against their will. But what could they do? The gentleman of the house saw nothing wrong with it. After all, they were only criminals who'd escaped the noose."

I remembered Pomeroy's words from this afternoon when he expressed no worry about a man being hanged for a crime he didn't commit—*They're paying for something else as bad they done in the past.*

"Did Egan report this when he returned?" I asked.

Grenville nodded. "They swore him to secrecy, but Egan is a journalist first and foremost. He did write about it, but the newspapers that usually print his pieces refused the story. He also sent a letter to a magistrate regarding the bouts, and the next day was waylaid by toughs and barely escaped. He's gone back to writing his books, he said, keeping his head down. This happened a sixmonth ago, but when I asked him about Jack Finch, it reminded him, and he told me the curious tale. And now I've told you."

I sat back, chilled. Gentlemen staging exhibition matches for the entertainment of guests was not unusual, but I'd not heard of convicted men brought out of prison for sport. I knew that it was not uncommon for people to pay to gape at the madmen of Bedlam hospital, or the detained prisoners in Coldbath Fields or Milbank, including the aforementioned chance to observe women being flogged.

As distasteful as I found the act of watching human misery for diversion, the prisons themselves admitted the watchers, controlled them, and collected the fee for the upkeep of the place. The gentleman who'd hired out the men from the hulks must be very sure of himself to bring the prisoners to his home.

I was surprised he'd let Egan in on the secret, but then, Egan had been warned off when he'd tried to reveal all, hadn't he?

"Hell," I said.

"Quite." Grenville nodded.

I wondered if Pomeroy knew about these goings on, and if he'd shrug and say it was the prisoner's just deserts.

Quimby had said he'd head to Sheppey and investigate Finch's past and how he might have returned to the country. I wondered if he'd already gone, or if I had time to put a word in his ear about the fights.

Were this any other case, I'd itch to go to Sheppey myself, but I had other worries crowding out my thoughts, hence my journey here tonight.

Music surged and the beauty of the voices onstage drew attention. Grenville turned away with Marianne to listen and watch.

Lady Aline creaked to her feet. "Come and pour me a glass of sherry, Lacey."

Grenville politely rose with me, but remained with Marianne while I escorted Lady Aline into the sitting room behind the box.

This tiny chamber, as sumptuously decorated as the house in South Audley Street, was a space in which one could take wine or even dinner during the intervals, or rest from the exhaustion of watching the performance.

In this jewel box of a room, I'd kissed Donata for the first time.

I poured sherry from a decanter on the marble-topped console table with lion feet and a brandy for myself. The strains of Mozart floated through the closed doors.

"I've held on to my patience," I said as Lady Aline settled herself in an armchair and took a large sip of sherry. I remained standing. "Now you must pay up."

"Of course, dear boy." Lady Aline inclined her head, feathers dancing. "I must beg your pardon, but your wife swore me to silence, and I have known the dear gel since she was in leading strings."

My lips twitched against my wishes. "Her orders outrank mine, you mean."

"They do. But I have also decided that you should not suffer.

I wish Donata to be happy, and happiness in marriage generally means placating the male side of things. I do *not* know precisely where Donata is, I am sorry to say, but I do know why she went."

"Because Stanton St. John wants to get his claws on Peter."

"Indeed, yes, and he does not care who knows it." Lady Aline's blue eyes snapped with rage. "He's hired a nasty solicitor to take his side—wants to prove Donata an incompetent mother and you an upstart who only wishes to lay hands on the family fortune."

"A popular opinion, in the case of myself," I said, tamping down my fury. Stanton was an odious pig to accuse Donata of neglecting her children. She doted on them and didn't care who knew it.

"Only to those who do not know you well, my dear fellow. I admit this leaves much of the world to speculate on your motives. A marriage for the pleasure of it is a puzzling notion to most. Small wonder romantic novels are the rage—marrying for love and friendship is regarded by many as the stuff of fiction."

"Cousin Stanton has much fuel," I observed. "So many are angry at me for coercing Donata into my clutches, Donata's cousins on her family's side most of all. Do they truly believe she'd have thrown in her lot with them if I hadn't happened along?"

"They do, though you and I both know she would not have. Donata knows her own mind."

"That she does," I said feelingly.

"Anyway, Cousin Stanton came 'round to this box and tried to speak to her that night," Lady Aline went on. "As soon as you departed. He must have been waiting for you to go. They did have a conversation, but the performance onstage was loud, and I could not hear all they said. By the look of it, he was threatening her. Finally Stanton storms off, and Donata, quite upset, asks to go home with me—I mean to my house, not her own.

"Once there, she paced and fretted for hours, refusing any food or drink, until finally she sent one of my footmen off to find your man, Brewster. He came, she closeted herself with him, then off she went with him in a hired coach. The last I saw of her. I know she has taken Peter to a place she believes is safe." She gave me an inquiring look, as though begging me to confirm her speculation.

"Brewster won't reveal the location, blast him." I began to pace as Donata had, the thump of my walking stick muffled on the carpet.

"Donata's orders to him outrank yours as well?" Aline asked.

"Apparently they do. Damnation."

Brewster had promised me that Donata and Peter had the best protection he could arrange, which he could not have done without Denis's permission. Which meant Denis knew where my wife was, and I did not.

I vented my feelings a bit longer. I could not deny, however, that if Denis had a hand in this—which he assuredly did—then Donata and Peter were safe.

I had realized some time ago why Denis's men trusted him. The lot of them were ruffians, some killers, who could rise up and crush him any time they wished.

But Denis held them because he was fair. He paid high wages —Brewster had not lied when he'd said he wasn't destitute. Denis made sure they had every reason to stay in his employ.

He also was not arbitrarily cruel—he did not torture a man who disobeyed him, or string out his punishment. He was far more direct. If a man endangered him or one of his other men, that man was dealt with, swiftly. I'd seen that in my very first encounter with him.

"Damnation," I said again.

"I agree." Aline set aside her empty glass. "I expect you to send me word the moment she returns. Now, shall we have more opera?"

~

As much as I liked *Figaro*, I could not concentrate on it and soon made my apologies and took my leave. Aline said she would depart with Grenville and Marianne, moving on with them to another entertainment at the interval.

I had Hagen take me home. I briefly toyed with the idea of seeking out Denis and pummeling Donata's whereabouts from him, but I knew such a thing would be useless. His men would simply carry me out and deposit me in the street.

I did write a note to Denis that I would like to meet with him, and I sent a similar missive to Pierce Egan. I wanted to know more about this pugilist match in Kent. Last, I wrote to Sir Montague, telling him the tale of the convicts forced to fight at a gentleman's pleasure—leaving Egan's name out of it, and suggesting he give this information to Mr. Quimby, if he had not already departed.

Before I retired for the night, I went upstairs to look in on Anne—simply watching her sleep in her cot made me feel better. The nurse snored in a bed next to her, ready to assist any time the babe awoke.

I retired for the night, hoping Donata would return while I slept and greet me in the morning. I'd rush to her boudoir to find her seated on her chaise, a silken dressing gown flowing over her legs, her hair wrapped in a bandeau. She'd give me a calm look over the rim of her coffee cup and ask why I was tearing about so.

So strongly did this vision seize me that when I woke, I slid on my dressing gown and stepped quickly through the chamber between our bedrooms. Disappointment hit me hard when I found the boudoir beyond quiet and empty.

Bartholomew meanwhile had entered my chamber to fill my bath and shave me. He was the only bright note in the gloom of the morning, with his light-colored hair, crisp blue suit, and enduring vivacity. I stepped into the hot water and gave myself to his ministrations.

"We did find where Mr. Finch took his lodgings, Captain," Bartholomew said as he pulled the blade across my face in a series of precise strokes. "With a lady, a fairly young one, and quite pretty. Didn't want to talk to me and Matthias, though." A fleeting look of moroseness crossed his face.

I'd started when he'd made the announcement, and Bartholomew pulled the blade away so he would not cut me. I forced myself to calm.

"Immune to your charms?" I asked, keeping my voice light. "Or afraid?"

"Not easy to say." Bartholomew continued the shave. "Matthias spoke to her—he was the one who pried her whereabouts out of the landlord of the nearest tavern." He set aside the razor and covered my face with a hot towel. "Landlord didn't want to talk about Finch, no one did, but Jeremy the footman is his sister's lad, and so landlord told us about the lady on the quiet. Didn't want to get into no trouble, he said. But at least we found the rooms."

"Excellent." My spirits at last lifted. I set aside the towel and rose with haste, soap and water splashing all over the floor. "You have succeeded where Brewster and a very competent Runner have failed."

Bartholomew shrugged, attempting to look modest. "It was just asking questions and talking about family. Jeremy's kin are proud of him working for such a distinguished lady."

Bartholomew did not have much more to relate. He and his brother had heard plenty about the evils of Finchie, as he was known, but not much about what he'd been up to since he'd arrived in London. No one had wanted to know.

I planned to breakfast quickly and return to St. Giles to question this young lady. My meal and perusal of newspapers was interrupted, however, by a commotion in the foyer.

Before I could leave the table to discover what was amiss, Stanton St. John barreled into the dining room, Bartholomew and another footman unable to restrain him.

I rose to meet Stanton as he charged around the table, and I brought up my walking stick to fend him off.

"Where the devil is he?" Stanton bellowed at me. "What have you done with Peter? I'll have the law on you, damn me if I don't!"

CHAPTER 13

I withdrew the sword partway from my cane as I faced Stanton, but I kept my voice chilly.

"Young Lord Breckenridge is well," I said. "And safe from you."

I realized at that moment that I truly believed my words. Donata, Brewster, and Denis would make certain Peter was well.

"You admit you've abducted him?" Flecks of spittle stained Stanton's lips. "He's not yours to do with what you please. He's a St. John, not a *Lacey.*" He spat the name. "Peter belongs to *me.*"

"He belongs with his mother," I said, my cool tone worthy of Grenville or Denis. "What is your sudden interest in him, by the bye? Breckenridge has been dead nearly three years, and I've been married to his mother for a little over one. Why are you only coming to us now?"

Stanton's face reddened to tell me I'd scored a hit. I'd been trying to throw him off balance, but I'd succeeded too well.

Which made me wonder—what *had* happened to generate Stanton's interest?

"I'll have you for abduction," Stanton spluttered. "I wager I can make more disgusting charges stick. You are by all accounts *very* fond of the boy."

"As a father," I said in a hard voice. "And as a father, I am certainly not about to turn Peter over to you."

"But you are *not* his father. Never can be. You can never get sons of your own on Donata, so I hear, now that you've made her barren."

Behind him, Bartholomew stifled a noise of outrage. The open doorway and hall outside had filled with the rest of the servants, male and female, led by Barnstable, who was half choking in fury.

I caught Stanton by the lapel of his finely tailored coat, letting my sword come all the way out of the walking stick.

"Do not think to insult my wife in her own house," I said in a tight snarl. "Do not think to insult her—*ever*. Do not even dare to speak her name."

Stanton sneered even as he eyed my sword. "I see she has you tamed. Does she put you on a lead when you go out?"

I shoved him at Bartholomew and rested the tip of my sword on his throat. "I will be kind and not call you out," I said. "But if you appear here again, I will ask you to name your seconds."

And if he did accept the challenge, I'd kill him. I was a dead shot. Stanton would die, and I'd flee ahead of the law to France or Italy.

For that reason, I did not call him out on the spot. I was loathe to make Anne the daughter of a fugitive because of such a man as Stanton. But I would definitely kill him if we dueled.

Stanton shook off Bartholomew's hold. "This is not Donata's house. It is Breckenridge's. She ought to be living in your broken-down pile in Norfolk, or your grimy rooms in Covent Garden. Or in a brothel."

I punched him. Stanton's head snapped back satisfactorily and blood streamed from his nose.

He recovered quickly and raised his fists in a practiced

pugilist's stance. We'd all had lessons at Gentleman Jackson's salon.

However, I had learned, not only in my ill-spent youth and in the army, but also from Brewster, how to fight dirty. I side-stepped, and when Stanton turned to meet me, I thrust my foot behind his ankle and pushed him hard. As he flailed for balance, I laid my fist into his gut.

As Stanton bent double, Bartholomew and Jeremy caught him and spun him around. They shoved him from the dining room, across the foyer, and to the front door. He'd obviously thrown down his hat when he'd entered the house, and Barnstable picked it up off the floor and jammed it onto Stanton's head.

Bartholomew and Jeremy, with two other footmen, towed him out by his elbows and dropped him to the pavement. They skimmed back inside, and Barnstable slammed the door and turned the key in the lock.

I remained in the dining room doorway, sword in hand, my knee smarting from my acrobatics, while the staff grinned at each other for a job well done.

"Thank you, gentlemen," I said. "I believe a spot of ale all 'round is in order."

～

I WAS NOT SO FOOLISH AS TO THINK WE'D SEEN THE LAST OF Stanton. He could easily have me arrested for assaulting him, and my servants even more easily for daring to touch a gentleman of the upper classes.

I would counter by bringing him to court for forcing his way into the house, and I believed a magistrate would be sympa-thetic to me. The house was legally Donata's to live in, and a man had the right to defend his home.

For the moment, I forced myself to push Stanton from my

thoughts and follow the information Bartholomew and Matthias had turned up—the young woman Finch had stayed with before he'd met his death.

I jotted a quick missive to Grenville telling him I'd gone to question the young lady, whose existence he'd have already heard of from Matthias. I also thanked him for the story Pierce Egan had told him and invited him to join me when I spoke to Mr. Egan about it.

When I finished and gave the note to Bartholomew to deliver, I found Brewster outside, sipping coffee he'd purchased from a vendor's cart. He drained the cup when I emerged and returned it to the cart and climbed into the hired carriage with me.

The rain had cleared, and the clouds were puffy white in a sky of blue—when the sky occasionally showed itself above the smoke. The air was softer, promising spring.

All hint of spring left us as we journeyed into the rookeries. The houses shut out the sky over the narrow streets, flapping linen creating a tent to further obscure it. I had a sudden fancy that the people here lived in deep crevices far from the surface of the earth.

The house Bartholomew had given me the direction to smelled strongly of unwashed bodies, tobacco smoke, and un-emptied chamber pots. Brewster scowled as he led the way upstairs and banged his fist on a cracked wooden door.

I heard swearing inside, and then a large young man wrenched open the door. He was tall and perhaps twenty summers or so, and wearing only a pair of homespun breeches. He took in Brewster, halted as though thinking better of attacking, folded his arms, and glared at us.

"What ya want?"

Behind him I saw a flurry of movement and heard the unmistakable sound of a sash going up.

"Oi, she's out the window," Brewster growled. "I'll run her down, guv."

So saying, he moved past me and raced down the stairs with remarkable speed.

This left me facing the belligerent young man. The pale skin on his bare torso reddened from the chill breeze pouring through the house. He swept his gaze over my well-kept suit and crisply shaved face, and a look of cunning entered his eyes.

"Apologies for disturbing you." I tipped my hat and retreated to the stairs.

"No, ya don't." The man grabbed me by the shoulders. "I need somefink for me trouble."

For his trouble, he got my walking stick across his face and a tumble down a flight of stairs to the landing. I lost my balance in the process and kept to my feet only by clinging to the stair railing.

The man shook himself, started to rise, fell again, and decided to remain seated. I turned my back on him and stepped into the cluttered room, which boasted a pallet on the floor and one rickety chair.

Snatching up the coat I saw on the chair, I carried it down to the young man and dropped it onto his bare chest.

"Are these your rooms, or hers?" I asked him.

"Hers," came the grudging reply.

"But you stay in them?"

"You her toff?" The lad turned inquiring light green eyes up to me. "I know you ain't her dad. He's been and gone."

I stared. "Her dad?"

"That's right. At least he said he were."

"And what was that man's name?" I asked, air barely filling my lungs.

"Finch. The old fighter. Heard of him? I ain't."

"Jack Finch is your young lady's father?" I said in amazement.

"Aye. So he said. She didn't deny it." He struggled to his feet, sliding his big arms into the coat. "If you're her toff, you already know she's a tart. Couldn't see your way t' handing me a shilling, could ye? For me breakfast."

"Out," I said firmly.

I stepped past him and continued down the stairs and out of the house. From the sounds of shrieking and scrambling I tracked Brewster around the corner to a dim passage.

No one stopped me or offered to help. Most people took no notice of the commotion, as though reluctant to become involved.

Brewster stood at the end of a muddy lane, very little light filtering down from above. He held a squirming, kicking young woman who appeared as a bundle of skirts and flailing limbs.

"Stop before I give ye a good thrashing," Brewster was shouting.

The woman's reply was foul, screeching, and filled with fear. I reached them and planted myself in front of her to block her escape.

"No good fighting him," I told her, resting my weight on my walking stick. "He's very strong, and I also believe he's your uncle."

Both Brewster and the lady stopped, two pairs of eyes fixing on me in astonishment.

The young woman recovered first. "And who are you? Me grandad?"

"Hardly," I said. "If Jack Finch is your father, then Brewster here is your uncle by marriage. He's married to Finch's sister."

She gaped at me then switched her accusing glare to Brewster. "That true?"

"Finch is your dad?" Brewster asked in shock.

"For me sins, yeah."

Brewster regarded her skeptically. "Who are you, and why don't we know about ye?"

"I'm Charlotte, ain't I?"

Brewster released her, but warily. Charlotte pulled a quantity of thick brown hair from her face and peered at us with light brown eyes.

She was very young—sixteen or seventeen at most. Her clear face and slender limbs told me that, as well as a beauty that hadn't yet been marred by lack of decent food and living in squalor.

"Charlotte Finch?" I ventured.

"That's what I call meself. Why you so interested?"

Brewster looked her up and down, ready to grab her if she tried to run. "Who's your mum then?"

Charlotte shrugged. "She were a whore. Dead now these three years."

I saw grief in her eyes before she quickly hid it.

"But Finch acknowledged you?" I asked.

Her face hardened. "If ye can call it that. More like he came 'round when he needed something, mostly money or a place to stay. But yeah, he admitted I was his daughter. Sometimes brought me little toys." She trailed off wistfully.

The idea that Finch had been thoughtful enough to bring his daughter a wooden doll or cloth animal or some such did not fit with the brute of a criminal others had painted him.

"Most like he stole them," Charlotte said. "But he brought 'em, didn't he?"

"What'd he bring you this time?" Brewster asked. "You know he's dead, do ye?"

I had not intended to say this directly, wishing to discover whether Charlotte knew of the death first, but Brewster was ever straightforward.

The effect was sharp. Charlotte stared at Brewster, her eyes rounding, and all color left her face. She swayed, and I reached to steady her.

Charlotte threw off my hand, her breath flowing back into her.

"Oh, God, that devil killed 'im!"

She whirled around, her drab skirt swinging, and tried to run, but Brewster easily caught her.

"What devil?" he demanded. "What you going on about?"

Charlotte balled her fists, her words a hoarse shout. "The bloody bastard what sends me out of nights. Me dad beat him something terrible."

"Who?" I asked, my anger rising. "That pale varlet that was in your rooms?"

"What?" Charlotte looked confused. "Naw, that's Ned. He's harmless, is Neddie. I mean Hobson. He has a hold of all the girls around here. Dad blacked his eye ever so fast." Her face fell. "But ye say me dad is dead?" She struggled against Brewster's hold. "I'll kill him. You just let me at him."

"We don't know what happened to your father," I said quickly. "We have no idea who killed him. No witnesses or evidence."

"Ye don't need witnesses or evidence! Ye shake Hobson until he tells ye what he did. Then ye drag him to the gallows, and the girls of St. Giles will sing your praises."

"Where can we find this Hobson?" I asked. The idea of pounding on the man who forced young women to sell themselves appealed to me.

Brewster was shaking his head *no*, but Charlotte said, "In Hart Street, just 'round the corner. Come on, I'll show ye."

CHAPTER 14

*C*harlotte yanked herself from Brewster and ran down the lane, the holes in the bottoms of her slippers flashing.

Brewster started after her, and I brought up the rear, my pace slower. I caught up to them when they'd reached a house whose mortar was green with mold and fungus, the wooden trim rotted and splintering.

Charlotte slapped open the door and charged inside, Brewster a step behind her.

By the time I reached the stairs in the house and began to climb them, Brewster had managed to get in front of Charlotte. He broke open a door above me.

I heard a woman scream and a man curse, much as when we'd come to Charlotte's lodgings. I reached the top of the stairs and caught Charlotte's wrist in a firm hand.

"Let him," I said as she tried to jerk away. "He's an expert."

A very young woman with a long fall of blond hair held a sheet to her naked body and screamed loud enough to shatter glass as Brewster hauled a man with a bruised face up by the throat. The fellow's bare body dangled as he clawed at Brewster's fingers.

A knife flashed in the man's hand—probably he'd dragged it out from under his pillow while Brewster was barreling inside. I cried a warning as he swung the blade at Brewster's ribs, but Brewster already knew. He caught the hand in his great fist, and I heard the sound of bones crunching.

The man wailed. The woman rushed at Brewster, but Charlotte wrested herself away from me and grabbed the woman in a competent wrestling hold.

I looked to Brewster, ready to aid him, but I saw it wouldn't be necessary. Brewster released Hobson, who fell back to the bed, cradling his hand and trying not to weep.

"You killed me dad!" Charlotte yelled at him from where she still held the woman. "Ye rotten bastard, ye killed me dad!"

Hobson rocked back and forth. He was a fleshy man, and the sight of him without a stitch was not pleasant.

"Shut your gob, girl," he snuffled. "I never did."

Brewster raised his fist to hit him again, but I waved him off. "You obviously know who her dad is," I said to Hobson. "And that he is dead. Tell me how you know."

"You Runners?" Hobson eyed us dubiously. "I ain't talking to no magistrate. I ain't done nothing."

"Except exploited girls younger than my daughter and forced them into prostitution," I said in a hard voice. "Being no better than a madam is a crime."

Hobson glared at me with bloodshot eyes. "You a solicitor? Drumming up business for your barrister?"

I leaned closer, trying not to flinch at his foul breath. "I'm a man who likes punishing men who hurt ladies. Tell me all you know about Jack Finch."

"He be dead," Hobson said.

Charlotte screamed between her teeth. "I told ya. He killed 'im."

"I never did," Hobson spluttered. "Found him like that, didn't I? I never knew Finchie were her *dad*."

"You had better explain," I said. "Or I *will* take you to a magistrate."

Hobson spluttered a sob, holding his useless hand. "I caught him at Charlotte's. I went at him, thinking he was sampling without paying, and he gave me this." Hobson pointed to a black bruise on his temple that spread below his eye. "Finchie laughs at me, tells me to give him any blunt I made off Charlotte. I said I didn't have it on me, and he says he'll come back tomorrow, and off he goes. Next morning, I see him being carried into a house down the lane and left there. I thought he were drunk—didn't see who was the man what dragged him. I go in to tell him I ain't sharing the spoils of my business, don't matter he's Charlotte's family. I picked the lock easy enough and find him on the floor. Cold and dead."

"Liar!" Charlotte yelled. "When he came here, you turned tail and ran off to get the money then and there. You were going to give him all your blunt. You weren't brave enough to stand up to him."

"Already dead?" I asked, making my voice loud enough to break through Charlotte's railing. "Are you certain?"

"He weren't breathing and he had a knife stuck into him," Hobson said. "Face were gray, eyes staring. Dead as a fish."

"And what did you do?"

"Legged it, didn't I? I wasn't going to be found with a man's dead body. I shut the door, locked it again, and ran off."

"Did you take the knife?"

"What you think I am, a fool? There's a dead body and I'm carrying around the bloody knife what killed him? I'd be swinging for the murder by Monday."

"What did the knife look like?" I asked.

"A knife. What'd you think?"

Brewster shook Hobson, just hard enough to jostle the man's broken hand and make him cry out again.

"Answer the man," he commanded.

Hobson shrugged, trembling. "Ordinary knife. What blokes brought back from the war. Hilt about as long as me hand. Leather-wrapped handle. Blade about an inch wide."

He knew much about it to have left it. I highly suspected he'd stolen the thing, but by now he might have sold it, and unless it was still covered with Finch's blood, it wouldn't tell us much. A good many men discharged from the army with nowhere to go ended up in London's slums. There must be a number of men in St. Giles and Seven Dials who owned such a knife.

"Did you know Finch?" I continued. "I mean, before you saw him in Charlotte's rooms?"

"Yeah, I knew 'im. Not well, thank the Lord. Didn't cross him, if you were smart. I hadn't seen him in years, and I'm glad he's dead now."

"He's me *dad*." Charlotte thrust the woman away from her and lunged for Hobson. "Don't you say you're glad he's dead. Coward. Bastard."

She spat at him before Brewster caught her around the waist and lifted her away. The other young woman collapsed to the floor, pulling the sheet around herself and weeping.

"None of that," Brewster snapped at Charlotte. "You go on home. *I'll* speak to Mr. Hobson."

"Are you going to kill him?" She asked with terrible eagerness.

"Haven't decided." Brewster set Charlotte on her feet. "Let the captain see you home."

I held out my hand. "Best come with me."

Charlotte looked from Brewster to me and finally deigned to clasp my arm.

"You shall escort me, sir," Charlotte said with false hauteur. She squeezed my elbow. "You're a fine one, ain't ya?"

"None of that," I said sternly.

I took her out and down the stairs. Behind us we heard Hobson cry out again, and Charlotte laughed, a vicious sound.

Then she sobered. "It don't matter if Hobson gets roughed up. He'll just beat the joy out of me when he feels better."

"Possibly not," I said. "I believe Mr. Brewster is explaining that you are now under his protection."

"I don't want to be under any man's protection," Charlotte growled. "Why don't you all just leave me alone?"

She made to jerk away from me, but I pressed her hand, holding her gently in place. She was little more than a child, fine-boned and delicate, though I knew that if she'd been a daughter of the *ton*, she'd likely be wed by now.

"It is not the way of the world," I said. "A young lady needs a strong protector, be he husband or brother, father or uncle. The world is unkind to young women on their own."

"The world be blowed," Charlotte said decidedly. "But I know you're right. Me dad were a bad man, yeah, but he were me *dad*."

I had no answer for her. When we reached her doorstep, the young man called Ned, dressed now in a tattered linen shirt and frock coat too small for him, came loping out of the shadows. "You all right lass? Where's the big man?"

"I'm well, no thanks to you." Charlotte dropped my arm and took Ned's. "It's all right. The big man is me uncle, it turns out, and this is his friend. They're going to look after me now."

"Yeah?" Ned eyed me narrowly. "What about me?"

"I look after *you*." Charlotte nestled into him and kissed his cheek. "Now go on and fetch me some breakfast."

❧

I LEFT CHARLOTTE IN NED'S CARE AFTER I ASKED HER A FEW MORE

questions about Finch. Brewster was waiting for me at the end of Hart Street when I emerged from the lane where Charlotte lived, and we made our way out of the warrens to Great Russel Street.

"Did you leave Hobson alive?" I asked as we walked.

"Oh, aye," Brewster said. "Knocked him about some, but he'll mend. He won't be bothering Charlotte again."

He said nothing more, but I had faith that Brewster had put the fear of God into Hobson. I wondered if a reminder who Brewster worked for had sealed the bargain.

"I'll tell Em to look in on her," Brewster said. "Em will be chuffed to know she has a niece."

"Charlotte seemed fond of Finch, in spite of her manner," I reflected. "All others we've come upon, including you, either loathed or feared him. The way Charlotte paints him doesn't fit —to her, Finch is a father who acknowledged a girl child he'd sired out of wedlock, a man who brought her gifts."

"It's interestin'," Brewster conceded. "A hard man but one what dotes on his daughter? Seems unlikely. 'Course, you're the same."

"You think me a hard man?" I asked, nonplussed.

Brewster gave me a sideways look. "You dress proper and pretend to follow the rules of the gentry-coves, but you throw away the rules whenever they don't suit you. It takes a hard man to cross Mr. Denis, but you do it."

My brows rose. "I don't cross him these days. He tells me to do a thing, and I do it."

"No, you don't." Brewster snorted. "You do what he asks when it's convenient to you and for your own ends. Don't think he don't understand that. Take me word, guv, he knows ye for a hard man, and a dangerous one."

He fell silent, leaving me bewildered.

"Charlotte told me Finch turned up about a week ago," I said after we'd walked without speaking a few moments. "Stayed with her but didn't say much about where he'd been or why he was in London."

"Huh," Brewster said. "I'll wager she knows more than she lets on. I'll have Em talk with the girl. Charlotte might tell Em what she wouldn't tell you."

"Even though I'm a hard man?"

"But with a softness for the ladies, as I said. A girl like Charlotte will know that first thing. Wrap you right around her finger."

"Seven days," I said, ignoring him. "Three days ago, he was killed. Did he come to London to meet someone? Or did he simply wish to visit Charlotte?"

"Or Shaddock, maybe," Brewster said. "The man was terrified when we mentioned him, which he shouldn't have been if Finch were safely away across the ocean. And didn't Mr. Oliver say Shaddock turned everyone out a few months ago, like he was afraid of something? Maybe he'd heard word that Finch had escaped and was heading home."

"Why did you fall out with Shaddock?" I asked in curiosity as we turned to Great Russel Street. The bulk of the British Museum rose before us, a temple to antiquities from all over the world. Lord Elgin's marbles, raw and naked, reposed there to shock the gentry out of their complacency. "Did he stage fights even then?"

Brewster nodded. "I was young and high-minded in those days." He let out a sigh, as though regretting the folly of his youth. "I started my fighting life because Shaddock took me in hand. He thought if I became a pugilist it would stop me thieving, save me from an early death at the end of a rope. He were right—I'd have been caught and strung up or transported sooner or later. I wanted to prove I was up to his standards, that he didn't make a mistake helping a boy from the streets. No matter how outraged he told you he was about White's and Finch's demands that he cheat for them, he did it himself long before he met them. Wanted me to go down in a fight, but I wouldn't do it. I left him in disgust."

"It is difficult when you learn your mentor has feet of clay," I said in sympathy.

I remembered becoming more and more frustrated with my own mentor, Colonel Brandon, and his hold over me once I'd made captain. He'd begun demanding my gratitude, though my promotion had been given to me because of deeds I'd performed in the field.

I'd grown angry with myself, wondering what was wrong with me that I would cease to have faith in him. And this was long before he'd believed me having an affair with his wife.

"You mean when you find out they're as crooked as anyone else?" Brewster asked. "I suppose I didn't go easy on him. But Shaddock taught me a skill and gave me a purpose in life—I wanted to be a good boxer. Learned I didn't have to rely on stealing, so I'm grateful for that."

I knew Colonel Brandon had given me a huge leg up when he'd helped me volunteer in the army and assisted in funding my uniforms, horses, and my first rank of lieutenant. If not for him, I'd have remained in Norfolk, poor and listless, possibly relieving my ennui in excessive drink. If I'd stayed home, sooner or later I'd likely have lost my temper and murdered my father.

It came to me in a flash as Brewster spoke that, yes, I was a hard man, and that I owed Colonel Brandon much, in spite of him turning out to be rather weak-willed.

"Where to now, Captain?"

I forced myself to focus on the present. "We need to discover exactly who Finch met and spoke to upon his arrival in London. What his plans were. If we follow his path, I'm certain it will lead to his killer."

"I know you have this curiosity," Brewster said. "But why not leave it up to the Runners? Mr. Quimby believes I didn't knife him, so I'm in the clear. Why care who killed a man like Finch? *Good riddance*, everyone but Charlotte has said."

I shot him a frown. "You are by no means cleared. No matter what Quimby says, most magistrates would be quite willing to fit you up for the crime. If they can't find the correct culprit, then you'll do nicely. After all, you're a known villain."

Brewster looked skeptical. "His Nibs will never let me swing."

"Only if it's expedient for His Nibs to save you. You'll be safe when we discover the real killer and make sure he's given to Quimby or Pomeroy to arrest."

Brewster studied me in puzzlement. "But why should *you* mind? I'm just a thug what follows you around on the orders of a man you despise. Why is it any interest of yours whether a cove like me lives or dies?"

"Because you're a good man." I punctuated my words with a slam of my walking stick to the pavement. "An honorable one. You've saved my life several times. If I could not repay that by keeping you from Newgate, I'd be a hard man indeed."

Brewster continued to be unconvinced. "I ain't even your class. You're a gentleman. Not my world."

"What has that to do with anything? I'll not throw you to the wolves, Brewster, whatever you might think. You almost died because of me and my bloody family, so cease looking so amazed. And I don't despise Denis. Disagree with him as to his methods and his morality—or lack of it—but I do not despise him. The world made him what he is, as it made you, and made me." I drew a breath and gave a little laugh. "That is enough pontificating for one day. I have appointments, and you need to tell your wife she has a niece."

Brewster blinked slowly as I ended this speech. "All right, guv," he said. "But I'm making certain you get home first. 'Cause I'm doing me job."

He snapped his mouth shut and led me toward a hackney stand, a belligerent scowl on his face.

Poor chap. I do believe I embarrassed him.

~

WHEN I REACHED HOME, I FOUND REPLIES TO BOTH MY NOTES. Pierce Egan agreed to meet me and Grenville at Jackson's boxing rooms tonight, and Denis agreed to see me at three this afternoon.

It was half past two by the time I received the messages, so I donned a light coat and walked down South Audley Street to its end, and to the home of James Denis.

CHAPTER 15

When I was admitted to number 45, Curzon Street by the aging butler, I saw that some of Denis's men lingered in the house. They did not congregate in one place but drifted in and out of back rooms, and I heard voices in the dining room behind the closed door.

The butler gave me a sharp look at my curiosity but said nothing as he led me up the stairs.

Denis was in his study, as usual, the room as coolly elegant as he was. The self-portrait of Rembrandt watched us with interest as I took my customary seat, and the butler set the customary goblet of brandy at my elbow.

"Before you ask, I will not allow you to question my men at will," Denis said, regarding me over the blank space of his desk. "However, I have found two who knew Jack Finch well, and they will speak to you."

He indicated a man at the window, one of the rotation of guards that stood there whenever Denis received visitors.

"I did not come about that," I said.

Denis had placed his fingertips together as he rested his

elbows on his chair's arms, and his fingers twitched the slightest bit. "No?"

"No. I came to bid you tell me where my wife is."

There was a silence. Denis's hands didn't move and neither did his eyes.

"I must decline," he said.

I gripped the arms of my chair, making myself hold on to my temper. I'd gain nothing by berating him. "I know it was Mrs. Lacey's own idea, and Brewster's. I do not blame you, but I must know. Surely you can understand my thoughts on this matter."

Denis remained silent. The clock on the mantel, an onyx piece by Vulliamy, which I had not seen here before, ticked into the quietness.

Fabric rustled as Denis lowered his arms. "If I reveal her ladyship's whereabouts, and more importantly, the whereabouts of her son, you will immediately rush to them or send someone in your stead, believing you are practicing prudence. Either action will place them in danger. So I must decline."

Anger heated me as he spoke, but I had to admit he was correct—my first instinct would be to go to Donata or at least send Bartholomew or Grenville to make certain all was well.

I cleared my throat. "If I give you my word I will say nothing, do nothing, will you tell me? You must know that this is more than I can bear."

Denis made a minute shake of his head. "What you cannot bear is that you do not know. Her ladyship is perfectly well. There is a reason she sent Brewster to *me* for help, not you."

The carvings on the chair's arms pressed my palms as I forced myself not to leap across his desk and grab him by the throat.

"She knows I am impetuous, you mean," I said tightly.

Another shake. "She knew I'd have the resources to adequately hide her and keep her son safe. There are limited places you could take them where his lordship would not be found before this is resolved."

True. Stanton knew of my Norfolk home and my rooms in Grimpen Lane. He'd already nobbled Donata's home in Oxfordshire by recruiting her cousin Edwin. As Viscount Breckenridge, Peter had an estate in Hampshire and one in Kent, in addition to a house in Brighton, but of course Stanton knew all about those too.

I let out a measured breath. "I am trusting you with my wife and son's well-being."

This earned me a cold look. "Forgive me, Captain, but this has nothing to do with you. Lady Breckenridge is protecting her son from an opportunist, fearing he will resort to kidnapping to enforce his claim on the young viscount. *Your* part is not to betray, by any act or word, the viscount's whereabouts, and to let her ladyship's man of business reinforce her husband's will with the courts."

I swallowed the first hot words that came to me. "You are telling me to step out of the way in a matter closely concerning my wife and stepson."

"Yes. It is very important that you do so."

"Because," I said, trying to keep my voice steady, "if it is made to look as though *I* took Peter away, Stanton will use that for fuel in his case. Stepfather not to be trusted, will do anything to put his hands on Peter's money …"

"Just so."

"Damn it all." I loosened my grip on the chair so I could run a tense hand through my hair. "Quiet happiness is all I asked for. I thought that marrying Donata, sharing my life with her, would make me the happiest of men. All I've done is bring trouble to her door."

"Trouble would have come with or without you," Denis said. "She is a wealthy widow, and not a timid creature. An unscrupulous man might have coerced her into marriage by embarrassing her after she had an affair with him, or otherwise threatened her and her son. You were a safe gentleman to ally herself with."

I gave a short laugh. "And here I'd convinced myself she'd fallen in love with me."

"She is very fond of you, I believe."

Denis said this without changing expression, and I laughed again.

"What a romantic you are. Everyone is to marry for practical reasons only, are they?"

"Marriage has been, since ancient times, a legal contract. Men and women have treated it as such ever since."

"Very philosophical." I sat back in the chair, forcing myself to relax. "Did you ever consider marriage yourself? As a purely business arrangement, of course."

"Once," Denis surprised me by saying. "And not for business or legal purposes. But I was very young, and fortunately came to my senses in time."

A surge of avid curiosity cut into my worry. "I'd be very interested to hear *this* story. Never tell me that you, James Denis, fell in love."

"Infatuation and the folly of youth." A faint smile quirked his lips, but I saw darkness in his eyes. "I learned, alas, that she was a fraud and a confidence trickster, and had expected to defraud *me*. I had a lucky escape, but learned a lesson."

"Good Lord." I blinked. "I'd think you'd have asked her to join your enterprise."

"I pondered the idea, but realized quickly she could not be trusted. She would have considered it leverage to be my wife, and it would have been a grave mistake to let her have that. And so I disappointed her."

"I see. What happened to this young lady?" I asked in some trepidation.

Denis spread his hands. "I do not know. She moved on—to

another victim, presumably. No, I did not exact vengeance or do anything sinister to her. As I say, I was young, and more credulous than I realized. The incident did *not* cast a pall over my life, or make me the cynical man you see before you. I was fairly cynical before I met her, as you know. But it taught me much about trust. Perhaps letting your son's whereabouts remain secret will give *you* a few lessons in trust."

I admired how neatly he turned the conversation back around to me and my shortcomings.

His story gave me much to think about, however. Denis with a thwarted love in his past was intriguing. I wondered very much about the lady, and concluded she must have been an excellent trickster to gain the interest of Denis. And very charming indeed if he let her go, doing nothing to punish her for her sins.

I did not entertain the notion that he was bowed by the tragedy of it, nor had he turned into a cold-blooded criminal to take his revenge on the cruelty of the world. Such was the stuff of opera. Denis had once told me of his life as a child and what he'd had to do to survive. I believed him when he said he'd been plenty cynical before he'd met the lady.

"You once told me the best way to keep a secret is to share it with no one," I reflected. "Will you give me your word that Donata and Peter are perfectly safe? And will come to no harm?"

Denis looked directly into my eyes, his dark blue ones cool but still. "You have my word."

I let out a long breath. "I will have to be content with that."

∾

DENIS HAD ARRANGED FOR THE MEN WHO'D KNOWN FINCH TO speak with me, one at a time, in the dining room.

The first in was a small man called Lewis Downie, who was

older than most of Denis's men. I'd spoken to him before, in Norfolk, when I'd been helping Denis track down a killer. Lewis had been at ease with me then, and he was happy to speak with me now.

"I knew Finchie," he said comfortably. "Went on circuit with him—oh, years ago. I was a lightweight and he a heavy, so I never fought 'im. But he were a brute all right. Gouged out a fellow's eye in the ring, then broke the same man's arm for good measure. People booed him as a villain and won great packets of money on him at the same time."

"What did you think of him outside the ring?" I asked.

Lewis grinned. "I tried not to. He had his circle—I had mine."

"What I'm coming around to asking is who you think could have killed him or had him killed. This man who lost his eye?"

Lewis shook his head. "A fighter he beat fair wouldn't have. When we go into the ring, we expect to be hurt. We just hope it's not enough to end our careers. Mine ended when I broke all me fingers. They healed but I never could give a good punch again." He held up a scarred hand that I remembered very capably holding a sledgehammer. "Happily I'm good with the nags and other things. Can still be useful."

He rested his hand unselfconsciously on the table.

"But what if Finch *didn't* beat a man fairly?" I asked.

"Then that man would be well paid. Not all of us believe we're the best pugilists in the world. Sometimes it's sensible to take a few coins to go down when we probably would have gone down anyway. There are a few champions, but most of us are just fighters. Another day in the ring."

"Mmm." I carefully considered my next question. "Any time you have been a—guest—of His Majesty, were you taken to do exhibition fighting? Say at a gentleman's home?"

Lewis's face darkened. "You've heard about that, have you? I'll tell you something for nothing, guv. Once you're slung into a prison or a hulk, ye cease to be human. I hear tell of a prison what's built in a circle, where those in a tower in the middle watch ye all day long—ye can't see them, but they see you. The reformers who like this idea think it's taking the violence out of ye, but it ain't natural." He shuddered. "Don't know what's worse, a guard what will beat you for the enjoyment of it, or bloody reformers who think they're helping ye by breaking your spirit and giving ye nightmares."

His horror was real. I could not decide whether he'd experienced this for himself or had only been told by his fellows, but I did not ask.

"And having convicts participate in exhibition bouts is part of their reform?"

"Ye misunderstand me, guv. That's hushed up, that is. An amount of money passes from a gent to ones high up and a selection of men come out of the hulks and box for the gent's pleasure. They choose trained fighters and also those what have no training to see what will happen. They bring out only able and strong men, to keep it sporting, but the blokes have no choice. They're fought until they fall down and can't get up. If any die, ah well. They're robbers and the like, bad 'uns all."

I heard the echoes of Pomeroy's words.

"Has this happened to you?" I asked gently.

"Naw, I'm too small to be of much use, and I told you, I can't punch anymore. But I hear. Men used like fighting mongrels, only worse."

Marianne had likened the events to dog fights. "I imagine the magistrates do not know about these matches?"

"I imagine they do." The man grinned. "I *imagine* they're taking cash to look the other way. The gents what buy the prisoners for a day are often the local magistrates themselves."

"This is a well-known occurrence, then?"

"Known." Lewis shrugged. "Not talked about, though. I'll sit in Mr. Denis's house and discuss it with ye, but I wouldn't run to Bow Street and proclaim it at the top of me lungs. Or stand outside the Houses of Parliament and buttonhole me MP about it—if I even knew who he was. This is more of a *keep quiet if ye know what's good for ya* sort a' thing."

I had concluded as much. "Perhaps Mr. Finch decided not to keep it quiet?"

"Don't know why he wouldn't. A day out fighting wouldn't be anything he'd object to, would it?"

I had no idea. And now that Finch was dead, I might never know.

"Tell ya who you could talk to about Finchie, though," Lewis said, holding up a bent forefinger. "He had a friend, maybe the only one in all the world. A tough man, like Finchie was, but they seemed to get on. He's called Blackmore. Sydney Blackmore. He knew Finchie better than anyone. If ye want Finchie's history, apply to him."

CHAPTER 16

I regarded Lewis with eagerness, my interest piqued.

"How do I find this man?" I asked in hope. Friends fell out and could become passionate enemies, well I knew. I might have just been given the name of Finch's killer.

Lewis shrugged, to my disappointment. "Who knows, guv? Blackmore's a villain too. Could have been hanged, transported, or buried in a prison himself by now. I met the man once, long ago. Once was all I wanted." He rose, finished with me. "If ye do find Blackmore, ye take Tommy Brewster with you to speak to him. Tommy and about six other blokes, all well armed. Understand?"

With that, he left me, breaking into a cheerful whistle as he departed the room.

~

THE SECOND MAN—THE GUARD WHO'D BEEN IN DENIS'S STUDY—gave me no more information than Lewis. He'd fought Finch himself, and had the torn hamstring to remember him by. He'd heard of Mr. Blackmore, but never met him and didn't know where he was now.

The butler entered when I'd finished speaking with the second man, standing pointedly beside the open doorway. Before I departed, I asked the butler to tell Denis to send me word of anyone who knew of Sydney Blackmore, and more importantly, where to find him.

I got a cold stare in response, but I trusted he'd deliver the message.

I pondered the situation as I walked home. Though I'd discovered much more about Finch today, I was no further forward on deciding who'd killed him.

Brewster had confessed to beating Finch when Finch threatened his wife, and that might be enough to convince a jury he'd lied about leaving Finch alive while he fetched his money. He could easily have stuck a knife into the man—why bother to pay him when it was easier to kill him?

I had a more horrible thought. Perhaps *Mrs.* Brewster had stabbed Finch in fear of her life, and Brewster had beaten his body and left him in the deserted house to cover for her. They sent for me precisely because Finch would be traced to Mrs. Brewster, and it would not look well for her if they said nothing at all. Because Brewster had once nearly lost his life for me, they knew I'd be on their side.

Even Denis's loyalty was not as certain as mine—I had honor where my friends were concerned, but Denis might think it better to cut his losses than risk helping. Brewster had much confidence in "His Nibs," but Denis had before rid himself of men who could have brought the law down upon him.

I imagined I did Denis a wrong in this thought, but my worry for Brewster and his wife had me wildly speculating.

I considered Charlotte, the daughter. She had been genuinely distressed when she'd heard of Finch's death, the only one so far to express sorrow. But she'd immediately turned our attention to Hobson, whom Finch had beaten for exploiting Charlotte.

Charlotte's lover, Ned, might have killed Finch in fear or anger—either believing Finch would hurt Ned for sleeping with his daughter, or that he'd convince Charlotte to chuck Ned out.

There was Mrs. Brewster's sister, Martha, though I could not picture her tracking Finch through the streets of St. Giles and stabbing him. But even small and sickly people could prove to have desperate strength, and she'd only need a lucky blow. She'd been as dismayed as Emily at his return, and he'd stolen her money. If Finch had already been insensible from Brewster beating him, it would have been easier for Martha to fell him.

Shaddock, Brewster's trainer, came next to mind. Deathly afraid of Finch and glad he'd met his end. Had Finch asked Shaddock to meet him to pry more money out of him? Shaddock had been a trained pugilist and he'd know how to defeat a man larger than himself. But would he still possess the strength?

Young Mr. Oliver had that strength. Was it coincidence that he, a student of Shaddock's, had been in St. Giles fighting right after Finch had died? And what about Mr. White? He and Finch both knew Shaddock—did Mr. White kill Finch for a reason connected to the trainer? Or out of fear—perhaps White was poaching on Finch's territory in fight fixing and blackmail.

Finally, I had this mysterious Mr. Blackmore. I had hopes of Denis in this regard—he knew the whereabouts of every criminal in Britain and even beyond its shores.

Quimby was busy investigating the hulks where Finch had been imprisoned, and possibly quizzing a captain who made arrangements to bring prisoners back after they'd been transported. A dangerous undertaking for Quimby—I hoped he'd be circumspect.

I stood in front of Donata's house for several minutes before I realized I'd reached it, so lost in thought I was. Jeremy had opened the door, peering at me as though wondering why I did not enter. I went inside absently, no more enlightened for all my musings.

I reflected as I handed over my coat and hat that I'd investigated murders when it seemed no one could be to blame. In this murder, so many people could have killed Finch—or at least, so many would have been quite willing to—that it was difficult to choose between them.

I did not wish to blunder and send the wrong man—or woman—to the gallows. Unlike Pomeroy's, my conscience, if I did so, would never rest.

~

As Bartholomew dressed me a few hours later for my outing to meet Egan and Grenville, he remarked, "I heard Mr. St. John has left London."

My heart chilled. "Has he? And gone where?"

Bartholomew plucked up a camel-hair brush and began to studiously flick it over every inch of the frock coat he'd slid onto me. "His house in Somerset."

I let out my breath. Gabriella would arrive tomorrow, but she'd come from the opposite direction, through Dover and Kent. Nor was Stanton rushing to Hampshire or Norfolk to harass the staff at those houses.

If I knew where the devil Donata was, I'd rest easier, but I reasoned that she would avoid Somerset if Stanton lived there.

"You're certain?" I asked, holding out my arms so Bartholomew could finish the brushing.

"Oh, yes, Captain. We've been keeping an eye on him since the first morning he came to threaten her ladyship. Matthias and I and Mr. Barnstable know every servant in Mayfair, and I asked my mates to let me know what Mr. St. John does every day."

"He hasn't ever gone to St. Giles has he?" Pinning Finch's

death on Stanton would be highly satisfying, though I knew it was quite unlikely.

"No, sir. Not that anyone has seen. But maybe you could push the murder onto him. Two birds with one stone, like."

Tempting, but I felt the need to negate the idea. "If we decided to pin a crime, any crime, on someone we didn't like, without proof, we'd be no better than barbarians. Fortunately, the laws in this country are a bit more civilized."

"Mmm." Bartholomew returned to brushing the coat. "Pity."

Thank God for the laws, I thought as I climbed into the landau not long later. If not for them, I'd happily give Stanton to Pomeroy and assuage my conscience by telling myself I kept Peter safe. I could spout lofty rhetoric, but I rather agreed with Bartholomew's views on simple justice.

~

JACKSON'S BOXING ROOMS IN BOND STREET ATTRACTED THE cream of the *ton*, who were instructed in the "gentlemanly" art of pugilism. This evening as I entered, a pair of thin aristos were standing in shirtsleeves, batting at each other with fists as Jackson, a broad-shouldered man who was double each of these gentlemen's weights, gave them pointers.

Grenville pulled his gaze from the match and raised a hand to me as I entered. Standing next to him was a slim man with dark hair, who nodded cordially as I approached.

"Captain." Pierce Egan clasped my hand in a firm shake. "Well met. It has been a long time since Astley Close."

"Indeed." I'd liked Egan when I'd met him—he'd been the voice of reason at that bizarre house party.

"My felicitations on your nuptials," Egan continued with good humor. "And your growing nursery."

I bowed, pretending my heart didn't expand at his words. "I am the most fortunate of men."

"I believe you. Shall you go a round?"

The pair of spindly gentlemen had shaken hands and moved off, discussing what they'd learned, their fists still moving in demonstration. Several more pairs of gentlemen took the floor.

"Not with this." I tapped my left leg with my walking stick.

"I have seen that such things do not hamper you when you fight," Egan said, eyes sparkling. "When you are enraged enough."

"That is true. However, I then spend the day after that in agony. So, I will be prudent and not lose my temper."

Egan sent me a grin. "What about you, Grenville? I have heard of your prowess with your fists. Shall you give someone a milling?"

"I'll have a go." Grenville was already in shirt sleeves and waistcoat, the discreet Gautier, his valet, waiting with other manservants on the far side of the room to reclothe their gentlemen. "I am certain a number of chaps in this room would be proud to give me a bloody nose—or as you might say, Egan, draw my cork and pour out my claret. Ah, Debenham, shall we box?"

Grenville went off with another sprig of aristocracy, leaving us in relative privacy.

Egan turned to me, interest in his lively eyes. "Grenville wants me to repeat my tale of pugilism in the wilds of Kent."

"With prisoners from the hulks as the entertainment," I said.

"Yes." Egan's amusement deserted him. "You know how devoted I am to the sport," he said as we strolled to the other side of the room. "I breathe it morning, noon, and night, and regale the populace about it in between. But this was unsettling. Reluctant men were bullied unmercifully, thrashed if they did not defend themselves. A number of them did not even know how to fight, not in the pugilistic sense. They brought a few men who, it could be seen, were not hardened criminals, and were reduced to a pulp for the fun of it. It was sickening."

"How did this gentleman who owned the house arrange it?" I asked, choosing my words carefully.

"You do not have to be coy, Captain. I did not give his name to Grenville, but upon thinking it over, I've decided to tell you. It was Lord Mercer." When I must have looked blank, Mr. Egan added, "An earl of very old lineage. The earls of Mercer have dwelled just south of the Isle of Sheppey, on the sea, since before the Conquest, to hear him speak of it. Mercer doesn't come to Town much, lives in a huge pile that must be left from Norman times, retaining the cold from every winter since. The matches were held in the garden—if you can call it a garden—within some very picturesque ruins of a large Greek temple. Those were new. Mercer has a genuine ruin out there, the remains of an old keep, where men waited, penned up and under guard until their turn to fight."

"One man was nearly killed, Grenville said."

"Yes, poor bastard. Not one of the untrained or reluctant fighters, as you might think. *They* proved they had mettle when they had to fight or die. One of the pugilists, big fellow. They forced him into so many matches he couldn't stand. If I'd not intervened, they'd have thrown him back in again and again until he died. Mercer thought I'd be pleased by the show. Lady Mercer stood proudly next to her husband through all this. Ghastly people."

I'd never heard of the Earl of Mercer, but if he rusticated in the country, it was not odd that I hadn't. And if he and his wife were as gauche as Egan painted them, their names would never pass Grenville's lips. He preferred to ignore those who irritated him.

"They swore you to secrecy, Grenville said."

"Threatened me is more like." Egan shuddered. "Lady Mercer sensed my unhappiness, took me aside, and explained things to me. I wasn't to ruin his lordship's bit of fun. Where was the harm? These men had done bad things—let this be their punishment."

My hand tightened on the head of my walking stick. I remembered Lewis's words in Denis's dining room—*Once you're slung into prison or a hulk, you're nothing. Ye cease to be human.*

"Grenville also said that you tried to report what had happened and were waylaid."

Egan's eyes glinted with anger. "Oh, yes. Taken aside on a dark London street and knocked about. Very competently. I heard Grenville had a sudden interest in pugilists, particularly Jack Finch, so I told him about it. And now you. I shall have to be careful on my way home tonight."

"I will see that you arrive safely," I said with sincerity. "Thank you for your story."

"What is your interest?" He watched me with keen attention, his journalist's curiosity apparent.

"My man found Finch dead."

"Ah, yes. Grenville told me as much. *Foul Murder in St. Giles,* newspapers say. And you do not wish your man to be blamed."

"Finch was in one of those hulks once upon a time," I said. "I assume Lord Mercer hosts these bouts regularly. Perhaps Finch fought in one, before he was transported. When he escaped, he might have threatened Mercer about them, and was killed by those who did not want the secret to get out."

Egan turned a shade of yellow-green. "Would Mercer go that far? Good Lord, I hope not, or I'm for it."

"It is worth finding out," I said with conviction. "For your sake if nothing else."

Egan swallowed but maintained his sangfroid. "I believe a visit to the Continent might be in order. Perhaps I'll write about pugilism in Paris for a bit. But I will comfort myself by believing you're wrong that this is the reason Finch died. The bouts were exactly the sort of thing a man like Finch would go in for. Oh, good show, Mr. Grenville."

Grenville had deflected Debenham's blow when it came at him, caught Debenham's fist, and spun the man around. Debenham stumbled and fell to one knee.

End of the match. Grenville stepped back, flushed and breathing hard, and helped his opponent to his feet. Pugilism at its most gentlemanly.

∾

AFTER OUR INSTRUCTION AT JACKSON'S MR. EGAN AND I adjourned with Grenville to his home in Grosvenor Street and took a meal. Marianne was out—visiting her acting friends, Grenville said, so we dined and drank hock and brandy in large quantities, as though we were carefree bachelors.

I had been a bachelor far too long to find anything carefree about it, but I did enjoy the excellent conversation with Grenville and Egan, and I learned more than I'd ever thought possible about horse racing and pugilism.

Grenville invited Egan to spend the night, which the man accepted with gratitude. Egan indeed fixed on a journey to Paris for a few weeks, and would leave in a day or two.

I walked home from Grosvenor Street with Brewster and told him what Egan had told me. He listened with interest, and he, like Denis's man Lewis, didn't seem surprised.

"I've never been sent down meself," Brewster said. "But a thief is the same as a murderer to some, and it's a shame any villain escapes the noose, they say," he finished bitterly.

"Would Finch have been outraged at these fights? Or embraced them?"

"I believe he'd have enjoyed himself. I didn't know he and Blackmore were such mates. Met Blackmore a few times in my day. Can't say it were a pleasure."

"I am hoping Denis knows where I can put my hands on him."

Brewster looked heavenward, where smoke and clouds blotted out the stars. "Which means I'll have to be next to you when you talk to Blackmore, me fists at the ready. And possibly a cudgel and a pistol too."

"I can ask Denis to speak with him first," I suggested. "Men tend to be calmer after a visit with him."

"His Nibs has the touch," Brewster acknowledged. "With Blackmore, you'll need it."

We reached the house. I was about to enter, but Brewster put a cautioning hand on my shoulder, and then I noticed what he did.

A footman was not at the door to admit me, which was quite unusual. The front door was unlocked and ajar, but it was unattended, as was the foyer and Donata's great staircase hall. In fact, the entire house was echoing and empty.

Donata's home was always teeming with servants, from the highly efficient Barnstable to the boot boy who blushed when I praised his work. The house was one of movement and industry, but tonight, all was silence.

I thought of Anne upstairs, small and vulnerable in her nursery. I made for the staircase at a run, never mind my injury or Brewster's attempts to hold me back.

I passed the first floor and its public rooms, which were as eerily quiet as the ground floor. Candles burned on the landing, but their light illuminated no one.

I moved to the second floor and our private rooms, where I at last heard voices—Barnstable calling orders and Donata's maid Jacinthe snapping at the housemaids and footmen.

Over these, I heard the unmistakable and acerbic tones of my wife.

CHAPTER 17

I shouldered my way past Brewster, who had managed to put himself in front of me, and burst into Donata's boudoir, scattering maids like startled birds.

Donata turned from the center of the chaos, she calm in a dull plum redingote, her hair cascading from where it had fallen from its pins. Her dark blue gaze met mine, and she flushed.

"Out!" I bellowed.

I rarely barked orders at Donata's servants, but my agitation made me harsh. Barnstable took one look at my face and herded them out.

The entire household must have been in this room and the dressing room beyond, because it took some time for the servants to exit. Jacinthe alone stood her ground, but Donata gave her a nod to leave us.

Jacinthe shot me a warning look as she went, one telling me that if I mistreated Donata, I'd answer to *her*. She exited through the dressing room and quietly closed the door.

Donata was already speaking. "Before you scold me, Gabriel, I was perfectly—"

Her words cut off with a gasp as I slammed myself into her and dragged her into my arms.

As passionate as Donata and I could be when alone in our bedchamber, she was still unused to my abrupt demonstrations of tenderness. She started, then relaxed and leaned into my embrace, her head on my shoulder.

Her redingote held the chill from outdoors and the scents of smoke and wind. I kissed her hair, burying my face in the warmth of it.

"Where the bloody hell did you go?" came my broken whisper.

"Dorset," she whispered back.

I lifted my head to look down at her in amazement. I'd expected Denis to hide Peter in some remote village in Scotland, maybe even in the Orkneys, or away across the Continent. Dorset seemed anticlimactic, and far too close to London for my comfort.

"A very fine house there," Donata's eyes were tinged with fatigue, but her back was straight. "Far from the main roads, with a nice view of the sea and the strand along the Fleet." She might be describing a house where she'd spent an excellent holiday.

"Peter remains there?" I kept my voice low—while I trusted Donata's servants, I also agreed with Denis's assessment that a secret is best kept when few people know it.

"Yes. I thought it a good idea."

A look into her eyes told me the decision to leave her son behind had been very difficult. But if Stanton heard of her return to London, he might believe she'd brought Peter back with her, and he'd focus on us here, leaving Peter in safety.

"Stanton went to Somerset," I told her. "So says Bartholomew."

"Good. May he fall into a bog. If they have bogs in Somerset."

"They have them in Norfolk," I said. "Perhaps if we retreat there, he will follow. I know where the deepest ones are."

Donata shot me an appreciative look, then unfastened her coat and peeled it from her shoulders. "If Stanton disappeared, everyone would suspect me, and that would not help Peter. Therefore, curb your murderous tendencies. My man of business will sort this out. Meanwhile, Peter is out of Stanton's reach."

"You must know I was mad with worry." I kept my words calm, but my hands folded into fists. I realized I did not have my walking stick—I'd dropped it in my crazed rush, and fiery pain began to lace my knee.

"Yes, I imagined you trying to shake my whereabouts out of everyone you could. I wanted to tell you, but Mr. Brewster advised me not to, in case the message was intercepted. I chafed, but knew he was right."

"Denis would not tell me when I shook *him*. Not even in a whisper, bloody man."

"Respect for him would dwindle if he did not follow his own rules." Donata dropped the redingote over the back of a chair and sank onto her chaise. "Sit down, for heaven's sake, Gabriel. You look all in."

"But the better for seeing you." I drew a chair close to her and seated myself, my throbbing knee very unhappy with me. "I must ask you to cease this tendency for disappearing."

Donata straightened her skirt with fingers that shook. "Thus speaks the man who vanishes on a whim when he is interested in something."

"You must know that I am furious with myself for not being at the theatre when Stanton arrived to berate you. Lady Aline told me what happened."

"I was glad you were not there," Donata said. "You might have sent him over the railing and gotten yourself arrested. I knew when Stanton cornered me that I needed to take Peter out of his reach, and quickly. I also knew that if you remained here and held Stanton's attention, I could slip Peter away. My foolish cousin is more worried about *you* bending Peter to your will than he is about me protecting him."

He was a fool indeed if he believed Donata an indifferent mother. "He'll not take Peter away from you," I said. "I promise you that."

"Yes, well, do not kill Stanton, please. I went through much trouble to marry you, and I would like to enjoy it for a few more years at least."

I thought about Denis's reasoning that Donata, as a wealthy widow, had chosen me as the safest man she could wed herself to, in order to keep more ambitious or brutal gentlemen at bay. But the look in her eyes when she spoke did not suggest her choice had been one of convenience.

"Stay home tonight," I said abruptly.

She blinked at me. "I am hardly in a fit state to go out. It was a long journey, and I am exhausted."

"You should retire, then."

Donata gave me a long and level stare. "An excellent suggestion. Call Jacinthe, and I will have her prepare me for bed."

I rose. But instead of reaching for the bell pull to summon the redoubtable Jacinthe, I turned the key in the door's lock. Then I returned to a waiting Donata, and readied her for bed myself.

∼

As SATURDAY MORNING DAWNED, I WOKE WRAPPED AROUND MY wife, emerging from the soundest sleep I'd had in days.

I realized why she'd returned as soon as a beam of morning sun sneaked between a crack in the curtains and brushed my eyes. The air in the house already felt lighter, warmer, brighter.

Gabriella would arrive today. Donata had come back for her sake, not mine.

As it should be.

Donata slept on, her hair tangled, her face flushed with sleep. She could sleep through a wild thunderstorm, I knew from experience. Very little disturbed her in the morning hours.

I longed to tell her all that had happened in her absence and pry more details from her, but that could wait. She'd had a long and trying journey, and I let her sleep.

I carefully slid my arms from around her, dropped a kiss to her hair, and climbed out of bed.

Reaching for the dressing gown I'd learned to keep in her bedchamber in case of a night of impulsiveness, I slid it on, padding to the dressing room to cross it to my own bedroom. Bartholomew was in my chamber, as usual, ready to give me a bath and shovel me into clothes.

I was down at breakfast three quarters of an hour later, digging into a pile of eggs and sausage, a large stack of buttered toast at my elbow. Coffee, thick and strong, cut through the fog in my head.

Before I left the house for my morning ride, penned a quick letter to Lady Aline, informing her, as I'd promised, of Donata's return.

I then looked in on Anne, to remind her that Gabriella would come today. Anne gurgled as I talked—I was convinced she understood every word I said.

When I finished, Anne said, "Bah!" in a voice that rattled the walls. Nothing wrong with her lungs, or her spirit.

At last I handed her back to the indulgent nurse and took myself to the mews.

The groom had my hunter ready, and John, the stable lad, brought out Oro. The dog had turned into a beautiful animal even in the last few days, strong and sleek, his ears perking as he saw me. His tail waved hard when I turned to him, and I scratched his head.

"He don't belong in a city," John said. "He'll be happy when ye take him out to Hampshire in the summer."

I agreed. I departed for my ride, very aware of Oro watching me go.

The ride was uneventful, which suited me. I let my mount run in the nearly empty park, twisting and turning him in cavalry moves that made me feel youthful again.

Oro was waiting by the stable door when I returned, wagging his tail so hard that his entire back end rocked from side to side.

John grinned as he led my horse off, and I found a ball for Oro to chase down the long line of the mews. He brought it to my feet every time, then dashed away again, waiting for me to throw it once more.

A few of my neighbors' grooms cursed me for sending my dog racing past their stables, but others came out to watch in amusement.

At last both Oro and I were panting, and I left him for John to water.

Oro was a fine hound, I thought as I returned to the house, far too fine to have been left to wander the slums of St. Giles. As I refreshed myself with a glass of ale Barnstable brought me, I wrote a note to Grenville, asking Bartholomew to deliver it to him.

My letter was short, written on a sheet I cut in half so I wouldn't waste the paper.

Ask Mr. Egan if Mercer complained of losing a dog. G.L.

❧

AT THREE O'CLOCK, GABRIELLA ARRIVED, ESCORTED BY HER uncle, Quentin Auberge and his wife, Adeline. I remained home all day and drove the servants mad making sure all was prepared.

I had not seen Gabriella since before my journey to Egypt. She'd returned to France before I'd gone, and by the time I found my way back to England in December, the weather was far too daunting for me to want her to make the journey to London. April was the date Donata planned for her return, and April it was.

I was in the staircase hall when Monsieur and Madame Auberge alighted from the coach in the street, and Monsieur Auberge reached back to hand Gabriella down. Both Auberges looked tired from the long journey from southern France, but Gabriella skimmed into the house on light feet.

"Father!" she cried, and then I was lifting her, whirling her, astonished that this tall young woman was my little Gabriella.

She finished with the embrace before I did and pushed away from me, but only to hold my hands and kiss my cheeks, in the French manner.

"Are you well?" she asked me at the same time identical words came from my mouth. We both laughed.

"Where is Peter?" Gabriella said eagerly. "And I want to meet Anne."

Donata chose that moment to regally descend the stairs. She'd hung back to allow me to greet Gabriella alone, and I was grateful to her for that.

The footmen and Barnstable were already taking the Auberges' wraps and seeing that they were comfortable. Gabriella's aunt and uncle would stay with Lady Aline, as the generous woman had many guest rooms in her larger house. Gabriella would reside here, in the bedchamber that had become hers.

I greeted the Auberges and made the usual inquiries about the journey and the weather. They gave me the usual answers, and then Barnstable ushered them into the drawing room, which was warmed by a large fire.

Madame Auberge sent Gabriella a smile that lit her plain face. "You run and see your sister and brother. Monsieur and I will enjoy our English tea and cushions that do not bounce. Captain, she has talked of nothing since the New Year about how much she wants to meet her sister."

Donata, sliding easily into the role of gracious hostess, guided Madame Auberge into the drawing room, conversing with her in fluid French.

"I am rude," Gabriella said as Bartholomew took her cloak, his smile of welcome nearly splitting his face. "My uncle and aunt are very tired, and I should see to them. But I am racing with you to the nursery instead."

"Donata is excellent at seeing to the comfort of her guests," I said. "I too am rude and feel not one whit remorseful."

Bartholomew disappeared with the wraps, while I escorted Gabriella up the stairs. She was far swifter than I, and was at the top of the house before her plodding father could catch up to her.

By the time I entered the nursery, Gabriella had lifted Anne, raising her high as I liked to do, before swooping her into her arms. Anne squealed in her ear-piercing way, and Gabriella laughed in delight.

"She is beautiful. I knew she would be. Good afternoon, Anne. I am your sister, Gabriella."

She'd break my heart. Gabriella had been very upset when she'd learned that I, not the French major who'd raised her, was her true father. But being the sensible young woman she was, she soon reconciled herself to the fact that she had two fathers.

My estranged wife and Major Auberge had produced a number of children between them, and Gabriella loved every one of them. I was pleased to see she would love this half-sister as well.

"But where is Peter?" Gabriella asked in bewilderment as Anne clutched Gabriella's finely embroidered fichu and tried to stuff it into her mouth. "I brought him some little soldiers—the French army, I am afraid."

"He is ... away." I glanced at the nurse, who pretended to be absorbed in straightening Anne's nappies on the other side of the room. She was a trusted woman, but I would take no chances. "Visiting. He will return soon."

Gabriella looked disappointed. "Ah, well. I will put aside the gifts for another day. I brought Anne some things as well. Is that all right?"

"Of course," I assured her. "Now let us sit, and you will tell me everything you have done since you left us last summer."

"But no." Gabriella rocked Anne, who was making burbling noises and dribbling saliva all over Gabriella's bodice. Gabriella used her fichu to wipe Anne's mouth with the ease of long practice. "You must tell me everything about Egypt. I have read your letters over and over, but I want to hear about *all* your adventures with Mr. Grenville and Mr. Brewster and Bartholomew."

"I will tell you more than you will wish me to, and you will beg me to cease."

"I doubt that very much."

She was kind. Donata's eyes glazed a bit whenever I went on about the pasha's palace and the stark beauty of the desert. But I could give Gabriella the gifts I'd brought back for her from Alexandria and Cairo.

"We will have to talk around the very many outings Donata and Lady Aline have planned for you, I am afraid," I said.

"I am sure it will all be splendid." Her face fell. "Do you think they will mind terribly if I do not accept a proposal when it is all finished?"

"They will be devastated," I said, smiling. "But *I* will not mind at all."

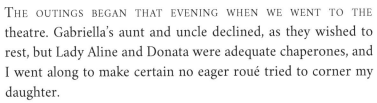

The outings began that evening when we went to the theatre. Gabriella's aunt and uncle declined, as they wished to rest, but Lady Aline and Donata were adequate chaperones, and I went along to make certain no eager roué tried to corner my daughter.

We took ourselves to Drury Lane to see *A Much Ado about Nothing*, which always seemed to me a silly play, full of misunderstandings, and characters unable to see through the flimsiest of disguises. But the actress playing Beatrice was spirited, and the troupe of tumblers between acts was quite good.

The young men who'd been Gabriella's hopeful suitors last year were in attendance, including Emmett Garfield, a young man I thought far too cocksure for his own good.

None of these gentlemen approached our box, however, only gazed longingly at Gabriella from afar. I was pleased to see that Gabriella didn't seem to notice any of them.

The next morning, I introduced Gabriella to Oro and also gave her the gold and lapis lazuli necklace I'd unearthed near the pyramids of Giza. Gabriella professed to adore Oro and clasped her hands in admiration when she beheld the necklace. I rather think she was more pleased with the dog, which did not upset me at all.

I'd had no time since Gabriella's arrival to consult with Grenville or Brewster about the murder and had to trust the pair of them to continue their discoveries.

Grenville did send me a reply to my question, which had reached me at breakfast.

Egan says Mercer never mentioned a dog, but that the man was careless about such things. Left all details of hunting and the farm to his steward. Egan is bursting with curiosity to know what a dog has to do with anything, but he is being polite and not tearing over to see you to drag it out of you.

I admit, I am curious myself. Your theory is that Mercer came up to Town, with his dog, and murdered Finch? Or sent his steward with said canine? An interesting idea, but I'm not certain I can credit it.

Freddy Hilliard told Marianne he saw you at Drury Lane last night with your daughter, and that she looked in fine spirits. He also said you sat beside her, fierce as a bulldog, snarling at any young man who glanced her way. Amusing, but I know how Freddy exaggerates.

I will speak to you more at our outing this afternoon, as I, at Lady Aline's command, will escort you and make dear Miss Lacey thoroughly fashionable.

The outing was south of the river, in Dulwich, where we would visit the public picture gallery.

The gallery was at Dulwich College, in a building designed by the architect John Soane, and housed a collection of paintings only recently opened to public view. The collection had an interesting history, Grenville told us—two gentlemen who had acquired many paintings for the unfortunate king of Poland were left with the entire collection when that king abdicated.

The two gentlemen could find no one who wanted to buy the paintings, though they offered them to the governments of Russia and Britain. Not long ago, both gentlemen passed away, leaving the collection to the widow of one of them, with the instructions that the paintings be made available for public viewing. Dulwich College was the fortunate recipient of the widow's bequest, and Soane redesigned the gallery there to house them.

Now, for a small fee, ordinary mortals could parade down the galleries and view paintings by Rembrandt and Poussin, van Dyke and Murillo, hung on walls of rich red.

Grenville, an expert on art, was our guide, explaining the merits of what he considered the most important pictures.

Gabriella, I could see, grew a bit tired of the extensive tour, but she politely listened and did not let her attention wander.

She and I exchanged knowing glances as Grenville ran on, but Donata was riveted and asked many questions.

We departed to find that the world outside had grown bright, as the morning's clouds had dispersed to give us a fine afternoon. The sunshine was warm, and Gabriella threw back her head to take it in.

"I say," came a voice across Dulwich green, followed by the spin of wheels and skid of hooves on a gravel path. "Oh, well met, cousin. Look Winston, it's our sweet coz, Donata. Dear lady, do stand still and let us greet you."

CHAPTER 18

*D*onata halted, her face flashing dismay before it settled into hardened resolve.

I looked down the path to the two gentlemen approaching, each in his own cabriolet—two-wheeled vehicles that were recently becoming fashionable, pulled by single, high-stepping horses. As it had grown warm, the cabriolets' hoods were drawn back to reveal the drivers, each a near perfect copy of the other.

The one who'd spoken tossed his reins to his tiger, the lad who rode along to hold the horses, and sprang to the ground. "And Mr. Grenville. How fortunate."

"Depends on one's point of view," Grenville murmured to me. He pulled out his quizzing glass and fixed his mouth into a slight sneer.

The man who'd descended wore a bright green coat over a pair of buff breeches, and a waistcoat of gold, green, and red damask. His collar was high, pushing his chin back so that he had to look down his nose. His cravat was wound in the same style of knot Grenville wore today—I had the feeling Grenville would instruct Gautier to never tie it so again.

"How are you, dear cousin Donata?"

"Robert," Donata said stiffly. She stood so still the feathers in her high crowned bonnet barely moved. "Winston," she added to the gentleman climbing a little more slowly from his cabriolet.

Robert and Winston St. John, the late Lord Breckenridge's nephews, were Peter's first cousins, referred to by Donata as Romulus and Remus.

Reckless rakehells, she also called them, two men very happy Breckenridge had produced issue so they'd not have the frightening prospect of inheriting the estate. They'd been left a generous allowance in trust by their late father and added to by Lord Breckenridge before he died—probably so they wouldn't constantly touch him for money.

"Funny we happened to be passing," Winston said, joining his brother. His suit was nearly identical, down to the tassels on his boots, though his waistcoat was more gold than green.

"Yes, it is interesting," Donata responded without inflection.

"Captain Lacey, how are you?" Robert said to me. He didn't speak to Gabriella, which was correct, as they hadn't been introduced. He glanced at her in curiosity, but I was not about to oblige.

"I am well," I said in answer to Robert's question. "Thank you. And you?"

"*Extremely* good health. Not like Cousin Stanton." Robert laughed, the sound like a neighing horse. "He looked as though he'd swallowed an entire orchard of lemons last time I clapped eyes on him."

"Yes, he had to rush to Somerset to recover," Winston put in. "Have you been aggrieving him again, fair coz?"

Donata refused to reward their obvious fishing for information. "I am sorry to hear it. I hope he recovers."

"You do not," Winston said joyfully. "You wish him to the devil. He fancies himself as Viscount Breckenridge—too bad he has three legitimate heirs in his way. Do take good care of little cousin Peter."

"I always do," Donata responded calmly.

I did not like the way Winston's eyes gleamed when he spoke of Peter. Had Stanton sent the pair to discover what had become of him?

Of course he had. Why else would these two dullards have made the journey across the Thames to a picture gallery, of all places? If my daughter had not been there, I might have invited Grenville to help me haul them off.

Brewster, who'd insisted on accompanying us today, lingered beneath a tree in the park beyond. He did not move, but his stance told me he was at the ready to come to my assistance should any hauling off be required.

"Surprised Peter's not with you," Robert said artlessly to Donata. "I'd think looking at dull old paintings quite riveting for the poor little chap. You lock him in the house so relentlessly."

Donata flushed. "What nonsense. Good day to you Robert. Winston."

She gave them each a cold bow. Gabriella remained mute and bewildered beside me, Grenville protectively on her other side.

The pair of buffoons did not move. They exchanged a glance, obviously trying to decide what to do.

Grenville came to the rescue. When the brothers did not withdraw, he raised his quizzing glass and stepped forward as though examining an insect that had caught his attention.

"*What* is on your chest?" Grenville continued to move smoothly to Robert, bending to study his gaudy waistcoat in minute detail. He rose, the quizzing glass fixed, while Robert waited in trepidation.

Grenville stepped back, flicking the quizzing glass into his pocket. "You call this a *waistcoat*, do you, Mr. St. John?"

Robert flushed. Winston started to laugh then broke off as Grenville gave *his* waistcoat a severe look.

Grenville said nothing more. He could devastate with his silences, leaving the gentlemen he critiqued to fill in the words.

The brothers could ignore him or laugh him off, but if they did, they risked censure from every other gentleman who recognized Grenville as the grand arbiter of male fashion. Or, they could rush to their tailors and beg for help mending their gaffe.

They chose retreat. "Ah, yes," Robert said. "My tailor is rather a cretin, and I shall have to have sharp words with him. Perhaps you'd attend with me, Grenville, and guide him."

Grenville only gave him a frosty look, and Winston jabbed Robert hard with his elbow.

Robert shot his brother a scowl, but he tipped his hat. "Well met, Donata. Enjoy the rest of your outing. Grenville. Captain."

He bowed to each of us in turn, including Gabriella in general but fortunately not singling her out. If he dared leer at her, I'd tear his face off.

Winston also made a neutral bow, and the two of them at last returned to their cabriolets, their voices rising in argument as soon as their backs were turned.

"I beg your pardon, Gabriella," Donata said with sincerity. "Breckenridge's cousins are ghastly. It's best to ignore them."

The two young men ascended to their seats, taking the reins relinquished by their tigers, still arguing. As one, they let their horses spring forward, wheels spinning in the gravel, and leapt away, leaving their tigers behind.

The two lads must be used to Romulus and Remus rushing off, because they started walking slowly after them.

"I see they're determined to race to the end of the park," Grenville said wearily. "Never mind the Sunday strollers out to enjoy the weather."

Dust spiraled up behind the large wheels of the cabriolets,

Winston standing in his seat to give his horses the office. Neck and neck, the vehicles raced down the narrow lane, forcing those walking on it to dash for the fields on either side.

"They are ever competing with each other," Donata said. "Hate each other yet are devoted at the same time."

Possibly why she called them Romulus and Remus. Romulus killed his brother in the end.

The cabriolets flew down the gravel, wheels bouncing as the horses stretched into a gallop. We watched, the five of us— Brewster from under his tree—mesmerized by the racing horses and the vehicles nearly floating off the ground. So must the spectators at the Circus Maximus have done as the charioteers charged their teams around and around.

I saw, as though the world had slowed, Robert's cab rise up and up, and then hit the earth again, just as one of the wheels snapped.

Screams sounded, as did the shriek of the horse as it fell in a flurry of limbs. The cabriolet twisted all the way around, breaking and scattering, Robert's body twisting along with it.

He hit the ground, arms outflung, and then the remains of the cabriolet, including the second large wheel, landed on top of him.

Winston, whose cab had continued at the same breakneck speed, frantically turned his rig, his protesting horse bucking and fighting. With surprising competence, Winston got the horse righted and around, a thick column of dust in his wake.

He raced back to his brother, slowing his cab enough to spring out and let the horse trot away, reins flying. The tigers sprinted forward, one rushing to catch Winston's horse, the other going for Robert's.

I was running as well, Grenville ahead of me, Brewster keeping pace with him.

Passers-by converged on the wreckage, pulling away the wheel, the black-painted boards, the canvas and wire hood.

"Robbie!" Winston was shouting. "Robbie!"

He fell to his knees, clearing the wreckage from his brother's body. Grenville and Brewster reached them, Grenville dropping to pry Winston away from Robert. Brewster lent his strength to lift away the last of the debris.

I stopped beside the group, my leg aching, my breath rapid. Robert's tiger had righted his horse, and the beast walked away with him, trembling. I could tell by its gait that, though shaken, the horse hadn't broken any limbs.

The same couldn't be said for Robert. He lay on his side, his head covered in blood, his right leg and one of his arms contorted into unnatural positions. His eyes were half open, his lips peeled back as though frozen in a shout.

"Robbie!" Winston sobbed, reaching for him.

"Is he dead?" One of the passers-by asked.

Grenville again lifted Winston aside so I could kneel beside Robert. "Grenville, your quizzing glass," I said.

He readily handed it to me, unclipping the chain from his waistcoat. I shoved the glass between Robert's lips.

At first nothing happened. We watched in silence, the tension heavy, Winston sobbing beside me. After a long while, I at last saw a thin film of mist coat the glass.

"He's alive," I said, releasing my breath. "But stunned senseless. He needs to be attended right away, or he will die."

Winston had gained his feet, but he ran his hands through his hair, his hat long gone. "What do I do?" he moaned. "What do I do?"

Brewster bent to me. "Tell me where to take him, guv."

"The college. They'll have a surgeon or know where to fetch one."

"I know," the gentleman who'd joined us said. "I'll tell him to be ready." He dashed away.

Brewster, with surprising gentleness, lifted Robert into his arms. He deposited him in Winston's cabriolet, the nearest vehicle, now brought around by Winston's tiger. Brewster began to climb to the seat as well, but Grenville stopped him.

"Let me. I'm probably the best driver here. Hop on the back, lad," he said to Winston's tiger. "I'll need help with him when we arrive."

Brewster readily stepped away, and Grenville sprang to the seat. He tapped the horse with the reins, and the cab sprang forward into a smooth but rapid pace. Winston walked forlornly behind it.

Donata and Gabriella reached me as I watched them go. Brewster had returned to the wreckage, helping others clear it up.

"Will he be all right?" Gabriella asked worriedly.

"Time will tell, as will the surgeon's competence," I said. "Grenville will see to things." I tried to sound reassuring.

"Bloody fool," Donata said. "I knew their ridiculous ways would bring them to grief."

Her face was white, her body stiff with agitation. It was one thing to despise a man, another to watch him be twisted and broken in the space of a moment.

"Guv." Brewster was at my side, a frown on his face.

I walked a little way apart with him, despite Donata scowling after me. "What is it?"

"This weren't an accident," Brewster said, keeping his voice low. "The wheel didn't break, it were loosened. Pin that held it cut short and replaced so none would see it had been done. That wheel were held on by a prayer. Could have fallen off at any time, giving all riding on it a tumble."

CHAPTER 19

I understand Mr. Brewster not wishing to distress me or Gabriella," Donata said. "But I do wish he wouldn't draw you aside and whisper like that. It is quite annoying."

We spoke in the upstairs room of a charming inn of white-washed stone covered with climbing roses that were just beginning to turn green with spring. I suggested we stay the night in Dulwich and not attempt the journey home when we were all unnerved by Robert's accident, and it was uncertain whether he would live.

I'd told Donata right away what Brewster had said, and I'd made certain Gabriella heard. I did not wish to upset her, but I also did not want to hide things from her.

Grenville had found the inn for us, having stayed here before on his way home from Brighton. The landlord was pleased to give us three private rooms and a parlor, as well as a hot supper.

"The poor man," Gabriella said as we took our places around the table. "I could tell you did not like him, but it is terrible."

"The surgeon seemed a competent fellow," I said. The sausage and soup with thick bread smelled appetizing, but I noted that all three of us only picked at our food. "He said he'd seen far worse than this on the Peninsula, and I concur."

Indeed, the surgeon, a big fellow with arms as large as a blacksmith's, had pronounced Robert's leg and arm broken—the arm in three places—and his ribs smashed, but he seemed confident he could bring him around.

Grenville generously had found Winston lodgings near the surgeon's then had given Winston laudanum and sent him to bed, promising to return to the surgeon and keep an eye on Robert.

Donata drew the tines of her fork through the juices that had dripped from her sausages. "Stanton has done this, hasn't he?"

"He could very well have," I answered. "I hardly see him sneaking into a stable himself to replace the linchpin on a wheel, but he could have hired someone to do it for him."

"Well, I shall certainly find out," Donata said decidedly. "Perhaps Brewster could be of assistance in this."

"I will ask him." Brewster at the moment was in the taproom, enjoying a meal and the local brew, probably with more gusto than we were.

"Is this why you sent Peter away?" Gabriella asked.

We had not mentioned Peter or talked much about Stanton, but Gabriella was good at putting things together.

"Yes," Donata said. "I am glad I did, more than ever. I had no idea Stanton was so eager to get his hands on the title. He was never so keen when Breckenridge was alive."

"Perhaps he has taken some losses recently," I suggested. "And is in need of money."

"In that case, why not simply ask? Why be so beastly? He could pry funds out of Robert or Winston without hurting them, without threatening Peter." She shuddered and laid down her fork. "With Robert and Winston gone, there would be no one between Stanton and the title but Peter."

I laid my hand on hers. "He will not touch him. This I vow."

Donata drew a long breath, but the fear in her eyes was real. "Stanton is as ugly and evil as my husband ever was. You know that Robert and Winston turning up here was no coincidence. Stanton sent them to follow us."

"Yes, I had guessed that."

Gabriella listened, troubled. "Can you not go to a magistrate? Tell him this cousin is threatening you? Is threatening my brother?"

"We'd need proof," I said. "I will, of course, apprise Sir Montague, but he, like his Runners, will not be able to apprehend the man if we have no evidence. The linchpin might simply have worn through."

"Brewster would not have mentioned it if it had worn through," Donata said. "Presumably, he knows the difference."

I agreed. "A Runner like Quimby and even Pomeroy is careful. I will send Brewster to Robert's stables to see what he can find."

Donata sipped her glass of sherry and grimaced at its taste. "Brewster will ask with his fists, you know."

"Very likely, or at least the threat of them." I managed to eat a bite of sausage, feeling a little better. "If the men in Robert's mews are innocent, they will not be the worse for wear. But if one of them is in the pay of Cousin Stanton, then he will deserve whatever Brewster gives him."

ROBERT DID LIVE, BUT HE WAS A POOR SPECIMEN WHEN DONATA and I went to visit him. His arm was wrapped in bandages, his leg in a splint, and he could barely part his eyelids to look at her.

He swiveled his eyes to take me in and croaked in a whisper, "How is my horse?"

"Well," I said, trying to sound calm and confident. "Grenville looked out for him. You know how good he is with horseflesh." Grenville had arranged for a stable and a groom for Robert's horse as well as Winston's horse and rig.

Robert let out a relieved breath. "Thank you."

We did not stay long. The surgeon's wife, who was caring for Robert, soon shooed us out.

"Poor fellow," Donata said as we joined Grenville in our landau and made for London. "I dislike him, but he did not deserve that."

"I feel bad that I twitted him about his waistcoat now," Grenville said. "Such a petty thing."

"But it truly was ugly, Mr. Grenville," Gabriella pointed out.

We laughed, but shakily. Robert would mend, and most would put the wreck down to an accident and the brothers' recklessness.

Chill bit me. Would Stanton try again? And where the devil was he? I decided I would find out whether he'd gone to Somerset in truth and exactly what he was up to.

When we arrived home, Donata wrote letters explaining why she and Gabriella had not turned up at the social engagements of the night before, but said adamantly that we must appear tonight.

Thus invoking one of our very loud domestic disputes.

"Shall we let my be-damned cousin ruin Gabriella's chances?" Donata demanded of me as we stood alone in her boudoir, the other servants having prudently withdrawn. "Or shall we show him he cannot cow us?"

"What is to stop him from trying to use you or Gabriella to coerce me into telling him where Peter is?" I returned. "Or him from threatening you to keep quiet about his attempt to kill Robert? It is too dangerous. You and Gabriella will remain home until Stanton answers for his deeds. Remember what one of your dear friends did to you over the Carlton House affair."

"That was different," Donata said. "I had no idea he was such a villain. With Stanton, I am well prepared."

"Until I find out exactly where the man is and how to keep him the hell away from you, you cannot possibly rush about London, especially with my daughter. When will the linchpin on *your* landau break?"

"I hope that Hagen and the men inside my mews are incorruptible," Donata said, eyes flashing. "They despised my late husband and all his family. Hagen keeps a sharp eye on all my rigs."

"Perhaps, but an attack might be something subtle, like pushing you in front of a coach when you alight at the opera. Or as blatant as shooting you on the street. Stanton apparently has the money to hire men to do bad deeds for him."

"Mr. Brewster will be on hand, will he not?" Donata asked. "He doesn't let you out of his sight."

"Brewster works for Mr. Denis, not me." My voice rose. "And not you."

"Brewster is an honorable man. I doubt he'd stand aside and let someone shoot me. I believe Mr. Denis would be most displeased if you were upset."

"Do not joke about this, Donata," I said fiercely. "Getting my daughter married off to a weedy young man is not as important as keeping her safe and well and as far from your husband's despicable family as possible."

"And will you hide her away again as soon as there is any whiff of danger?" Donata snapped. "That will be all the time, if so. It is not fair to Gabriella to keep her from having a marriage, children, and a happy life because of Breckenridge's horrible cousins."

"You have decided for her, have you? What if she does not

wish to marry these imbecilic boys you and Lady Aline have chosen, giving her no say in the matter—or me either."

Donata flushed, but her jaw tightened. "They are not imbecilic boys. They are intelligent and accomplished young men who have money and position and will become influential in time. You haven't bothered to talk at length to any of them, so how would you know what they are like? You can trust that I will not pair your daughter with a simpleton. She will be happy with whomever she chooses."

"You can foretell the future? Like the crone in Parson's Point who used to terrify everyone in the village? How the devil do you know what will and will not make Gabriella happy? She scarce knows herself. I want her to be near me, yes, but not if she is forced to marry an insipid Englishman who pays more attention to his horses than to her. If she's happier rusticating in France with the family she's known her entire life, I will let her remain there."

Donata's face changed from white to red to white again as I made this speech.

"First, I will thank you not to compare me to a crone," she said, her voice calm with fury. "Second, of course Gabriella does not know what will make her happy. Young women do not at that age. As I told you, *I* fancied myself madly in love with a handsome gentleman who turned out to be the worst sort of rakehell. Gabriella will never be in that danger. But if you shut her away this Season, these young men will find other ladies who are eager to marry, and there go her chances. She does not have much time."

"And the fact that *you* made disastrous choices does not mean you can right the wrong with Gabriella," I roared. "Do not shovel her into a marriage to soothe your own conscience."

The scarlet returned to Donata's cheeks with a vengeance. "I see, my *favor* to you is only to make up for my own stupidity and unhappiness? I care nothing for Gabriella, but only for myself? I am pleased you have enlightened me."

"I did not mean that, of course." Donata had the irritating skill of turning my words around on me. "You have been very good to her, but I question why you wish to endanger her to rush her into a marriage. Can it not wait a week?"

Donata lifted her chin. "Gabriel, I can forgive your ridiculous remarks because you have no idea how difficult it is to be a woman. If Gabriella is left on the shelf, either here or in France, she will be derided and shamed, pitied by kindly people and despised by cruel ones. The consensus will be that it was only to be expected, as Gabriella's father was a destitute army captain put on half pay for arguing with his commander. They will bring up what a wastrel *your* father was and speculate that the apple does not fall far from the tree. And Gabriella's ruined chances will have an effect on Anne's."

I knew that every word she said was true. I'd told Charlotte Finch much the same, that a woman needed a protector, be he father, brother, or husband.

At the same time, I knew my determined wife would argue rings around me until she got her way.

"Damnation!" I shouted. "I am not asking you to put her into a convent, I am asking you to stay home from the theatre and bloody soirees until I can break every bone in Stanton's body. She is *my* daughter, and I will not let her be paraded about against my wishes. And *you* are my wife. Tonight, you will *not* go out."

Donata's brows climbed, and her voice could have frozen a raging river. "I see. It has come to this, has it?"

"It has. I do not understand why you are being so stubborn about it."

"Because I am a broken woman dispirited by her first marriage," she said, her voice continuing to hold vast chill. "And I must prove that I am happy in my second to cease wagging tongues. But if my husband commands that I remain in the house, then I must do so."

I wanted to shake her, but because I would never hurt a woman, least of all one I loved, I balled my hands and made her a stiff bow.

"Your husband does command it. Because he knows his wife is being an obstinate mule, because she hates to lose an argument."

"She does," Donata acknowledged. "Especially when she knows she is right. She will not back down. Perhaps her husband regrets marrying her?"

"Never," I said in a ringing voice.

I knew that if I stayed, I'd say something unconscionably stupid and lose all I'd gained, so I turned my back and left her.

I slammed the door so hard I expected the wood to splinter, but this was a well-made house, and the door took the blow well.

∾

DONATA DECIDED NOT TO SPEAK TO ME FOR THE REST OF THE afternoon and evening, but Gabriella told me in a whisper that she was happy to stay in. She was distressed about Donata's cousin for his own sake, and not ready to face the chattering *ton*.

Gabriella and I dined together, which was a fine thing. Donata did not deign to come out of her chamber.

"She only worries for me," Gabriella said, defending her. "If I were an ordinary English girl, she would be correct. But me, I am not so worried for my chances."

Gabriella had heard our argument, of course. The entire household had. Gabriella was the only one who pretended not to.

I ought to have prodded Gabriella as to why she didn't fear

spinsterhood, but at the moment, I was only happy we were together, and so I made myself enjoy the meal.

Donata and I would make it up. We always did.

~

I HAD ALREADY SENT A LETTER TO SIR MONTAGUE HARRIS IN Whitechapel about my suspicions as to Robert St. John's accident, but I visited him the next morning as well.

When he received me, Sir Montague had disquieting news of his own.

"I have not heard from Mr. Quimby in days," he said. "Though he promised to send me a letter every afternoon. I wrote to the chief constable in Kent, and he said he has not seen Mr. Quimby at all, nor did he ever reach the hulks at Sheppey."

CHAPTER 20

*N*ever reached them?" I gazed at Sir Montague in bafflement, and he returned the look, his usual good humor absent.

I pictured Lamont Quimby, his neat appearance and diligent and logical inquiries. He was skilled at his job but not large and strong like Pomeroy. "Perhaps he decided to pursue a question and did not want to alert those he investigated."

I spoke the words with an optimism I did not feel. Finch, a brute of a man, had been murdered. Pierce Egan, a well-known and popular figure, had been waylaid and beaten. What would this killer do to Quimby?

"I fear he's run afoul of the villain called Captain Steadman," Sir Montague said. "We suspect he assists in prisoner escapes, though none have proved it."

"Quimby mentioned him," I said. Not by name, but this must be the same merchant captain Quimby had spoken of. Such a man would not want a Runner in his midst, and might take desperate measures to keep his business going and his neck from the noose.

Sir Montague's expression told me he shared my concern. "I

would rush to the end of Kent myself, but it is difficult for me to travel these days, and too many duties keep me here. Likewise I would send patrollers to discover things for me, but I cannot risk alerting magistrates who might be involved in what you tell me Mr. Egan has discovered."

"I will go," I said quickly.

"No." Sir Montague gave me a stern look. "This is beyond what you should have your hand in. Finch was a dangerous man, and yet he was cornered and murdered. Also, we do not know if Lord Mercer had anything to do with Finch's death. Finch had many enemies. Mr. Egan was only roughed up and frightened."

"Pierce Egan is beloved of the upper classes for his writings on sport," I said. "His murder would be thoroughly investigated, shouted from every page of every newspaper. Mercer knows to be cautious with him."

"Perhaps. But again, I say, Lord Mercer might have nothing to do with anything but using prisoners for his own ends. I would prefer to deal with him myself."

"I will go charging in like a mad bull, you mean." I gave him a grim smile. "And you wish to use a more delicate approach."

"It is a delicate situation. Lord Mercer is a boor, but he is also vastly wealthy and gives much money to maintain Britain's superiority on the seas and across the Empire. We cannot afford to anger him."

Officials like Sir Montague could not afford to, he meant. If Lord Mercer had friends in the right places in government, he could remove Sir Montague from his post. I did not believe Sir Montague clung to his power out of personal glory, but he enjoyed his work, and if he were retired he could not stop men like Mercer abusing their positions.

"I would like to make certain Mr. Quimby is alive and well," I said. "I feel responsible for bringing him into the investigation."

Sir Montague's eyes held a knowing glint. "I appreciate your solicitude. I will only sanction this journey if you take another Runner with you—I suggest Mr. Pomeroy. And only to discover where Mr. Quimby is and to bring him home, mind. Not to approach Lord Mercer or Captain Steadman for any reason."

Pomeroy would hold me to that, I knew. He did not want to lose his post either.

"Pomeroy," I said. "I will ask him. Not Spendlove," I finished dryly.

Sir Montague's large belly moved with his laugh. "Mr. Spendlove would certainly be a cat among the pigeons. He'd arrest half of Kent and be tossed into the Thames for his troubles. And still not understand that he'd angered every powerful man from here to the North Sea. No, I believe you and Pomeroy will do well. As for the other matter ..."

Sir Montague's smile vanished as he tapped the letter in which I'd told him about Robert's cabriolet and our suspicion that Stanton had deliberately damaged it.

"Stanton St. John is also an influential man," Sir Montague said. "As is the entire St. John family. He has many friends and connections, as well as wealth of his own. I wonder why he is so keen to inherit?"

"I speculated that he might have money troubles. Lost a packet in a wager he couldn't pay, or some such."

"Your Mr. Grenville would have heard something like that," Sir Montague said. "Debts of honor are everything in his circles. But it is a thought. I will look into it. Otherwise, unless you can prove the man had something to do with it, and that the pin was deliberately cut ..." He spread his hands. "Mr. St. John was in Somerset at the time?"

"As far as we know," I said. "I would like to find that out."

"Well, we shall have to send men running to the four winds, won't we? You and Mr. Pomeroy head to Kent. I will inquire whether Stanton St. John has truly gone to Somerset."

"I worry for my wife," I said hesitantly. "She is ... headstrong."

Sir Montague laughed again. "Her ladyship is exceedingly sure of herself, but from what I have observed, she is sensible and surrounded by many powerful friends. She should be safe enough at home."

I wondered. I'd made the decision to search for Quimby on impulse, but I knew Donata would never remain in the house while I was gone. I would either have to take her with me—into more danger—or make certain no one could go near her.

I thanked Sir Montague, said I'd inform Pomeroy, and left to journey first to Bow Street and then to Mayfair to speak with Denis.

POMEROY WAS PLEASED TO BE CHOSEN TO LOOK FOR QUIMBY. "I knew there was something bad in this case," he rumbled. "Don't you worry, Captain, I won't lose the thread and pursue other matters once we're there. Now, if I see a wretch stealing something before me own eyes, I'll have to nick 'im, but otherwise, I'm your man."

Mr. Denis, though again displeased with me for seeing him without an appointment, agreed to watch over Donata and Gabriella. They'd not stir a step without at least three of his men, and usually more, guarding them, whether they went to the shops, or the theatre, or a supper ball.

Brewster, however, would journey to Sheppey with me. Denis did not believe Pomeroy alone could keep me out of trouble.

Gabriella, when I explained I was to depart for a day or so and begged her to please stay in the house when not with Donata, nodded and said she understood.

"I am not so featherheaded as to rush about on my own," she

said. "I am no longer the innocent country girl, Father, as you know. And I saw what happened to Lady Breckenridge's poor cousin Robert." She shivered. "London is such a dangerous place."

She'd learned how dangerous the first year she'd come to me. I'd nearly lost her, and that memory made my throat tighten.

I pulled Gabriella into my embrace, holding her close and dropping a kiss to her hair. I would never let anyone hurt her again, even if I had to be in thrall to Denis for the rest of my life.

Donata took the news I was leaving coolly—that is, when I finally persuaded her to open her door to me.

"As always, you rush into danger while you try to pack me in down and tuck me into a cupboard," she said.

"As always," I answered.

She gave me a narrow look. "You are a great idiot, Gabriel, but a noble one. You have softened me up by making me worried about your Mr. Quimby. Go. I will keep my outings to a minimum, and not run about without Mr. Denis's hulking men. As long as they dress decently, I do not mind."

"I am certain Mr. Denis will ensure they are well turned out," I said in a mild voice.

Her eyes softened. "I am not so stupid as to believe Stanton will not try to do exactly as you say he might regarding Gabriella or me. I will take great care." Donata touched my coat, her fingers over my heart. "But *you* must take care. If you get yourself run through or shot then … Well, I shall be very cross with you."

I bent to show her how I appreciated her sentiment, then I took up the small bag Bartholomew had packed for me, and departed with Brewster to meet Pomeroy.

⁓

Grenville had very much wanted to come with us, but he assuaged his disappointment by saying he would continue investigating Stanton, and also Finch's acquaintances, including Mr. Blackmore. He would also watch over Donata, escorting her and Gabriella to every engagement. He would make tongues wag, he said, he would stick so closely by them.

He had my gratitude.

At any other time, I'd have enjoyed the journey. The spring air was soft, the country sky a light blue. Donata had insisted she pay for a private coach for us, which took us into Kent with speed and comfort.

Brewster rode on top with the coachman, wanting to put as much distance between himself and a Runner as possible. Pomeroy sprawled on the carriage seat opposite me and slept most of the way, his snore filling the small space.

We followed a road that led south of the marshlands into farm country. The fields were dotted with the strange, conical chimneys of oast houses, buildings in which hops were spread to be dried. It reminded me of Marcus, who wanted to turn the fields of the Lacey estate into barley to sell to the brewers.

That in turn reminded me I didn't know where Marcus was, only that he was off on an errand for Denis. One more person in the world I worried about.

Our journey took two days, with the horses changed often. By the end of the second day, we crossed the river Medway on a ferry and headed for the Isle of Sheppey, which was cut off from the rest of Kent by a thin piece of water called the Swale.

South and east of Sheppey lay the estate of Lord Mercer, so Egan had said, a prosperous piece of land stretching through rich fields toward the sea. I had promised Sir Montague I would not seek out Mercer, but I gazed southward, wondering if I'd be able to hold myself to my word.

Our first destination, however, was the island and the hulks there.

I paid for the ferry crossing to Sheppey, and the carriage rolled onto the flat barge to be floated across the Swale.

Flat land under large skies flowed around me, sunshine gleaming on the strip of water to either side of us. I was reminded of Norfolk, and the touch of homesickness the thought engendered surprised me. As a lad, I had not been able to rush from Norfolk quickly enough. Now I looked forward to summer and walking with Gabriella along the wide, gentle shore at Cley.

We disembarked from the ferry and continued along the narrow track to Queenborough.

The Royal Navy had been on the northern tip of this island for a century and more, ever since the entertaining Samuel Pepys had recommended shoring up the garrison in the late 1600s, thus guarding the entrance to the Thames. So said the little guidebook Grenville had thrust at me before I'd gone.

A gun tower stood on the very tip of the island, where the Medway and Thames met, in a place the locals called Sheerness. The tower had been built in the late seventeenth century but was in much disrepair now, said my book. As the long war with France was over, and Bonaparte had never managed to finish his plans to invade England, we'd likely not need such a thing for a long time.

Despite the April warmth, the wind coming off the sea and the mud flats was sharp. I huddled into my coat, watching fat clouds race overhead, as we found accommodation in Queenborough.

After a decent enough meal and ale and a sleep in tiny rooms under the slates, we headed the next morning two miles north to the Royal Navy docks and the hulks.

The houses we passed on our way to the point were tiny but neat and painted a uniform grayish blue. Women came out to watch us pass, and small children ran through the streets, shouting after us.

Brewster went silent as we descended the coach and received our permission to go out to the docks—which was given to Pomeroy, who acted as leader of our party. The navy men would reluctantly admit a Runner, we'd decided, but an army captain alone, probably not. Rivalries ran deep, and I'd met naval men who could be utter bastards to their army counterparts.

Brewster hunkered behind me, pretending to be my servant, his hat pulled well down around his ears.

We were given a guide, a young sailor whose cheeks were reddened by the wind, the youth eager to finish with port duty and head off to see the world.

I smelled the hulks before I saw them, two rudderless, mastless ships resting on a mud flat offshore, low tide keeping them out of the water. They were about half a mile apart, but the stench blown toward us made me regret eating such a hearty breakfast.

Human beings packed together, and waste, blood, disease, and death, combined into a miasma that was bad enough this far away. I hated to think of the men trapped there, breathing that air, praying they survived long enough to live on dry land again.

"They wait here about three months," our young guide, who gave his name as Jones, said. "Then the prisoners are shipped out to Van Diemen's Land. Long journey."

Many would die along the way, and those who made it to the far side of the world would be subjected to hard labor, often for the rest of their lives.

"Prisoners from France were kept in the hulks during the wars," Seaman Jones went on. "But when the Frenchies went home, the ships were needed for our own villains."

"Any ever escape from them?" Pomeroy asked with professional interest.

"They try. It ain't easy. They mostly attempt it at night, if they can get out of their shackles, and either they're shot or they go the wrong way and drown. Water's beastly cold."

Frigid. I'd bathed in the North Sea in my boyhood but I'd been hardened to the chill and it hadn't seemed so harsh then. My years in warmer climates and my injury had made me more sensitive to cold, as I was now, shivering in the brisk wind blowing over the mud and water.

We walked along the strand, turning our left sides to the sea to head toward the shipping docks beyond the naval ones. Commercial vessels put to sea from here, fairly small ones carrying cargo across the Channel to France or Holland, or perhaps south to Portugal and Spain, and larger vessels that trod the world.

The entire strand teemed with ant-like movement, as men worked in the yards, both naval and civilian. Naval ships rocked at the ends of moorings, and one ship was in a huge dry dock, a racket of hammering and sawing filling the spring day. On the commercial side, men ran up and down gangplanks with loads under their arms or guided winches to move nets full of cargo from decks and open holds to land.

Both sets of workers carried on without much cheer. The endless sky, endless water, and flat, flat land might have something to do with that. Such a landscape was hard on those unused to it.

Along a more deserted stretch of shore a line of men dug a trench in a desultory fashion. They were chained together, watched over by several large fellows with pistols on their belts, whips folded in their hands. One of the chained convicts gazed at us, his eyes devoid of expression.

Brewster glanced at them and away. I gave the man who stared at me a polite nod. He looked startled then quickly put his head down and went back to digging.

"Poor buggers," Brewster said in a whisper.

He might be here with those chained men if I did not clear

him of this murder. I quickened my steps to catch up with Pomeroy.

"Which ship belongs to Captain Steadman?" Pomeroy was asking as he strolled, his eye on the line of masts around the corner of the point.

Our sailor gave a visible start, and his face lost some of its pinkness. "He's out," he said quickly.

"When's he returning? I hear he assists fellows who maybe don't like it so much on the underside of New South Wales."

"Never heard that," Jones stammered.

"Ah, well," Pomeroy said. "Only curious. Did you give this tour to another Runner? Name of Quimby?"

Now our guide looked confused. "Never heard no one of that name. Never saw no Runner either. You're me first." He looked proud.

"Funny that. Quimby said he'd be in this area—would have arrived several days ago."

"I'm not always walking visitors around, sir," Jones said. "And Sheppey's a big place. He could have gone to Minster or Leysdon—Leysdon's on the south end of the island."

"True. Or he might not have come here at all. Thought I'd ask."

Pomeroy spoke offhandedly, as though Quimby's whereabouts didn't much interest him. I walked silently behind the two, the tip of my cane sinking into mud between the stones. Brewster crunched behind me, head down, his breathing loud.

We continued the tour of the docks, thanked the cheerful Jones and the sour-faced lieutenant who'd lent us Jones in the first place, and returned to our carriage.

Before I ascended, I felt eyes on me, and turned my head to see a large man in the shadow of a brick building, staring hard at me. He said nothing, only looked, and then turned as Brewster came up behind me.

We made our way to our lodgings with no further occurrence except that the wind sharpened. Clouds bunched up, bringing us rain.

We warmed ourselves with a pint of ale in our inn at Queenborough. "We've learned nothing," I said to Pomeroy as we sat in the inglenook by the fire. Brewster had remained in the yard with the coachman, keeping a healthy distance between himself and Pomeroy.

"Not necessarily." Pomeroy leaned back, resting his tankard on his wide chest. "We discovered that talking about Steadman made a young seaman nervous. He's been told to keep quiet, an order that could only have come from higher up. We also discovered he was truly baffled when I mentioned Quimby, so the man might never have set foot in the Royal Navy's shipyards. Might not even have made it to Sheppey."

In that case, where the devil was he? Waylaid on the road? Highwaymen were by no means completely a thing of the past. Captured by Lord Mercer? By this Captain Steadman?

"Guv." Brewster approached the table, holding a tankard which he'd secured before ducking out with the coachman. "Man what was watching you up by the shipyard is here. Think he has sommut to say."

Pomeroy began to rise, but Brewster's hand came up. "No Runners. He's here for the captain, not you."

Pomeroy sat back down without losing his bonhomie. "Tell me all about it when you return, Captain. Don't mind you doing my job for me."

I set down my pint and followed Brewster through the narrow hall of the inn to the yard. Brewster continued out of that into an alley as narrow as the inn's hall, a mere dirt path between high stone walls.

A man skulked in the shadows of the house at the end of this. Brewster, having divested himself of his tankard in the yard, moved quickly and had our fellow hemmed in.

The man's face was covered with bristly beard, the corners

of his eyes lined from sun and wind. He stood bareheaded in the rain, not seeming to mind that his hair was dripping.

"I know where your beak is," he said before I could ask who he was.

"Do ye?" Brewster didn't touch the man or even ball his fists, but the threat he exuded was clear. "Where is he then? And don't be touching the captain for coin."

"Don't want your coin." The man's accent was flat, a native of the coastal fens. "Ye want to know or not?"

"Please," I interceded. "Anything will be helpful."

"He's on the hulk, ain't he?" the man said. "They knocked the poor bugger about then dragged him there. Ten to one he's already dead."

CHAPTER 21

The rain took on a fiercer chill. "Hulk?" I asked the man, my lips stiff. "Which one?"

He pointed off to his right. His finger indicated the wall, but I understood what he meant. The easternmost one, the *Atonement*.

"How do you know?" I asked.

The man shrugged, but Brewster took a step to him, and he shrank back.

I assessed him. Our informer had the build of a laborer, but unlike the locals inside the tavern, who were loud, whether snarling or singing, this man barely parted his lips to talk.

His spirit had been broken. I'd seen such a thing in soldiers in the army, who had gone into battle once too often. They folded up into themselves, some continuing their duty as expected, but without any fear or hope—they felt nothing at all. Others slid off into the night and either deserted or ended their misery with knife or pistol.

"You've been there," I said. "On the *Atonement*, I mean. As a prisoner."

He gave me a nod. "Aye. Months. I think. Labored by day,

chained at night. Pardon came through just before I was to be transported. My innocence proved. Don't matter now, do it?"

Brewster stared at him. "What you still doing *here*? Me, I'd be galloping home were I free and clear."

Another shrug. "Nowhere to go. No money to get there. I work for my keep. Sleep in a stable. No irons."

His lack of inflection chilled me. He was going through the motions of life, not knowing what else to do. He might have no family or perhaps one that wanted nothing to do with him.

"You're certain you saw a Runner from London?" I asked. "On this hulk?"

The man's eyes flared with irritation. "I recognize a Runner when I see one. Like that big lout ye came here with. 'Sides, he told me. Was looking for old Jack Finch, what was transported years ago. Don't know what he thought he'd find. He said was chatting to a few sailors on a dock when suddenly they jump on him, beat him down and strip him, and row him out here. He were here, half insensible, when the rest of us came back."

"Good Lord," I breathed. I thought of Quimby, small and thoughtful, a smart man but not gifted with bulk. "Was he still there when you were let off?"

"Aye," the man said. "Thought he wouldn't last—a thief-taker in with hundreds of convicts? They went at him at first, those who could reach him, but he talked us round. Said it was only his due, and when we got to Van Diemen's Land, we'd save our pennies and buy us a fine house and have dances all night. He were a kind bloke, ye could see."

"What day did you see him last? How long ago were you released?"

The man shrugged. "Don't know. Three, maybe four days. Saw you and knew the yellow-haired one was another Runner. But you, sir, seem more amiable, like, so I decided to talk to you. You'd best get the other one out of there."

"So we shall." I dipped my hand into my pocket and pulled

out a few shillings. "You might want to find another town to rest in, in case someone takes umbrage that you spoke to us. If you can get yourself to Norfolk, on the far north end of it, go to a village called Parson's Point. Look up a man named Terrance Quinn, and tell him I said you can be hired to work on my house there."

The man blinked as though coming awake. He switched his gaze to Brewster. "Is he a madman?"

"Aye," Brewster answered readily. "But don't let that worry ye. He'll not steer ye wrong. Take his money, and his advice."

The man at last accepted the coins, clutching them in his fist as though fearing they'd disappear.

"Right you are, sir," he said, and then turned around and walked into the mist and rain, as though ready to trudge to Norfolk on the spot.

"Whew," Brewster said. "I don't like Runners, but I wouldn't wish that on one of them. Mr. Quimby is a good sort, for all he's a thief-taker. Are we off to rescue him?"

"Yes," I said. "Let us hope they don't chain us up and throw us into the hold as well."

POMEROY, WHEN WE BROKE THE NEWS OF QUIMBY'S CAPTURE, WAS ready to continue drinking and have a night's sleep, saying we'd investigate the former prisoner's claim in the morning.

"On your feet, Sergeant," I told him sternly. "One more night might kill him. If you were festering out there, you'd be grateful we didn't wait for the convenience of daylight."

Pomeroy refused to grow angry, though he did rise. "Ye keep forgetting I ain't your sergeant anymore, Captain. And on this little jaunt, it's me what's in command. Have ye thought this man from the hulk might be playing you for a fool, luring us out so we'll be cornered ourselves?"

"It occurred to me, yes," I said. "But you did not see his eyes when he spoke to us. The hulks nearly broke him. He had no reason to tell us about Quimby except concern for the man."

"Ye mean except maybe being paid to tell you." Pomeroy lifted his tankard and drained it. "You're right that if Quimby is there, he needs to be hauled out. But you let *me* talk to the turnkeys. Obviously the Governess didn't know how to put the fear of God into 'em."

I agreed that Pomeroy could bully the way for us, and we departed the inn.

Our hired coachman did not want to leave his warm billet and plenty of ale, but after I put a crown into his hand, he grunted and went to ready the horses.

The naval yard, when we reached it, was far from silent. Though carpentry work had finished for the night, plenty of sailors were on duty guarding the valuable ships and guns. Sentries remained on the lookout for warships, should the Austrian or Russian Empires take the whim to invade tonight.

"Good sir," Pomeroy called out to the guard with musket who halted us. "Fetch Lieutenant Ostman. I have a favor to ask him. A casket of best brandy to him if he does it, and have a cup yourself. The captain here will stand it."

I tried not to flinch, but at least the guard nodded and fetched another guard to lead us to Ostman's lodgings.

The lieutenant, who had reluctantly welcomed us earlier and assigned Seaman Jones to be our guide, was not happy to be pulled away from his dinner, his wine, and his mistress. He met us in the cold and dark foyer of his house, light and warmth waiting in the rooms behind him.

He was even less happy when Pomeroy asked for a boat to row us out to a hulk.

"Nothing to do with me," the lieutenant barked.

"It might, sir, begging your pardon." Pomeroy's eyes twinkled and his voice boomed like a cannonade. "Runners abducted and taken to the hulks, criminals escaping from the colonies, all under the Royal Navy's nose. Quite a scandal, sir."

Which everyone on Sheppey and beyond would know about, thanks to Pomeroy's hearty bellow.

The lieutenant flushed. "I will arrange it," he said stiffly. "But I have never seen this Mr. Quimby. You've a bee in your bonnet, man."

"It's buzzing quite hard," Pomeroy said. "Pass us off to your flunky and get back to your beefsteak and pudding." He gave the lieutenant a wink.

The lieutenant's countenance became more sour than ever. "I will arrange it," he repeated, and swung away, calling orders to his servants.

Seaman Jones arrived quickly at the lieutenant's door. The lad must have been pulled away from his supper as well, but he greeted us cheerfully.

"Got a boat for ye and good strong rowers. But I don't know why ye want to go out to the *Atonement*, sirs. Terrible place."

"Exactly why we're going, lad," Pomeroy said. "Lead on."

Jones took us from the officers' quarters and down through narrow alleyways to the water. We trudged behind him across the wet and slick shingle to a waiting longboat.

The boat was already in the water, straining at its tether tied to a ring in the rocks. We waded out to it, the brackish water freezing me through my boots. My knee throbbed.

"Never thought I'd be rushing *toward* a hulk," Brewster muttered behind me. "Can't be good luck, this."

"Nothing to worry about," Pomeroy assured him. "I won't order you clapped in irons, my good fellow, not until you're lawfully convicted. No need to jump ahead."

"He won't get his reward if there isn't an official conviction," I told Brewster, and Pomeroy laughed.

"Right you are, Captain. Always hit the nail on the head."

"Very comforting," Brewster said. "I'm sure."

The strong wind from the North Sea tried its best to push the stink of the hulks down the river, but all the tempests in all the world would not cleanse this place, I thought.

The ship called the *Atonement* rose like a black slab of rock not far from shore. High tide cut off the rudderless ship, anchored forever on a mud flat. A few lights winked on the stern deck, but the rest of the ship was as black as the night.

The fetor of bodies, urine, and filth clung to the ship like a mist. Men were crammed into these hulks by the hundreds, chained to the wall at night, some without a pallet to lie on. By day they were marched out to dredge channels or break rocks, or other manual labor.

I'd known men in the army who'd been taken from the hulks and given a second life as cannon fodder for the French, but they'd found the cramped quarters and second-rate food a sight better than they'd been used to. One man told me he'd had nothing but a dirty pair of under breeches to wear because the guards had stolen the clothes he'd been allotted. They also stole all the food and consigned the prisoners to live on rotten biscuits.

One of the guards on deck, cradling a musket in his arms, peered over the railing as we approached. "What you doing here?"

"We need to come aboard," Seaman Jones said nervously.

"Magistrate's business," Pomeroy called from the bow. "Just open up the hatches for me, there's a good fellow."

"Who're you?" the guard asked. The musket didn't move, and though, by the way he held it, I did not think it loaded, the man was large and would be tough. He'd have to be, to stand watch in this place.

Pomeroy rose to his feet, bracing himself on the gunwale. His tall bulk stretched his dark blue coat, and the wind caught its tails. He removed his hat, his fair hair a pale smudge in the moonlight. My former sergeant was a formidable sight, and he'd put the fear of God into better men than the hulk's guard above him.

"Pomeroy. Of Bow Street. I have letters if you want to see them. A pistol and a dozen stout naval men behind me if you don't."

I knew bloody well Pomeroy had no letters from his magistrate, or Sir Montague. I doubted the guard could read them even if he had, which I guessed was what Pomeroy counted on. He wasn't above a bluff, or a blatant lie, as means to an end. The naval men who'd rowed us out did not look pleased to be named as Pomeroy's rearguard.

"We can't have all you up here," the guard said. "Too dangerous. There's bad men here, didn't ye know?" he finished in an attempt at humor.

"And you're one of 'em," Brewster said in a tight whisper. One of the sailors coughed a laugh.

"Tell you what," Pomeroy shouted. "You let me up there with a couple of fellows, and we'll have a quick look about. Ten minutes, and then you'll be left in peace."

Two more guards had joined the first, including one with a pistol in his belt who seemed to be in charge.

"Let 'em up," he growled. "Magistrates should leave us to get on. What's a Runner want to look at convicted villains for anyway? You're done with 'em."

"We have our reasons," Pomeroy said. "You all right climbing the ladder, Captain?" he asked me. "Or shall I leave you down here all snug?"

"I'll manage," I said grimly.

The guard lowered a ladder made of ropes and wooden steps that looked cracked and brittle. Pomeroy, without worry, grabbed hold and started scrambling.

If the ladder took his weight, it ought to take mine, I told myself. I had no intention of letting Pomeroy board this hulk alone, as competent as he was. If they'd already imprisoned one Runner …

"You don't have to come," I told Brewster, who looked as though he'd be sick.

"The devil I don't." Brewster seized the ladder and jerked it from my grasp. "Not risking them shooting you as soon as you're over the gunwale or knocking you on the head and locking you up too. His Nibs would draw and quarter me and feed me my own entrails, just to teach me a lesson. I'm going up first, and you stick to me like a cocklebur once you're on."

He started up the ladder, moving quickly and competently, the lower rungs banging into the hull as he went.

Finally I positioned myself to begin the climb, and Seaman Jones kindly gave me a boost. After a few rungs, I learned how to lead with my good leg and not let my bad one hinder me too much.

The guards had seemed annoyed rather than alarmed that a Bow Street Runner had come to do an inspection. I'd expect them to be a bit more nervous if Quimby were here. Either the man outside the inn was mistaken, or these guards had no idea Quimby was in their hold.

Brewster caught my arms as I reached the ship's railing, and he dragged me the last few feet. I steadied myself on the deck, Brewster's hold assisting. He refused to let go even as we followed Pomeroy to the main hatch. A cocklebur indeed.

Some of the guards did have loaded guns, which they now primed and cocked while the others loaded their muskets. The head guard drew his pistol, checked and primed the pan, then held it at the ready.

He nodded at two men who unscrewed the bolts that held the hatch closed and then hauled up the grate.

The stench that boiled out of the hole made me step back and Brewster curse. Pomeroy remained calmly at the opening, looking down into the dark.

"If they're chained, why the worry, gentlemen?" he asked, gesturing at the guards' weaponry.

"Some have been known to get free," the head guard said, his voice like flint. "They charge the hatch. But don't worry, we'll close it on them, and they'll just mob until they drop."

He spoke matter-of-factly, as though talking about birds fighting for nesting space.

Pomeroy peered down into the darkness. "Should throw buckets of water down there once in a while to clean it out. Shine a light on the poor buggers for me."

One of the guards brought forth a lantern with a flickering candle inside it and lowered it into the hold.

No ladder connected the upper deck with the ship's interior —they must bring a ladder only when they needed to haul the prisoners up for the day or send them back down at night.

The swinging lantern showed me eyes, both rodent and human, glittering in the feeble light.

Equally unnerving were the sounds. Men cursed, their voices cracked. Some pled for water; others groaned in pain. Behind this came the rustle of chains, clink of iron, skitter of claws, and movement of bodies against damp wood.

Brewster, next to me, had gone very quiet. Unlike Pomeroy, who made remarks about men packed in like the rats with them, Brewster remained silent, leaning his hands on his knees, his eyes fixed.

Pomeroy looked upon the men below with the serenity of one who believed he'd never meet their fate. Brewster, on the other hand, knew that only the grace of God had kept him on this side of the hatch.

Pomeroy scanned the faces illuminated by the lantern. "Quimby?" he bellowed. "You down there?"

"There are three levels in the hold," the head guard said coldly. "If you're searching for a man, give me his name, and I'll look up his number."

Pomeroy ignored him. "Quimby, lad! Shout out if you're here!"

More groans and a few cries came in response.

"Put out the light, damn you," one man yelled. "Don't ye know I need me sleep? Must look me best in the morning."

Laughter, tired, came, drowned out by another man telling the first to shut his gob.

Over this, I heard a thin voice. I held up my hand as Pomeroy drew breath to shout again.

"Mr. Quimby?" I called. "It's Captain Lacey. Is that you, sir?"

"Ah, Captain," came the weak response. "I must extend my apologies. I am not my best to receive callers at present, I am afraid."

CHAPTER 22

The guards refused to go down. They'd descend in the morning, they said. Once the men were chained up for the night, they wouldn't go into the hold even to remove a dead body. It waited until daylight.

I snarled at them and demanded a ladder and more light.

"You've locked up a Runner," I told them in a hard voice. "Who brought him in?"

The head guard stared at me. "What the devil are you on about? I know every single man down there. They're listed in my book."

"I wager this one is not," Pomeroy said. He stood aside as a ladder was lowered, the guards pointing their guns into the hole.

"You should wait until the lot is brought up in the morning," the head guard tried again.

"I should," Pomeroy said, swinging himself into the hatch. "But when the captain commands, I obey. Habit of a lifetime."

Brewster knew he could not stop me climbing down after Pomeroy, but he said, "You let me go first, guv. And don't you stray a step from me."

I agreed it would be prudent for Brewster to lead me. I waited until he and Pomeroy reached the floor below before I carefully descended, my knee aching.

I half expected the guards to slam the hatch and lock it as soon as we were below decks, but they remained vigilant, muskets and pistols at the ready.

The prisoners, at least the ones I could see, were indeed chained to the walls. Pomeroy flashed the lantern around, and the men cringed from the light.

They wore leg irons, and each had one hand shackled to a chain that ran to the wall. The chain was long enough to at least let each man lie down, but they had no beds, only a thin layer of dirty straw that covered the board floor. I saw no blankets of any kind.

Men of all description lay before me—large, small, spindly, stout. Their heads were shaved. Most wore shirts and tattered breeches, but they were barefoot and had no coats.

I took care not to breathe through my nose, but the stench of filth and sweat was overpowering even then. More than one man coughed, clearly ill.

"Did ye bring the water, guv?" one groaned.

I had no water, but I stopped and opened my flask of brandy, giving the poor fellow a drink.

He coughed then swallowed and grinned, showing rotted teeth. "Thank ye kindly, good sir. Better than water, I'm thinking."

In this place, that was probably true.

Brewster glared at me as I stood again. "Not one step, I said," he growled.

"I don't think these fellows are going to rise up and have a go at me," I told him. "It would serve them no purpose even if they did."

I heard one or two chuckles. Brewster let out an aggrieved sigh. "For a man so worldly, ye're an innocent one, guv."

Ahead of us, Pomeroy strode with confidence, lantern high. "Quimby? Sing out again, man."

I heard Quimby answer down the row. Brewster and I began to follow.

"Tommy?" a weak voice sounded at our feet. "Love a duck. It *is* you, me old china."

Brewster halted and peered down into darkness, Pomeroy's light receding. "Slocombe?" he asked in astonishment. "What the devil are you doing in here?"

"Broke a bloke's arm." A smile gleamed. "Should a' killed him and run, because next thing I know he brought me up before the beaks. Said I were a dangerous man. Only reason I didn't swing is judge didn't like the bastard. Reckon judge wanted to break his other arm before it were over." He heaved a breathy laugh.

"Hard luck." Brewster's sympathy rang true.

"Aye, well. Time for a change of scenery, I think. They say a man can make his fortune out in the Antipodes."

If he didn't die from the years of labor before him, it was possible, so I had heard. But more likely he'd expire from disease and exhaustion before he served out his sentence.

"Did you see our bloke brought in?" Brewster asked him. "Small fellow, blue eyes, looks like a schoolmaster?"

"He's who you're after? Someone threw him down here when we were out doing our day's digging on shore. Was waiting when we came in, but guards wouldn't let him out. Chained him up with the rest of us." Another breathy laugh. "They're for it, are they?"

"Seems like."

Slocombe's eyes narrowed. "But what you doing going about with Runners, Tommy? Turned traitor, have you? His Nibs won't like that."

"His Nibs would have already strung out me insides to dry if I had—you know that. I ain't working for no Runners. I'm helping the captain here prove I didn't kill a bloke."

"What bloke? *Did* ye kill 'im?"

"Oh, so you want me to put me hands up when I'm already inside a hulk?" Brewster said with a nervous chortle. "Naw, I didn't kill him. The bloke was Finch. Jack Finch."

The man next to Slocombe stirred. "Finchie?" he asked in bewilderment. "He's dead?"

"As a doornail."

"Whew," the man said. "You looking for the cove what did it? Why, so ye can give him a reward? Finchie was one evil bastard."

"Did you know him?" I asked the man.

"Aye, bad luck for me. He was transported a few years back. Good riddance. He returned to England's shores, did he?"

"He did," Brewster said. "How's that work? Ye arrange with a man here to pick ye up there and sail ye back?"

Slocombe's grin returned as his neighbor fell silent. "Not something we're saying with a Robin Redbreast or two scuttling around."

I hadn't expected an answer. "Did either of you know Finch's friend?" I asked. "Man by the name of Blackmore."

Slocombe shuddered. "A still more evil bastard. A grand day when *he* went into the dock, but now I'm terrified I'll catch up to him on Van Diemen's Land."

"Ye won't," the other man said, brows lowering.

"Why not?" Brewster asked him.

"Cause he be dead," the man spat. "In't he?"

I blinked in amazement. "Sydney Blackmore is dead? Are you certain?"

"'Course I am. He were part of the gang what went to the posh gent's to fight. I was there too—nearly got me head bashed in. Twisted bugger, that aristocrat, laughing like a monkey to watch us going at each other. Blackmore got hit so hard, he died."

Brewster and Slocombe were as agape as I was. "S'truth," Slocombe said. "What did the posh gent do then?"

"Hushed it up, didn't he? Had his lads haul poor old Black-more back with us in the boat and dump his body in the sea. End of a villain."

"Cor." Brewster's voice was hushed.

My anger tightened. If Lord Mercer had insisted the body be disposed of as the prisoners were taken back to the hulk, it meant the guards were certainly in on it. Probably getting paid by Mercer to bring him the choicest candidates to fight in his matches.

Was this why Quimby had been locked in the hulk to be mistaken for a convict? Even if Quimby hadn't received word about Mercer's fights until after he'd begun his journey, he could have easily found out about them. Rumors about it would be rife, and if Lord Mercer had let Pierce Egan in on the secret, probably to impress the famous writer, he'd have let it slip to others as well.

Sir Montague had told me to avoid Mercer, but I knew that was so I wouldn't stir up trouble before Sir Montague was ready for it. Time to get Quimby out.

"Where did Blackmore live?" I asked Slocombe's neighbor. "Before this address, I mean?"

The man's scowl lessened at my joke. "Seven Dials. I hear the rats would run away when they saw him coming."

Seven Dials, within the parish of St. Giles and not far from where Finch had been found dead. Bloody hell.

"Thank you, good sir. If there is anything I can do for you ..."

"Nip of that flask wouldn't go amiss."

I obliged him, and also Slocombe.

Pomeroy's light returned. He carried it in one hand and had his other arm around the waist of a stumbling, heavily breathing Mr. Quimby.

"Good God." I caught Quimby, supporting his other side.

Quimby's dark brown hair was matted with dirt, sweat, and blood. His face bore many bruises, and his left eye was swollen shut. The neat suit I'd seen him wear had been replaced by a pair of linen breeches and nothing more. Bruises and cuts marred the flesh of his bare torso.

"Up you go," Pomeroy said cheerfully, hauling Quimby to the ladder.

"A moment." I slid off my greatcoat and wrapped it around Quimby's shoulders. "Wind's bitter."

Quimby nodded his thanks. He grasped the ladder, hands slipping in his exhaustion, but with Pomeroy's help, firmed his grip.

A cheer went up as Quimby climbed to freedom. He clutched the ladder with shaking hands, but managed to nod back down at us. "I thank you for your hospitality, gentlemen."

They shouted encouragement—a hulk full of convicts hailing a Runner. Mr. Quimby certainly had a way with him.

The guards above pulled Mr. Quimby the final yard to the deck. Pomeroy made me go next, and I too was cheered. Then Brewster, and finally Pomeroy. He got curses and jeers, but he waved back good-naturedly.

The head guard glared at Pomeroy as the big man emerged into the wind and spattering rain. "How the devil did you get him free?" the guard demanded.

He'd refused to send down the keys, fearing Pomeroy would be mobbed, the keys stolen, a mutiny commencing.

"Picked the lock," Pomeroy said cheerfully. "I'm very good at it."

NOT UNTIL QUIMBY WAS ENSCONCED AT OUR INN, HIS WOUNDS tended and bathed, and a hot meal and ale inside him, could he tell his story. I lent him my nightshirt and dressing gown, for which Quimby thanked me cordially.

"Such luxury," he said fingering the dressing gown's velvet placket.

We'd have to buy him secondhand clothes in the morning. He was far too small for anything Pomeroy, Brewster, or I had.

"Well, gentlemen," Quimby said after he'd scraped clean a plate holding a cutlet, potatoes, greens, and a hunk of brown bread. "There isn't much to tell. As you know, I came to investigate how Mr. Finch could have escaped his captivity and returned to these shores. We know that men not only depart from here but also return, and we are pretty certain how, but we have no proof. I didn't do much more than linger in pubs, listening to conversation. All discreet inquiries—well, I'd believed I was being discreet—led, as I suspected they would, to Captain Steadman."

"Yes," Pomeroy said. "The merchant captain that made Seaman Jones very nervous when mentioned."

"Exactly. Captain Steadman is, not to put too fine a point on it, a smuggler. He is a legitimate merchant, registered, sails around the Horn every year to India and islands in the Pacific. Does a good business, in his own small way, without treading on the toes of the East India Company and others. He pays them a bit of compensation, from what I gather, and avoids the markets they are most possessive of. But he'll pick up things here and there and bring them back, without bothering to list them on the cargo manifest, if you take my meaning. Silk cloth, exotic animals, men."

"Ah." Pomeroy's smile spread wide. "Got him."

"Not necessarily." Quimby took a slurp of ale and made a noise of satisfaction. "He's regarded as something of a hero among the locals. He transports escaped slaves to the free land of Britain, brings back men—innocent ones, he claims—who have been sentenced to hard labor in the penal colonies. He's quite a colorful figure, so they say, but others mutter about him. He doesn't help these men and slaves escape out of the goodness of his heart. He gouges a large fee from them and is hard on those who don't or can't pay."

"In other words, they go from slavery to indentured servitude," I said. I ran my thumb over the head of my walking stick. "Perhaps I should speak to this captain."

"No, ye don't," Brewster said at once. "Exactly the trouble I'm paid to keep ye out of."

"I tried to," Quimby said with a little smile. "Was able to make an appointment with the great Steadman. I went to the dock at the appointed hour, and was waylaid forthwith. I fought gallantly, or so I supposed, until I was disarmed, thoroughly beaten, my clothes stolen, and then had a very smelly bag put over my head. When I came to, I was in the hold of a mostly empty ship with one or two men too sick to rise."

"Hard luck," Pomeroy said as Quimby paused for a sip of ale.

"Indeed," he said. "Not long later the other prisoners were driven down, their day at an end. The guards took me for one of them and chained me up, no matter how much I protested— some of these bruises are from them. And there I was. The next morning, I tried to explain again, but was clubbed for my trouble. So off I went to dig out a ditch in the shingle with my fellow prisoners, watched over by a very disagreeable man, quite ready with a whip. Cut me for daring even to speak to him." He took another hasty drink. "I could only hope Sir Montague would notice my lack of correspondence and the fact that I did not return to London—that is, *before* I was shipped off across the seas."

"He did," I said. "He was most worried about you, and sent Pomeroy to seek you."

"Captain Lacey found the last piece of the puzzle," Pomeroy put in generously. "Good thing I brought him along—he's expert at prying information out of men who won't talk to the likes of Runners."

Quimby gave me a grateful nod. "I assure you, Captain

Steadman would be quite loathe to speak to any gentleman who approached him. I kept my identity as a Runner to myself and behaved as a man looking to move cargo. But he saw through that readily enough. I don't believe he cared whether I was a Runner or a prince of the realm. I asked too much about his business and he took steps." Quimby lifted his tankard to us. "I thank you, gentlemen."

"The naval lieutenant and his pet sailor did not like us asking questions," I observed. "But I would swear they knew nothing about your capture. Seaman Jones had not heard your name."

"Possibly they had no idea. The thugs who took me were not of the navy. I believe Steadman pays those at the naval docks quite well to ignore him, but I do not believe they assist him. I heard no talk of that."

"Safer to leave them out of it," Brewster grunted. "If he had navy lads doing things for him, he couldn't be sure they wouldn't talk when they were out of his reach. Even if unintentionally."

"I agree," Quimby said. "Steadman runs his own empire. The lads in the hulk knew much about him, though. Said that for the right price, he'd send a boat to pick up men from the penal colonies who could get free of their shackles and outrun the guards. A large price, but some, like Mr. Finch, could pay it. Or at least be certain of raising the sum once they reached England again."

"Huh," Brewster said. "Explains why Finch came to touch me and Em for blunt. And why he wanted the same from his youngest sister and his own daughter. He needed to pay his fare."

Quimby's eyes widened, his professional interest pushing aside his exhaustion. "Daughter?"

"Found her after you departed," I said. "Charlotte put him up for a few days and doesn't know whom he met in his final hour."

"Thinks her man what sends her out on the streets killed him," Brewster said. "Bloke called Hobson. Could have been."

"Hmm, worth looking into," Quimby said.

"Let the poor man sleep, Captain," Pomeroy broke in. "He's all in. We can finish interrogating him tomorrow."

I returned Pomeroy's gaze with a neutral look. His solicitude was not so much concern for Quimby's health as the fact that he did not want me giving Quimby further clues. He was still annoyed with me for not bringing the case straight to him.

However, Pomeroy did have a point. "Quite right," I said, rising. "Sleep well, Mr. Quimby. You should have a commendation for your courage."

"For walking into a trap and getting banged on the head?" Quimby touched his hair, damp from the water pump in the yard. "Not very clever of me."

But he'd come through it with equanimity and without panic. There were plenty of hardy men who would have despaired in his place and possibly already died. I had cultivated great respect for Mr. Quimby.

WE DECIDED ON A SWIFT RETREAT TO TAKE QUIMBY TO SAFETY, and left in the early hours of the morning. We didn't know what kind of forces Steadman had, and as only two of four of us— Pomeroy and Brewster—were able-bodied fighters at the moment, we concluded that prudence should prevail.

I could have wished time to visit Lord Mercer, in spite of Sir Montague's warning, but perhaps it was best we went.

Pomeroy insisted on asking the landlord to deliver a cask of brandy to Lieutenant Ostman, by way of the gate guard from last night. Always good to keep a promise, Pomeroy said. I agreed, and paid over the cost, to the landlord's delight.

The drive back to London was too slow for my taste, but a

faster pace might have been difficult for Quimby. Pomeroy, who again snored loudly most of the way, didn't seem to mind, and neither did Brewster, who once more kept the coachman company.

When we reached London, Quimby insisted on going straight to Sir Montague. It was late, but that man received him, and Pomeroy and I sat in to listen as Quimby outlined what he'd told us. Quimby added what he'd learned about the convicts being taken from the hulks to fight in pugilist matches for Lord Mercer. Apparently this happened once every couple of months, with a new set of convicts every time.

I contributed my information that Finch's friend, Mr. Blackmore, had been killed at these games, which made Sir Montague's eyes sparkle with both anger and canny determination. Lord Mercer bringing convicts to his house for a day's entertainment was one thing—getting a man killed for his sport was another.

I did not remain long at the magistrate's house as I wanted to return home, and Brewster chafed to be off to his wife. Pomeroy said he'd see Quimby home, and the two left together. Brewster insisted on riding with me all the way to South Audley Street before he bade me good night and disappeared.

Donata was in, Barnstable told me as he calmly admitted me, but I saw when I reached the sitting room that she'd been out that evening. Her gold silk gown with its bodice sliding a long way down her shoulders was something she'd only wear to a soiree or the theatre.

She was in the sitting room, because Grenville was with her, as was Marianne in a similar shoulder-baring gown.

"There you are, Gabriel." Donata came to me as though I'd merely been out visiting a friend. She kissed my cheek. "No doubt you'll want one of your hot baths, but Grenville has interesting news."

"Indeed, I do." Grenville seated himself close to Marianne

and resumed the goblet of brandy he'd set aside to politely rise when Donata did. "We were correct that Cousin Stanton did not go to Somerset at all. He went to Lincolnshire."

He took a sip of brandy, mirth in his eyes.

He knew I'd fume at his abrupt message with no explanation, and he was right. "Out with it, man," I said. "I am too exhausted to guess. Why the devil did he go to Lincolnshire?"

"Simple." Grenville smiled, enjoying himself. "He swore up and down that you had gone there ahead of him. With Peter."

CHAPTER 23

$\mathcal{A}$s weary as I was from the long ride, pressed between Pomeroy and the carriage wall, my blood began to tingle at Grenville's words.

"Are you certain? How do you know this?"

"So said Mr. St. John's mistress," Marianne answered. She also had brandy, and took a calm sip. "She's an actress from my old company, a lady who never used to speak to me, but of course she will now." Her blue eyes held an equal measure of disgust and triumph. "She was not happy that Mr. St. John decided to rush north and at the same time told his acquaintance that he was off to his estate in Somerset. She knows all about Mr. St. John wanting to become his young lordship's guardian, and that he is sure that you, Lacey, and Lady Breckenridge, were trying underhanded ways to keep him from doing what was right."

"She confirmed that Stanton has indeed run through much of his fortune," Grenville added. "She is uncertain how, as he does not confide in her about his business, and she apparently has no interest. I have begun making inquiries, and I'm optimistic they will bear fruit."

"The lady has a low opinion of you, I'm afraid, Lacey," Marianne said. "But I doubt this will harm you. Her opinions aren't much valued. She, however, is adamant that Stanton should be the next viscount. His due, she says."

"She is confident he went to Lincolnshire?" I asked.

"Oh, yes." Marianne's face was girlish under her fair hair, but years of struggle had given her wisdom. "He heard a rumor that you had rushed quickly to Lincolnshire, somewhere on the sea. As your home in Norfolk isn't far from this coastal village, I suppose he found the story plausible. He assumed you'd taken Lady Breckenridge's son there for nefarious purposes."

"I must wonder who put this rumor about." I turned to my wife, who could be devious in her own way.

"Nothing to do with me," Donata said, lifting a hand. "I wish I'd thought of it, but I did not."

As she spoke, I believed I knew exactly who had thought of it, and why. I would have many errands in the morning.

Grenville rose. "Off to bed with you, Lacey. Sleep away your fatigue and tell me of your adventures tomorrow. I am agog to learn of them but not so cruel as to keep you awake to satisfy my curiosity. Rest well, old chap."

He led Marianne out, her arm through his, the two murmuring, heads together, even as they went.

"She is good for him," Donata said after Bartholomew had closed the door, leaving us alone.

"Marianne?" I made for the sofa and stretched out my aching leg. "I agree with you. I was thinking she looked happy, but I see he does as well."

My wife pulled an ottoman to me, sat upon it, and began removing my boots.

"I'll ruin your frock," I said, unable to move.

"No matter. Lady Hertford wore a similar one tonight, and it looked dreadful on her, so I will no doubt have it altered or give

it to Jacinthe to do with as she pleases. I take it you found poor
Mr. Quimby? You'd be much more melancholic if you hadn't."

"Yes. Found him. He went home, and by now is likely
sleeping the sleep of the just. He ran afoul of dangerous men."

Donata slid the boot carefully from my injured leg and
briskly rubbed the back of my stiff knee. "Dangerous indeed if
they thought nothing of capturing a Runner."

"They might not have known he was one. He told no one."

My wife sent me a disparaging look. "A stranger in a village
asking many questions? Of course they'd believe him a Runner,
or at least a gentleman sent by the magistrates, or possibly a
foreign spy poking around the dockyards. Most people do not
take well to others prying into their business."

I grunted as my knee loosened. "They threw him into a
prison hulk. I'd say they were displeased." I gave her a brief
version of the tale, some of my words groans as she continued
her massage.

When I finished, Donata released my leg and moved to the
sofa to sit with me. "I hope this Captain Steadman will be
immediately arrested."

"Sir Montague will see to it, if Steadman didn't slip his
moorings the moment we rescued Mr. Quimby."

"You are a good man, Gabriel." Donata rested her head on
my shoulder and smoothed my shirt under my unbuttoned
waistcoat. "I believe I knew that the moment I met you."

"No, you did not," I said. "You thought I was a toady of
Grenville's trying to curry his favor."

"Very well, then I knew the moment you knocked Breckenridge on his fundament. I wanted to cheer. You *are* good,
Gabriel, though such declarations embarrass you. You could
have left Mr. Pomeroy and Sir Montague to deal with this, but
Mr. Quimby might have been dead if so. You are too modest to
admit such, but I know it was your doing that found Mr.
Quimby and got him out so swiftly."

"I thought that was stubborn ruthlessness," I said. "And being foolish enough to charge in where others practice prudence."

"No, indeed. Prudence is all very well, but when no one else will act, sometimes ruthlessness is what is needed."

"Mmm, well." I was too tired to argue. "How is Gabriella? Has she been enjoying your outings?"

Donata was quiet a moment, long enough to alarm me.

"What is the matter?" I asked, sitting up. "Is she ill?"

"Goodness, no." Donata soothed me back down. "She is quite a strong young woman, like her father. But I am not sure she is enjoying herself. I do not mean she sulks and broods like some young ladies do—she is very polite, and she does like the plays and musicales. But she accompanies me and Lady Aline out of duty, I can see."

"I do not believe it is the company she objects to, but the purpose," I said gently. "She is not in a rush to marry."

"No girl is. We believe we can flirt and dance and be a diamond of the first water forever. But it does not last, and I do not want to see Gabriella lonely and unhappy. She is lovely and is well-mannered, and she will make a very good wife. She can be a grand hostess in a year or two, with only a little help."

"Perhaps she has no desire to be a grand hostess."

Donata raised her head. "Forgive me, Gabriel, but as I have said before, you are a man and cannot understand. Unlike gentlemen, we ladies are not allowed to pursue a political career or join influential circles in your clubs that keep us out. But we *can* hold grand suppers or musicales to mix the right people and encourage lords and MPs to make the changes we would like to see. Or we hold discussions of books and plays, and let such things lead to talk of reform with the very lords and Cabinet ministers who can make that reform happen. *That* is the power of ladies. It is not inconsiderable, our power." She drew a breath, quieting. "This is what I am trying to give Gabriella, to marry her into the correct families so that her influence, and her happiness, will be at its greatest. Not an easy feat, I must say."

I gazed at Donata in surprise. I knew she deemed Gabriella's marriage important, but I hadn't realized the depth of her objectives.

She wanted to give Gabriella a career, the life of a prominent lady, the sort of life Donata had achieved, despite her bad marriage. Though Breckenridge had been personally horrible, his family and title bestowed upon Donata, as Lady Breckenridge, much influence and power. That power would help Peter grow up to be a successful peer and not a feeble branch of the family tree.

"I beg your pardon," I said with sincerity. "I suppose you are right that I saw your purpose as a bit frivolous. Believe me, I do want to see my daughter happy."

"Good," Donata said in relief. "Then perhaps you can begin to help me."

I winced. "You mean by greeting guests and swanning about in suits that do not allow me to turn my head, do you not?"

She patted my chest, her hand warm. "You will do splendidly."

~

I WAS AT LAST ABLE TO BATHE AND TAKE MYSELF TO BED, AND MY wife joined me, to my gratification. In the morning, I was sore from jouncing over hard roads, but I made myself go out for my usual ride. The remedy for aching muscles, I've always found, is to use them.

I felt a trifle better when I returned. Donata was still asleep, and Gabriella was as well, since Donata now had her keeping late hours like a lady of fashion.

Brewster arrived, looking none the worse for wear for our journey, and asked what I'd be getting up to today. He did not look happy when I immediately said I needed to speak with Denis.

"If His Nibs has me thrashed for letting you bother him day in and day out, Em won't be happy."

"Your task is to keep me whole and alive so His Nibs can have me run errands for him, not to keep me from badgering him when I please," I said as we walked down South Audley Street past the brick walls and arched, clear windows of Grosvenor Chapel. The chapel was very much along the same lines of St. Giles-in-the-Fields, austere but elegant, pleasing to the eye.

"He'll differ with you there, guv."

"If he proves to be busy or out, I will fix an appointment instead of insisting to be admitted. Will that soothe you?"

"Probably not." Brewster eyed me. "You're in a bit of a temper, I can see."

"I am quite annoyed with Mr. Denis, yes."

I closed my mouth, saving my breath for the walk.

When we reached Curzon Street, I saw Denis alight from a landau, its top up against the rain, and stride inside his house. His men surrounded him, so that I barely saw the flash of his greatcoat and hat between carriage and front door.

I'd once reflected that I pitied a man who had to be guarded in his own house, who could never ride alone in a city park or tramp through country fields as I did without thinking a thing of it. Even a ride through the city was perilous, never mind any time he descended from his coach.

The empty landau was rolling off by the time we reached Number 45. The butler opened the door before I could raise a hand to knock.

"He saw you coming," the man said stiffly. "Inside. I'm to let you up in a few minutes."

He indicated I was to wait in the lower hall, and then he walked upstairs with a heavy tread and vanished. Brewster deserted me as well, heading for the backstairs, likely off to see his cronies.

I paced the hall, not resting on the upholstered settee with gold carvings and crimson cushions as the butler had obviously wanted me to. I had not seen the settee here before, and I paused to study it. It was not a copy, I realized, or a modern piece made to look like something from an ancient civilization. I would wager it had come straight from the Ottoman Empire itself, possibly a gift from a grateful vizier.

The butler emerged in the upper hall and gave me a curt gesture. Obediently I climbed the stairs, holding on to the railing, and nodded in passing to the painting of the maid with a cream jug on the landing.

Denis sat at his desk, reading a book. He continued to read as I came in and took my place, though today I was offered no brandy.

Presently, Denis came to the end of a chapter, marked his place with a strip of paper, and closed the book.

"A treatise on the properties of gasses," he said, sliding the book aside. "I find it most interesting. Now, Captain, from your expression, you have come here to berate me. What about this time?"

The mild curiosity with which he asked stirred my already uncertain temper. "Marcus Lacey. You sent him to Lincolnshire to lead Stanton St. John there. Didn't you?"

He gave me one of his brief nods. "I suggested to Mr. Lacey that you and your wife would be pleased if Mr. St. John took himself elsewhere, and remarked upon the resemblance between you. Mr. Lacey thought it a fine idea, and made a show of hiring a coach for a village on the Lincolnshire coast. From there one can arrange passage to Amsterdam, I believe."

"And so Stanton, believing me absconding with the viscount, hied to Lincolnshire to stop me." I sat back, my anger dispersing. "A neat plan."

"Just so."

"Did you offer Marcus a fee for this task?"

"Of course."

Bloody hell. I was annoyed with the pair of them, but I had to admit the ploy had worked. "Marcus does not know his danger, agreeing to work for you."

"Mr. Lacey is a man of the world, possibly more than you, and has survived on his wits a long time."

I knew I could not keep control of Marcus, and I likewise knew I had no right to. "Are you also helping him prove he is the Lacey heir?"

Denis shook his head. "I am not interested in that dispute. He insists his story is true and that he can produce documents. But whether he is indeed your cousin or an illegitimate son of your father or other male relative means little to me. I judge each man on his own merit."

"I believe you," I conceded. "Well, you have solved the problem of Stanton—temporarily. Were you aware that he tried to kill his cousin, Robert, by deliberately damaging his vehicle?"

"Mr. Brewster told me. Mr. St. John is dangerous. What do you want done about him?"

"I'd like to have him arrested and tried," I said impatiently, though I knew this was a forlorn hope.

"He would evade justice," Denis replied. "Especially if he can prove he was nowhere near Dulwich or even London when the accident occurred. A more permanent solution must be found, or he will certainly try to harm his young lordship."

I shifted in my chair. "As much as beating him to a pulp would satisfy me, I cannot condone murdering another man. I would be as bad as he is."

"No," Denis said, a dry note in his voice. "You have too much honor."

"Which is a worthless thing in these times, I know. Nevertheless, I must think of something. We cannot keep Peter hidden forever, poor lad. He will have to grow up and take his place in the world."

"And learn of the world as he grows," Denis said. "It is the best way to survive its slings and arrows."

"He will have many arrows because of his position and his family, and the way his father abused people, not to mention the rumors surrounding his stepfather ..."

"He will have many to help him weather it," Denis said, finished with the discussion. "Your stepson may stay where he is until you decide how to settle things with Mr. St. John. I heard that you climbed into a prison hulk and took away Mr. Quimby, who had been forced there."

I could not feel surprised that Denis already knew every detail. "Yes, poor chap. He is a resilient fellow. What do you know about Captain Steadman? He had his men seize Quimby and row him to his fate."

Denis did not change expression. "I have heard of Steadman —the merchant who will smuggle humans for a price. I have never met him, nor do I employ him, before you ask."

"He apparently charges high fees for his services and is merciless to those who cannot pay. It explains why Finch approached the women of his family for money. I suspect he went to Mr. Shaddock, Brewster's trainer, for the same. Shaddock was quite fearful when we mentioned Finch, and relieved he was dead. Perhaps Captain Steadman had Finch killed because he could not come up with the money for his passage."

Denis rested one hand on his book as though wishing to get back to it. "Steadman would not kill someone who owed him— he would beat and terrify a man into paying instead. He prefers money to bodies he'd have to dispose of. But laying hands on a Runner and throwing him into a hulk, even for the amusement of it ..." Denis shook his head. "I believe I will speak to Captain Steadman."

He studied the air behind me as he said this last, as though slotting the thought into a pigeonhole in his mind. I'd noticed that Denis rarely wrote anything down, likely so that there would be no record of his involvement in whatever happened in his demesne.

"Have you or your men found anything more about Mr. Blackmore, Finch's friend?" I asked. "I discovered that Blackmore is dead, killed in an illegal pugilist match in the garden of Lord Mercer."

"Yes, that information came to me as well." Denis moved the book an inch closer to him. "Blackmore and Finch were both pugilists, as you know. They formed an unlikely friendship, but from all accounts, they were loyal to each other. When Finch was arrested five years ago and sentenced to transportation, Blackmore carried on their habit of thieving and extorting, and at last was also arrested and convicted, a few months ago. Sentenced to transportation, spent a few weeks in Coldbath Fields, then was taken to the hulk at Sheppey. There, as you discovered, he died."

"Perhaps that is the reason Finch died as well," I said, turning my cane as I thought this through. "Finch escapes his imprisonment in Van Diemen's Land, procures a passage to England on Steadman's ship, and journeys to London, only to find that Blackmore has been arrested and sentenced. Finch investigates Blackmore's whereabouts—or perhaps he found all this out before he ever left the docks at Sheppey—and discovers Blackmore is dead. More importantly, *how* he died. Though Finch is angry at what happened at Lord Mercer's, he still must pay Steadman. So, he comes to London to collect money, planning to give it to the captain, and then take his vengeance on Mercer for Blackmore's death. Lord Mercer gets wind of this, and sends someone to kill Finch."

"That is possible," Denis said. "I do not know how Finch thought to murder Lord Mercer in any quiet way. That would get him hanged without doubt, and Finch had just gone to the trouble to find passage back to England. Murdering a peer of the realm is a different thing from killing a man in a scuffle. Even if Finch decided to beat Lord Mercer to relieve his pique, it would be an unwise decision. Finch even being in England would send him to the gallows."

"A man enraged might not think this through," I pointed out.

"You certainly would not." Denis gave me a cold smile. "Finch had gotten away with many crimes before he was caught. He'd be canny."

"Which makes me wonder how Finch managed to be arrested and convicted at all," I said, my thoughts beginning to stir through my tiredness. "Pomeroy told me the judge was afraid of him, but I don't know the exact circumstances of his arrest. Did one of his victims finally have the courage to prosecute?"

"You can inquire," Denis said, giving me a pointed look. "Your magistrate friends will know those details, as well as the circumstances of Blackmore's arrest and trial."

They would indeed. My interview here was at an end. Denis slid the book all the way in front of him and opened it again, ignoring me completely.

I craned for a glimpse inside the book as I rose, and saw that the page was covered with equations and diagrams. It might indeed be a treatise on chemical gasses as he claimed.

I departed, Brewster joining me as soon as I walked out of the house in greatcoat and hat. The social whirl I was now expected to attend would not begin until later today, so I decided to act upon an idea.

I returned home briefly, and then set off in another hackney with Brewster and Oro.

Brewster thought me highly amusing. "You expect to have the dog track the killer with his nose? After a week, when it's been raining? Because he happened to stray into the street that day?"

"He knows something." I patted Oro's head where he sat at my feet, warming my legs better than a rug. "He likely witnessed the entire affair. Was he Finch's dog? Or the killer's?"

"Jack Finch with a dog?" Brewster snorted. "He'd kick it, more like."

I rubbed Oro's ears, and his tail gave a thump. "The killer's then? He's a well-bred water dog, even if he was rough when we found him. Perhaps when the killer ran away, Oro couldn't follow for some reason. He remained at the door, waiting for his master to return, except his master never did."

"Maybe in an opera, guv. Or one of them Greek stories you go on about."

"Not quite the same thing," I said. Or was it? Would Oro, like Odysseus's dog, have waited twenty years for his master?

We descended at the church and wended our way through the warren to the lane where Finch had been killed. It was as usual, deserted. Even the inhabitants of this area did not like this passage.

As we neared the black-painted, worn door of the narrow house at the end, Oro stopped. I tugged on his lead, but he would not take one step forward. He sat down on his haunches and began a strange, whining howl.

"He remembers, all right," I said.

"Captain Lacey?" A voice came from behind us. "Mr. Brewster? Thought that was you."

Oro ceased his cries. He turned around with us, calming as the young man who'd called out came toward us. It was Mr. Oliver, the boxer who'd been Shaddock's student.

He walked toward us in curiosity, as though wondering why the devil we'd come down here, but his gaze riveted to the dog, his perplexity growing.

"Captain Lacey, whatever are you doing with Mr. Blackmore's dog?"

CHAPTER 24

*H*e's Blackmore's dog?" I asked in astonishment. I stared down at Oro, as though he could answer whether Oliver spoke the truth.

"Aye." Oliver put his hands on his hips as he studied the dog. "He took it everywhere he went. We all know Demon."

Oro waved his tail once. He looked up at Oliver, his forehead wrinkling.

"Demon?" I repeated. Oro moved his tail again. "A dog less deserving of the name I've never met."

Oliver grinned. "Blackmore liked to call him that, pretend he was vicious. When he weren't, of course. He's a friendly chap."

While I disliked the name Blackmore had hung on Oro, the fact that he'd taken care of the dog was a point in the man's favor. Oro had been scruffy and flea-ridden when I'd found him, but not starved, hurt, or terrified.

"Where on earth did Blackmore get him?" I asked.

Oliver shrugged. "Dunno. Blackmore just turned up with him one day. Demon would sit and watch the matches."

"What matches? Blackmore was still fighting?"

The young man flushed. "No. The ones Mr. White organized. Blackmore was in on it with him, wasn't he? Mr. Shaddock didn't want nothing to do with him, or White. Wanted well out of it. Don't blame him. But a bloke has to make a living, don't he?"

I recalled Denis's man, Lewis, saying, *Sometimes it's sensible to take a few coins to go down when we probably would have gone down anyway. There are a few champions, but most of us are just fighters.*

"Blackmore and White," I said, as pieces fell together in my head. "But Blackmore is dead now, killed a few months ago in a boxing match in Kent. Tell me, Mr. Oliver, did Mr. White organize the matches for Lord Mercer? The ones using convicts from the hulks?"

Oliver's flush deepened, and he swallowed, as though realizing he'd said more than he should.

Brewster surreptitiously stepped behind him, blocking his way out of the lane.

"He did. Only never tell him I said so. But you ain't a Runner, are you?"

"No," I said. "I am only interested in keeping Mr. Brewster from becoming one of the convicts on the hulks. Did Lord Mercer hire Mr. White? Or is this a long-standing association?"

"You'd have to ask him that," Oliver said, troubled. "But yeah, Mr. White goes about the country, organizing matches for all sorts. Mr. Blackmore used to go with him, 'til he were arrested himself."

"For what?" I asked.

Oliver shook his head. "Never heard. But he were a thief and liked to use his fists to get his own way. Might have punched the wrong man, or hurt a bloke so bad the Watch or the Runners had to arrest him."

I would indeed have to find out the particulars. I had the feeling that Denis, with an eye on every incident in London, probably already knew why both Finch and Blackmore had been arrested, who'd come forward to accuse them, what judges had tried them, and the exact wording of their sentences, but he'd left it to me to plod slowly along.

"Is this why Mr. Shaddock closed his school?" I asked. "Because of Mr. White and Mr. Blackmore?"

"I dunno," Oliver said. "He argued with Mr. White, yes, yelled at him to go away. But Shaddock weren't scared when he talked to him. When he told us he were retiring for good, *then* he was afraid. I never found out why. Mr. Shaddock wouldn't speak to me after—angry I'd taken up with Mr. White. But what else could I do?"

Had Shaddock grown fearful because he'd heard Finch had escaped and was returning to London? Quimby had told me they were sent notices when a convict broke free, even from as far away as the penal colonies. Steadman would take his time sailing back—he'd stop to carry on his trade—and the notices could have reached England before Finch.

Perhaps Shaddock had heard the news from a magistrate or someone he trained having seen the notice in a magistrate's house. He'd dismissed his students and shut himself away, planting his garden so his wife would not have to leave the house often.

"Mr. Oliver, will you take my advice?" I said. "Stay well away from Mr. White and men like him. Go back to Shaddock and ask for more lessons. Find matches that aren't rigged or for prurient entertainment. Life will be far less complex for you."

Oliver, his brow furrowed, nodded. "You're probably right, Captain Lacey. White left me in the dust, as you saw, anyway. Think Shaddock will speak to me?" He directed this last at Brewster.

Brewster didn't soften. "You can only ask him. He's an old man, and he's done bad things, but maybe he can steer you right."

Oliver squared his shoulders. "I'll take a chance. Thank you, sir. Captain Lacey." He tipped his hat, a squashed affair, and pulled it straight on his head.

Brewster moved aside. "Go on, then."

"Mr. Oliver," I said as Oliver prepared to make a dash for it. He turned back, wondering what I was on about now. "If you ever wish to speak to me about Lord Mercer, please do. You can leave a message for me at the bake shop in Grimpen Lane, Covent Garden. No one has to know my information came from you."

He looked relieved. "Right you are, sir." He saluted us again then jogged around the corner and was gone.

As he disappeared, Oro sat down and began to howl. He kept it up until I stroked his head and ruffled his ears, saying words to soothe him. Finally Oro blinked, as though coming to himself, and lipped my hand in apology.

"Depend upon it, he witnessed the murder," I said with conviction.

Brewster only grunted, still skeptical.

~

THE NEXT PERSON I WANTED TO VISIT WAS CHARLOTTE FINCH. Oro was quiet and curious as we walked the few streets to her rooms.

Again, we caught Charlotte in bed with her young man, but from the groggy look Ned gave me when he opened the door, they'd only been sleeping. Charlotte was heavy-eyed and cross when she came to discover what we wanted.

"Yeah? Caught who killed me dad yet?"

"Not yet." I stared at Ned until he stepped back and let me in. Brewster followed, scowling at the pair of them.

Charlotte's expression turned to puzzlement when she saw Oro. I told him to wait, and he sat down, obedient, as I closed the door.

"Did your father have that dog with him when he came here?" I asked her.

"He did," Charlotte said, still puzzled. "I made him sleep in the street—wasn't having no dirty dog in my room."

"My wife would agree with you," I said. "So he was your father's?"

"Suppose so. He were looking after 'im, anyway."

"For his friend, Mr. Blackmore, who'd been killed?"

"Yeah." Charlotte's brows drew down. "How'd you know?"

"I tend to find things out. Did Mr. Finch talk about Mr. Blackmore?"

"Happen he did." Charlotte planted herself on the one chair and folded her arms over her bright dressing gown, a thing of yellow silk with blue Chinese-looking embroidery. "Dad asked me, if you please, like I'd know anything about it, what happened to Mr. Blackmore. He'd been arrested, hadn't he? For thrashing a bloke." She fluttered a hand. "Didn't happen around here. Off Mr. Blackmore goes to Newgate, and we never see him again. Dad went to Blackmore's digs and found the dog, and comes back here in a rage. He was even more angry when he came home a few nights later, saying Blackmore was dead. Dad was powerful cut up. He and Blackmore were great friends."

Brewster rumbled. "Were Finch and Blackmore more than friends? Seems like there weren't two greater villains alive. Why were they so chummy?"

Charlotte blinked. "I dunno. They were just mates. Weren't bent or nothing. They got on, is all, like me and Neddy."

Ned, in breeches and a loose shirt, stood behind Charlotte with his hands on his hips, trying, and failing, to look intimidating. Charlotte had full command of this partnership.

Ned and Charlotte had the sort of relationship Brewster meant, but I could see that Charlotte considered Ned a friend, not just a bedmate. Bedmates to her were business, but for some reason the washed-out Ned was special to her.

"You said your father asked you for money," I prompted.

Charlotte nodded. "He needed it, he said. Bad. Why he thought I'd have any, I don't know. I had to give it all to Hobson. Not now, though, thanks to Uncle Tommy." She grinned up at Brewster, her demeanor far less hostile. "That's why Dad thrashed Hobson, to get my money out of him."

Because he had to pay Steadman his exorbitant fee for bringing him out of bondage, I'd already surmised. "He succeeded in getting the money from Hobson, I believe," I said. Hobson had certainly been bruised and furious.

"Oh, yes. No one stood up to me dad for long." Charlotte sounded proud. "But he were good to me. Always, like I said. And he didn't have to be. He brought me this." She slid her hand down the silk gown. "Guess he stopped off in China."

Or helped himself to goods on the merchantman returning from Asia that gave him passage. Finch could have sold such a gown for several guineas, but instead he'd bestowed it on his illegitimate daughter, and was distressed at the death of his friend. The terrifying man was proving to have a soft heart, or at least a close thing to it.

"Did your dad still need money after he got whatever Hobson gave him?"

Charlotte nodded. "He were worried, so whatever he needed it for must have been important. But he said he had an idea where to get it, so all would be well." Her face fell. "And then he died."

"Before or after he found this source of income?" I mused, half to myself.

"Well, I don't know, do I?" Charlotte said angrily. "I didn't know he were dead." Tears filled her eyes and caught in her voice. "He said he'd come back for me, and he never did."

"Aw, Lotty." Ned leaned down and wrapped his arms around her, and Charlotte sank back into him, sniffling.

"I'm very sorry about your father, Miss Finch," I said gently.

She looked up, eyes streaming. *"Miss Finch.* Like I'm a lady." She swiped at her wet cheeks. "Find out who murdered him, Captain." Her voice turned fierce. "And then string him up until his balls turn blue."

WE LEFT CHARLOTTE AFTER THAT. ORO WAITED PATIENTLY FOR me on the landing, and he fell into step with me as we went down the stairs.

"Why don't you look in on your wife and meet me in Grimpen Lane?" I said as we strode back to the hackney. "I thought I'd stop off and speak to Pomeroy."

Brewster scowled. "I'll come with ye. I don't trust you not to get yourself into mischief between here and there."

He remained outside when I went into the magistrate's house at Bow Street, leaning on the wheel of the hackney and holding Oro's lead.

Pomeroy was in, but my request startled him. "I'd like to speak to Spendlove," I said.

His fair brows climbed. "Would you, Captain? What the devil for?"

"I want to ask him about Finch's conviction. I wish to discover who was Finch's accuser, and Spendlove would know. Save me some time."

"If he'd speak to you. But he's out. Went to Reading after a pair of counterfeiters. Might be back tomorrow."

"You have records here. A room full of them." I'd once stood among boxes upon boxes in the dust of the cellars.

Pomeroy heaved a sigh. "I can ask. Wait here."

He barreled out, leaving me alone in his room. The chamber

was neat but plain, with a table for a desk, a second chair and another, smaller table, and not much else. The window, I saw as I went to it, looked out over a tiny yard. A small shed in the back served as additional jail space, I knew. I'd once viewed a corpse laid out there.

I waited for half an hour. I fully expected Brewster to become impatient and disappear, dog and carriage and all, but a look out the window across the hall showed him still below, in conversation with the coachman and another man I couldn't identify. From above, what I mostly saw was hats.

"You're in luck, Captain." Pomeroy's voice boomed back into his room before he did. "One of the magistrate's clerks remembered the case, at least when Finchie were brought in by a very proud patroller called Spendlove. It were something of an occasion. Finch was arrested for beating a man called Leeds, who said he would prosecute. Spendlove caught Finch in the act, near the church in St. Giles, and there wasn't much chance he'd get off. I suppose that gave this Leeds bloke courage."

"Who *is* Mr. Leeds?" I asked, trying to keep my eagerness at bay.

"Devil if I know. Clerk of some kind, I'm told. Probably didn't get out of Finch's way on the street one day, and paid the price."

"Hmm." I very much wondered. "Thank you, Pomeroy. I'll stand you a pint for that."

"And I will make certain you pay. Oh, and tell Tommy Brewster that his friend, Slocombe, I think his name is, and the other bloke what helped you on the hulks were pardoned of their misdeeds and set free." He shook his head. "Stop interfering, Captain. If it were up to you, no men would be banged up, and we'd be overrun with villains."

"We already are," I said, clapping on my hat. "They're sitting right now in the Houses of Parliament."

"Ha." Pomeroy's laugh rang through the tiny room. "Very amusing, Captain."

I departed, his merriment and the words *Houses of Parliament* following me down the stairs.

~

I NOW HAD TO RETURN HOME AND KEEP MY PROMISES. ONCE there, I sent a note to Denis, asking if he could find out anything about a Mr. Leeds—*possibly a clerk,* I scribbled—who had prosecuted Jack Finch.

I also wrote a letter to my friend, Sir Gideon Derwent, a reformer, describing the conditions in the hulk, the *Atonement.* While I did not, as Pomeroy had implied, wish to set free every convicted man, I could not agree with treating them worse than rats.

Sir Gideon was a reformer with a strong voice and much influence. He likely already knew about the hulks, but I penned him a vivid description of what I'd seen. I also mentioned Lord Mercer's practice of taking men out of the hulks to fight in savage matches, and Blackmore's death because of it. Sir Gideon, who was quite powerful in his own way, would not fear reprisal from Mercer. While Sir Montague might be slow and careful about Mercer, Sir Gideon would simply expect the man's crimes to be punished, no matter how much money he gave to the Admiralty's purse.

I'd already relinquished Oro to the stables, where Brewster had a bite of dinner with the coachman and lads, and then I had to give myself to Bartholomew to be stuffed into a new suit.

The coat and trousers were well made and hung easily on my big frame, but I'd refused to let the tailor add a colorful waistcoat, overly wide lapels, or shorten the trousers to show off my boots. I had never been, and would not now be, a fop.

Bartholomew kindly tied the cravat so that I could actually

turn my head and look up and down with a bit of effort, but he made certain that I was free of every speck of dust before he let me out of his sight.

I had to admit that escorting my wife, who was a beautiful lady in her green and gold silk, and my daughter, equally lovely in a simpler gown of cream trimmed with blue, was not a difficulty. The gentlemen tonight would look upon me with envy.

Our outing was a supper ball at a Grosvenor Square mansion. The house was enormous. A connection had been built between it and its stables, and now it sported a roof garden on top of the extension. The ballroom, reached by a grand staircase from the entrance, opened onto this roof garden, which was lit by lanterns. A high wall cut off the view from the roof to the houses across the narrow road, so we could make believe, but for the noise, that we were somewhere in the country.

I escorted Gabriella inside, while Grenville had Donata on his arm. Marianne had not been invited—not to a society ball given by a countess with unmarried misses in attendance. Marianne, ever practical, would not be annoyed, but Grenville was.

"Rules put too much emphasis on *who* a person is," he'd muttered to me outside. "And not enough on what they are like inside. The dear girl is intelligent, resilient, courageous, and has far more sense than half the people on the guest list. And yet, she is forbidden and always will be, unless she's invited for her talent, to entertain us all."

"Mr. Fox married his Mrs. Armistead," I reminded him.

"And they retired to the country to putter about their garden," Grenville growled back. "I dislike puttering."

"He was getting on in years by then," I said. "But the match was more or less accepted."

"Because she was once the Regent's mistress, and he was a great statesman," Grenville said. "Again, connections were more important than character."

I withdrew from the field, and we spoke no more about it.

When we emerged into the ballroom, I saw Gabriella's suitors brighten and begin to surge our way. With some dismay I noted that Emmett Garfield, the most confident of them, had filled out since last spring, and looked less of a youth and more of a man. Young ladies in the ballroom cast coy glances at him.

Not Gabriella, I noticed with some relief. She seemed to ignore the gentlemen and scanned the room for the young misses who had befriended her last Season.

I had to spend some time greeting the hostess and other ladies and gentlemen of Donata's acquaintance, including Lady Aline. Gabriella at last was led off by Donata with Gabriella's new female friends and their mothers, leaving me relatively alone.

"There is more masculine entertainment in the drawing room," Grenville said at my elbow. "Cards and brandy, and also a few fellows who know Lord Mercer. Shall we adjourn?"

CHAPTER 25

The drawing room was grand, with a ceiling I judged at twenty feet, plenty of paintings of ancestors on the walls, built-in cabinets full of books, and eight card tables, most of them occupied.

Grenville led me to a table with two empty seats, the gentlemen already there waiting for us to make a foursome for whist. Fortunes could be lost in such casual games. I would have to wager with care or at least make certain I won.

I'd met one of the gentlemen before—Viscount Compton, a neighbor of Grenville's, elderly and a bit short-sighted, but sharp of mind. The other man I knew vaguely as Mr. Fitzpatrick, the second or third son of an earl. In his mid-thirties, he mostly lived to race horses and enjoy himself, having a large allowance and not many cares.

"Mercer," Mr. Fitzpatrick said after the play had gone around the table a few times. "Dear Lord, never tell me you've made friends with him, Grenville."

"Not at all." Grenville feigned horror. "The captain is busy finding things out again, don't you know, and he is curious about Mercer. We all agree Mercer is fairly awful."

"He's very odd, to be sure," Fitzpatrick said to me. "He's a neighbor of mine, in Kent. I have a house there, where I've got some beautiful racers—two-year-olds who will go to Newmarket this season."

Mr. Fitzpatrick clearly was more interested in talking of his horses than Mercer, but Grenville steered him back to the matter at hand.

"I have heard he's more than odd," Grenville said. "Disgusting rather."

"Disgusting is a good word for him," Fitzpatrick said readily. "He invites people down and more or less forces them into the garden to watch men bash each other until they can't stand. Then he throws the injured fellows into a cart and has them rolled back from whence they came. Wherever that may be."

"The nearby hulks," Grenville said. "That is supposed to be a deep, dark secret."

Fitzpatrick's brown eyes widened. "Truly? I'd never heard that. But come to think of it, these fellows do look dirty and barbaric. And resigned. I always wondered why some were rather reluctant fighters. Mercer has to have someone scream at them to ginger them up. Very strange and quite unsavory."

"Who did he have scream at them?" I asked. "His gamekeeper, perhaps?"

"Hmm? Oh, no, nothing like that. The chaps who bring the others do the shouting. One is sort of a herdsman, I suppose you'd call him, keeping an eye on the fighters, and another fellow, Mr. White, to take the wagers. I only went to one of these gatherings, and decided never to go back." He shuddered. "It does not take much incentive to avoid Lord Mercer. He doesn't even *ride*." The last was spoken in a tone of shock.

"A fellow was killed at one of these matches," I said. "A former pugilist, probably fighting men half his age."

Mr. Fitzpatrick's brows went up. "I hadn't heard that, either, but I cannot confess I am surprised. I say, Grenville, you ought to put it about that Mercer is not quite the thing. Perhaps he'll move to the Continent and trouble us no more."

"Rather hard on the inhabitants of France or Switzerland, or wherever he ends up," Grenville said.

"Too true." Fitzpatrick chuckled. "The sacrifices we make for our fellows."

"Mercer killed a man," Viscount Compton said abruptly. He peered at his cards, then at those on the table, squinting until his eyes were nearly closed.

Grenville, who rarely permitted himself displays of emotion in public, blinked in amazement. "I beg your pardon?"

Compton plucked out a queen and laid it down. "When he was younger, just down from Oxford. He beat a footman with a poker. Killed the chap. No one knew why. Possibly didn't bring him his brandy quickly enough."

"Good Lord," Grenville said. "Was he never brought to trial?"

Compton shook his head. "He lied through his teeth, made out it was an accident, but we all knew. Mercer buries himself in the country because decent people won't stick him. His wife is a baron's daughter, but by all accounts, she's no better than a courtesan. I don't mean a courtesan like yours, Grenville, who is a lady who must live by her wits. I mean a whore who enjoys it. Leads her husband around by his what-sit. Damn it all, I've played the wrong card. Meant to put down the queen."

"That *is* a queen," Fitzpatrick said, his voice faint. "You've taken the trick, which means you've won the hand."

"Ah," Lord Compton brightened. "So I have. Perhaps we should change the disagreeable subject. It seems to have put you gentlemen off your game.

~

WHEN WE FINISHED PLAY—I WON ENOUGH HANDS TO KEEP FROM

having to pay Lord Compton too much—Grenville and I
returned to the ballroom.

Grenville stood up with ladies whose social standing needed
a boost and continued to express approval of my daughter.
Gabriella was already well-liked, as she had a natural charm and
a friendliness that said she did not view the other young ladies
as her rivals.

I happened to know she had no interest in the gentlemen,
which was to my liking. What was not to my liking was that Mr.
Garfield was particularly attentive.

He was deferential to me but a little too certain of my
approval—Mr. Garfield had helped me on a problem last year,
and I suppose he thought this meant I would accept him as a
son-in-law.

Mr. Garfield danced once with Gabriella, and they chatted
in a polite way that wasn't overly familiar. Only one dance, I
was pleased to see.

Grenville escaped the ballroom, pretending he was aged and
exhausted, and led me to a small chamber on the next floor,
away from the noise.

Our host had left brandy there, and Grenville poured out. I
sank gratefully into an armchair, my leg tired.

"Well, now we know what sort of man Lord Mercer is," he
said after a long swallow of brandy. "A foul, violent bastard. You
can always put your Mr. Pomeroy onto him. *He* won't care the
man's a peer. Mercer would be tried in the House of Lords, but
whether or not they acquit him, it would ruin him forever."

"Yes," I said absently.

"What are you thinking?" Grenville asked with interest. "I
see cogs spinning."

"Trying to put the entire picture together," I said, easing my
cramped knee. "Finch is arrested and transported for roughing
up a fellow called Leeds—whoever he is. Once Finch is gone, his
friend, Mr. Blackmore forms a partnership with Mr. White, the

unscrupulous bookmaker. They arrange pugilism matches for Lord Mercer using convicts from the hulks, or true pugilists, or both. At one of these bouts, Blackmore makes friends with one of Mercer's dogs and takes it away with him. Mercer, not a sporting man, according to Fitzpatrick, except for his fondness for boxing, does not notice. The kennel master could have been too afraid of Mercer to report the loss, or perhaps he did and Mercer did not care. Or Mercer gave him the dog as payment."

"Or the dog wasn't Mercer's at all."

"Possibly, but Oro is a gentleman's dog, not a mongrel from the streets. Mercer's estate is a likely place from which Blackmore could have acquired him."

"I take your point." Grenville gestured with his goblet. "Go on."

"Blackmore continues his partnership with White, until Blackmore is arrested for assault and condemned to transportation. Lord Mercer hears of this and is pleased to bring Blackmore to his house for one of the matches that Blackmore used to arrange." I closed my eyes, picturing the scene. "Blackmore was a pitiless man by all accounts, and perhaps he'd bullied Mercer or demanded much for his services. The fighting grows rough, and Blackmore is killed. Or perhaps Mercer killed Blackmore himself, as he did to the footman long ago, and blamed it on the fighting."

I opened my eyes again, letting the colors in the comfortable room drive out the bleak images in my mind. "About this time, Finch has managed to escape his confinement in Van Diemen's Land and arranges passage on Captain Steadman's merchant ship, stealing a silk dressing gown along the way as a gift for his daughter, whom he has not seen in years."

"Perhaps Captain Steadman discovered the theft," Grenville put in. "And demanded still more money for the journey."

"Possibly. Or it was done so neatly that Steadman knew nothing about it. Merchant ships usually carry bolts of cloth, not made garments, so Finch might have stolen it elsewhere. In any case, he brought the gown to Charlotte.

"Finch arrives in London and of course wants to look up his old friend, Blackmore. He goes to Blackmore's lodgings, discovers he's been arrested and sentenced. The dog must have been left behind, perhaps with a neighbor, and Finch decides to take care of it for his friend. He wants to work out what happened to Blackmore, or help him escape and give him back the dog, as a friend would do. And now I move into sheer speculation."

"All of this is," Grenville pointed out. "But best fits what we know. Pray, continue."

"Perhaps Finch returned to Steadman, not only to pay him, but to ask him for help rescuing Blackmore from the hulks. He discovers, maybe from Steadman, maybe from someone else near the shipyards, that Blackmore has been killed.

"Steadman, meanwhile, must be paid. Finch likely didn't pay him in advance, as it would be difficult to come up with the fee while he was in captivity. Captain Steadman, we have been told, transports his passengers and then stands on them for the money. Finch must not only pay for his passage, he wants to take vengeance on Blackmore's killer. Because he is not supposed to be in this country at all, he will need still more blunt to find the murderer, possibly kill him, and then flee."

"Which is why he came to Mrs. Brewster and her sister, demanding cash," Grenville finished. "Did Steadman, or his collector, catch up to him and beat him? Perhaps going too far? Finch struggled, and they had to knife him to get away?"

"And therein lies the speculation. Finch was in London to gather funds. It could have been Steadman's man who killed him, or it could have been Mercer, learning that Finch was furious at Blackmore's death. Perhaps Mercer out of fear, sent someone to silence him forever."

"Or Hobson," Grenville suggested. "Angry that Finch beat

Charlotte's takings out of him. He claims he saw Brewster conveying Finch, unconscious, into the house. He walks in, stabs Finch, and walks out again."

"Yes, that is possible. I had also thought of Charlotte, but she was genuinely distressed when we told her Finch was dead, and she seems to have been fond of him. And he of her."

"Unless she didn't realize she'd killed him." Grenville clicked his empty glass to the polished table beside him. "Suppose she followed Finch when he went to see Brewster, angry with him for frightening her chap, Ned. They argue, struggle, and she pushes him off with her knife and runs for it. She has no idea the knife has gone in as far as it has."

"A lucky blow. It struck exactly where it could kill him instantly."

"Such things can happen." Grenville tapped his fingertips together. "I do not want it to be Charlotte, because, like you, I have sympathy for her. Also, can a man who'd look after a friend's dog and remember to bring his daughter a gift when he's running for his life be as horrible as he's painted?"

"Difficult to say," I said. "I've met thoroughly disagreeable, even frightening gentlemen who would never let any harm come to their horses."

"As have I," Grenville said glumly. "Their grooms they'll beat until bloody, but not one hair on their darling hunter's head must be mussed."

"Here we are, then," I said. "I have considered Mr. White as well. A cheat of a bookmaker—perhaps he worried that Finch would peach on him for Mercer's games, or vent his feelings on White for getting Blackmore killed, in a roundabout way."

"Yes, here we are," Grenville said. "There are other possibilities. Mr. Shaddock, very much afraid of Finch. The fellow who got Finch convicted—Leeds—fearing that Finch would come after him. Perhaps Finch did. And I hate to say this, but the Brewsters. Mr. and Mrs."

"I have thought of that," I said reluctantly. "I believe in Brewster, but he loves his wife and will do anything for her."

"Well." Grenville sat up straight, resting his hands on the gilded arms of his chair. "There are any number of people who wouldn't mind offing Finch. Now we need to prove which of them *did* kill him."

"We?" I asked.

"Of course, my dear fellow. I also do not want to see Brewster hang. The chap has grown on me." He let out a breath. "So, what do we do first?"

~

FIRST, WE HAD TO FINISH THE BALL AND TAKE GABRIELLA HOME. Mr. Garfield bowed to Gabriella when he said good night, but he was carefully polite. Her other suitors were as well.

Gabriella was tired, but she stated she had enjoyed herself very much. She didn't gush, but said it with truth in her eyes.

She went directly to bed upon our return home. I did not wish to discuss Gabriella's possible husbands with Donata—I knew I'd lose my temper—and so I said good night to my yawning wife and took myself to bed.

As I breakfasted the next morning, Barnstable glided in and set a letter by my plate.

I recognized the slanted handwriting, broke the seal, and unfolded a letter from Denis.

Jack Finch was arrested in February of 1814 for robbery with violence. He was prosecuted by the victim, Josiah Leeds, who claimed he'd been set upon by Finch and another man not identified, and robbed.

In the dock at the Old Bailey, Mr. Finch pleaded for his life, saying he had a daughter to look after. This apparently moved the jury, and the verdict was returned as guilty, with a recommendation for trans-

portation. The judge, who was from all accounts, made nervous by Mr.
Finch, convicted accordingly.

The man not identified I would guess was Sydney Blackmore. Why
Mr. Leeds did not accuse him by name, I have not discovered.

Mr. Leeds is a clerk at the Bank of England, where he has held a
position for nearly twenty years. The position is not an important one,
and he is not a wealthy man. He resides at 23 Birchin Lane, not far
from his place of employment.

JD

The missive took up half a page, with the second half blank. Out of habit, I tore off the empty part to save for my own correspondence. Donata could afford as much paper as she wished, but I always thought it imprudent to waste it.

I used the page immediately to send a note to Grenville, asking him to accompany me to the City. I wanted very much to know why Mr. Leeds, a clerk of no importance, out of all the populace of London, was the only one not afraid to bring Finch to court.

I went riding, as usual, happy for the wind in my face after the stuffy ballroom of last night. When I returned, I found a reply from Grenville saying he could be ready in an hour.

Accordingly, at eleven of the clock, I faced Grenville in his carriage. I allowed him the forward-facing seat, in deference of his motion sickness. When the carriage moved slowly, however, as it did today, he was not as much affected.

"We have not had much chance to speak of anything but murder," I said as we headed toward Piccadilly. Brewster accompanied us, but rode with the coachman, so we were private for the first time in a while. "You have not told me how you fared in Paris. I imagine the city is much changed since I lived there in '02."

"Paris is eternal." Grenville gave me a faint smile. "But yes, there have been some changes. The restored monarchy is trying to add to the collection at the Louvre, as many pieces Bonaparte procured as he rampaged through Europe were returned after his defeat. I was frequently asked my opinion on what was best to acquire. Otherwise, people are adjusting to the aftermath of defeat. A strange time, but the French are a resilient people. I imagine they will rise to greatness again."

"In other words, you enjoyed yourself."

Grenville's smile turned to a grin. "I did, as a matter of fact. It was refreshing. Marianne and I were received everywhere— there a man's mistress does not have to be his secret shame. Or at least, his obvious fondness of her does not have to be a secret. We became quite chummy, Marianne and I. She is very bright, as you know, and eager to learn all about art and music. She has a deep knowledge of the theatre and classical plays, no matter that she was relegated to the background in them. She can discuss their themes and history more readily than most of my Cambridge cronies."

"Does this mean you will be fleeing London for permanent residence in France?" I spoke lightly to hide a pang of sadness. I would miss him and our friendship.

"Oh, I doubt that very much. If I were to put myself in exile, I'd choose Florence, or Venice. I believe you'd enjoy Venice, you and Donata."

"She'd never leave England to reside on any other shore," I said with conviction. "Donata loves her life here, no matter what she might state."

"Perhaps not to reside forever, but a visit for some months. Like our Egyptian excursion, but in fine hotels with our ladies at our sides."

It did sound appealing, as did a return to Egypt. The heat and sands called to me—Mr. Belzoni, the famous strongman turned antiquities collector I'd met there, had told me it would. But a visit to the ancient city of canals and art with Donata might also be enjoyable.

Grenville talked more of Paris and what he and Marianne had seen and done until we reached the Bank of England.

That edifice, referred to by wits as the Old Lady of Threadneedle Street, dominated the turning from Poultry Lane, dwarfing the buildings of the Exchange across the road. Scaffolding covered part of the bank, which was again being remodeled. I had read that John Soane had redesigned much of it. I seemed to be visiting all his buildings.

I had made no appointment with Mr. Leeds. The usher inside the door of the lofty hall was surprised I asked for him, but after consulting his fellows, he found a pageboy, a lad of about thirteen, to take us upstairs to the clerk's room.

We climbed several staircases, which tasked my injured leg, to a cramped hallway at the very top of the building. The page led us down the corridor to a door at the end.

This he opened to reveal a large room with small windows in which many desks had been fitted. Standing at these desks were gentlemen scribbling away or consulting books, or whatever it was banker's clerks did.

"Mr. Leeds," the pageboy called.

Several gentlemen looked up, and then all but one lost interest and returned to their tasks.

The gentleman who gazed at us in puzzlement had dark brown hair, straight and sleek, caught in a very short, old-fashioned queue. He was slim and looked to be about Grenville's height.

He regarded us with eyes of pale blue, then he abruptly dropped his pen, whirled from his desk, sprinted to a door on the far side of the room, and disappeared through it.

CHAPTER 26

I stood, stunned, as the far door slammed. The pageboy stared in shock, and the other gentlemen in the room ceased working, gazing first at the door through which Mr. Leeds had disappeared and then back to us.

"I'll fetch 'im," the pageboy declared and darted back into the hall.

Grenville and I exchanged a glance and followed, Grenville making a bow to the room. "So sorry to have disturbed you, gentlemen," he said.

The pageboy flew on youthful legs through another door and down a flight of back stairs. Grenville, faster than I, rushed off on his heels. I followed the best I could, using the wall in the narrow stairwell to steady me, as there were no railings.

At the bottom, a door led out into the street, and I wondered briefly why I'd bothered to climb all the way to the clerk's aerie.

When I emerged I saw that the pageboy had seized our fleeing gentleman by the coat tails and was holding on to him. Grenville reached them and began speaking rapidly to Leeds—I could not hear what he said over the noises of the street.

Leeds gave Grenville a puzzled look, and then deflated, no

longer attempting to run. By the time I reached the group, Mr. Leeds leaned against the wall of the bank, trying to catch his breath.

"I beg your pardon, gentlemen," he said, wheezing. "I am of nervous disposition. Go on, lad. You may return to your post."

The pageboy frowned, as though uncertain Mr. Leeds should be left on his own, but I gave him a reassuring nod and a coin. The lad quickly slid the coin into the pocket of his bright red coat and vanished into the bank.

"Very well met, Mr. Grenville," Leeds said, wetting his lips. "I fancied you were the bailiffs, you see." He gave a nervous laugh. "I am ever owing money."

"Well, you shan't have to worry about landing in the Fleet today," Grenville said soothingly. "We have come to speak to you about a point of law, but nothing to do with debts. We all have *those*, dear sir. Perhaps there is a place we may speak, one not in a passage filled with horse droppings."

Mr. Leeds nodded. His worry had turned to curiosity, and he led us around the corner to a tavern already doing a brisk business.

We found a relatively empty corner in which to sit, Grenville drawing many stares from the clerks and coachmen who occupied the place. Grenville asked the barmaid for three of their best bitters, earning a breathless thanks from Mr. Leeds.

"Now then, gentlemen." Mr. Leeds lifted his glass, looking much more confident. "Why did you wish to speak to me? I have much information about the bank's investments, I'll have you know, though gentlemen usually send their man of business to seek my advice."

"Mr. Finch," I said without preliminary. "You prosecuted him."

Mr. Leeds choked. He set down his glass hastily and snatched a handkerchief from his pocket. He coughed into this for some time, his eyes streaming.

Grenville thumped him on the back. "All right, sir?"

"Yes." Leeds wiped his eyes. "You caught me off guard, Captain, you did. What about Mr. Finch? He's gone. Transported, thank God."

"No, he is dead," I said, watching him.

Leeds looked startled, then flushed. "Truly? Ah, well. It may sound cruel, sir, but I cannot be sorry. He was a wicked man."

"You prosecuted him," I went on, "for robbing you. Can you tell me exactly what happened?"

Grenville said nothing, resting against the back of the settle and sipping his beer. He knew when to ask gentle questions and when to let me be straightforward.

Leeds wiped his mouth once more, stowed the handkerchief, and took a fortifying drink of bitter. "He and his friend beat and robbed me, *that* is what happened. It was my good fortune that a patroller from one of the magistrate's houses happened by, and he nicked Finch. The other chap ran for it and got away, I'm afraid."

"Probably Finch's friend Blackmore," I said. "Who is also now dead."

Leeds jumped again, but I'd at least waited for him to swallow this time. He gave me a shaky smile. "Again, I cannot say I am sorry. They hurt me very much."

"Why did they waylay you?" I asked. "Not to offend you, but I can understand two such ruthless villains rolling Mr. Grenville on the street and stealing all he had. His coat alone would be worth much, and a thief would guess that his pockets were full. But you must not be a rich man."

"I am not, no." Mr. Leeds rested his hands on either side of his half-drunk glass. "But I walked alone in an insalubrious part of the metropolis—visiting a sick friend—and they set upon me. I suppose even the tuppence in my pocket and my linen handkerchief was enough to make such men tackle me."

I kept my expression quiet. Finch and Blackmore were

villains, yes, but I could not believe they'd risk capture by robbing so poor a target like Mr. Leeds. Finch had frightened large quantities of money out of men like Shaddock and who knew how many others. He'd have no need of the few pennies and a linen handkerchief carried by Mr. Leeds.

"Who was the friend?" I asked.

Leeds blinked. "Pardon?"

"The friend you visited. Did he live in St. Giles?"

"Oh." Leeds' brow smoothed out. "Yes. A chap who'd fallen on hard times, and yes, he dwelled in St. Giles. I had gone to sit with him. He is dead now, poor fellow."

"Another clerk?"

"Eh? Oh, he was, yes. But illness forced him to leave his post." He shook his head. "It was very sad."

"The name of this friend?" I asked.

Mr. Leeds shot me an angry look. "Look here, Captain, what is your interest? It was a very long time ago. That bastard Finch robbed me, I lost a friend, and Finch got what he deserved."

"My apologies," I said. "I did not mean to upset you. I am looking into the circumstances of Finch's death for ... er, a friend. I was surprised to hear you were brave enough to bring charges against him. He intimidated so many."

Leeds shrugged, his composure restored. "Well, the patroller who arrested him took him to the magistrate, who locked him away in Newgate. I had Finch dead to rights, so I agreed to prosecute. I wasn't brave, not really—there wasn't much chance he'd get off, so no danger for me." He gave us his thin smile. "Finch made up a story in the dock about having a daughter, and convinced the jury to feel sorry for him. He was transported instead of hanged, but that didn't matter. I'd never have to see him again."

He took another sip of bitter, everything well in his world.

"Did you know Mr. Finch had returned to London?" I asked.

Leeds started, but the start had come a second too late. "Did he? I thought you said he died in the Antipodes."

"No, he died here in London. A week and more ago. His daughter—he did indeed have a daughter—is quite distressed."

"Oh." Leeds flushed once more as these new ideas went through his head. "I did not realize the daughter was a truth."

"She is. A by-blow, but he had affection for her. Brought her gifts."

"I see." Leeds stared at his glass but did not reach for it.

"Was the patroller named Spendlove?" I asked. "The one who nicked Finch, I mean."

Leeds brightened. "Oh, yes. Courageous of him. Felled the man right enough. I hear Mr. Spendlove is a Runner now. Good on him."

Grenville and I exchanged a glance. I decided to say nothing more at present, and we finished our beer, Grenville switching the topic to mundane pleasantries.

We returned Mr. Leeds to the bank's side door. The drink and the end of my questions seemed to restore his confidence.

"I do hope we have not landed you in trouble, Mr. Leeds," Grenville said as they shook hands in parting.

"I am allowed a brief time for lunch or tea," Leeds assured us, bowing. "I thank you for the sustenance. And if you or the captain ever need guidance in investing, I do know more than most what goes on in the bowels of the bank." He tapped the side of his nose, gave us another nod, and skimmed inside, leaving Grenville and I alone.

"Well, well," Grenville said as he led us along the busy street. Brewster, who'd followed at a discreet distance, joined us. "What do you make of that?"

"What'd he tell you?" Brewster rumbled.

Grenville's coachman, Jackson, had pulled the landau into the street called Lothbury, in front of St. Margaret's church.

With Christopher Wren before me and John Soane behind me, I was surrounded by architectural genius in this narrow space.

"What I found interesting," Grenville mused once we'd settled in the coach, Brewster joining us to hear our tale, "was that Leeds told his story without hesitation, until you, Lacey, tripped him by asking the name of his sick friend. Then he fumbled about until he said the friend was deceased. So why was he in St. Giles the day Finch waylaid him? Leeds knew Finch had returned to the country, though he pretended he did not. I would swear he did not know Finch was dead, however. But very much relieved."

"All of which could be explained by his terror of Finch," I said, though I did not believe that was the entirety of it. "Fear that Finch would retaliate for Leeds getting him convicted. Relief he was dead."

"The friend was a fabrication," Brewster said with certainty. "An excuse for him being in St. Giles. Finchie and Blackmore would never waylay a man for a few coins and a cheap cotton wiper. But this Leeds bloke had to say *something* in the witness box, didn't he?"

"Mr. Leeds was keen to point out he knew much about the Bank of England's doings," Grenville said. "Perhaps he truly does know quite a lot, and perhaps Finch, being the extortionist and blackmailer he was, tried to get Leeds to give him money. Leeds meets Finch and Blackmore in St. Giles, won't pay up—or can't—and they rough him up. When Leeds spies a patroller, he seizes his chance and cries out. Pomeroy told you that Spendlove made his career chasing Finch, so he was probably following anyway. Spendlove is only too happy to drag Finch in, and bullied Leeds into prosecuting. Leeds is rid of Finch, Spendlove pockets a hefty reward, and everyone is happy."

I nodded, but I still wasn't satisfied. "Finch needed money, upon his return—perhaps he hoped Leeds might be a source of it …"

I trailed off. Finch had been tapping his family for funds to pay Steadman. Would he not also want to put his hands on Leeds, who could possibly get him gold, or silver, or whatever Leeds could give him, straight from the Bank of England?

Leeds knew his way in and out of the bank's back doors, and he had obviously been to St. Giles before. Not to see his friend, as he'd claimed—but for what? To visit a lady? To conduct shady deals of some sort?

I imagined Leeds facing Finch in the alley in St. Giles, Finch growling at him to deliver the goods, and Leeds plunging a small knife into his side.

"Hmm," I said. "I am trying to fit Leeds for the crime, but why on earth would Leeds agree to meet Finch in St. Giles the day Finch died? Why would Leeds not ignore the summons, lock himself in his house, flee town?"

"Finch had something on him," Brewster suggested.

"Ah," Grenville said. "That would explain it nicely. Finch knew something that could make Leeds's life hell—perhaps the fact that Leeds uses his inside knowledge to help others make money, as he offered to us? If Finch threatened to expose him, wouldn't Leeds rush to him and shut him up?"

"Very possibly." I tightened my hand on my walking stick. "Let us discover more about Mr. Leeds."

"We might have found our murderer," Grenville said. "Poor chap."

~

I RETURNED HOME, ALREADY COMPOSING LETTERS IN MY HEAD. I'D ask Sir Montague Harris to find out all he could about Mr. Leeds—perhaps there had been suspicion of him before, which would make him more susceptible to Finch's blackmailing.

I would also write to my friend Mr. Molodzinski, a man of business and very astute, who had rooms not far from Leeds' lodgings. Molodzinski had his finger on the pulse of whatever went on in the City, plus I liked him and was happy of an excuse to communicate with him again.

I would also ask Sir Montague if he could have someone look up the records for the house in St. Giles that Brewster found so handy to put Finch into. I had reasoned Denis might own it—he had various properties around London—but I was beginning to suspect he did not.

By the time I reached South Audley Street, it was late afternoon, and the house was thronged with callers. Flowers filled the front hall and the drawing room, which was full of people.

They were calling on Gabriella. The flowers were from young men, as it was customary to send a small bouquet to a lady with whom a young man had danced and from whom he'd received permission to call. I'd noticed Gabriella's suitors dancing with several young ladies, and I imagined the gentlemen's pockets were a little emptier today.

I managed to slip past the throng and retreat to my bedchamber. I was dusty and hot from a journey across London, hardly fit to be seen in polite company. I sat down at the small desk in my room and wrote my letters.

When I emerged an hour or so later, washed and changed, everything had gone quiet, to my relief.

I went downstairs to leave the letters for Barnstable to post. The flowers remained in the lower hall, wilting a little now, but the house was deathly silent.

I deposited the letters on the tray in the foyer and caught sight of a downstairs maid busily tidying up the drawing room.

"Mary?" I asked her, entering that chamber. "Where is everyone?"

Mary ceased dusting, came to attention, and gave me a curtsy, eyes downcast. "Her ladyship has gone out. Miss Lacey is in the library."

"Thank you," I said. "I beg your pardon for disturbing you."

I turned away to make for the stairs, but Mary cleared her throat. "Begging your pardon, sir."

I swung back, noticing that Mary was more subdued than usual. Donata's servants were always deferential, but not dejected.

"What is it?" Worry stirred. "Is Gabriella ill?"

"No, sir. Not my place, sir, but I thought you should know. Her ladyship left in a rare temper. And I believe Miss Lacey is crying."

What the devil? "Bloody hell," I muttered as dire foreboding washed over me. "Thank you, Mary. I appreciate your candor."

For answer, she curtsied again, clearly wishing me elsewhere.

I left the room and climbed the flight of stairs to the library.

I was the only person who used the library—though Donata enjoyed reading, she'd have her maid or Barnstable fetch her a tome to peruse in the comfort of her boudoir. I preferred to lounge among the books, with their scents of leather and aging paper, feeling as though the ancients and moderns who'd scribbled away at these texts were watching over me. Donata had some valuable books here as well, kept carefully in glass cases.

Gabriella liked the library too, and during her visits, I often found her browsing the shelves or sitting on the window seat, her feet drawn up, while she lost herself in a novel or book of poetry.

She reposed on the window seat today, a shawl about her shoulders, but no book lay in her lap. She'd half turned to look out the window behind her, and tears glistened on her cheeks.

"Gabriella," I said in alarm as I closed the door and quickly went to her. She rose to greet me, but I motioned her down again. "What is it?"

Gabriella sank to the edge of the window seat. She pulled the shawl about her more closely and studied the carpet at her feet. "Lady Breckenridge is very put out with me."

"Why?" I sat next to her on the wide cushion, the gold velvet warm from the afternoon sun. "Did you explain to her that you did not wish to marry?"

I allowed myself a touch of relief. After viewing the prisoners in the hulks and hearing about the horror that was Lord Mercer, my daughter's and Donata's clashing wishes were a storm in a teacup.

"Never mind," I said gently. "I'll speak to her."

Gabriella gazed at me in anguish, her brown eyes glimmering. "You do not understand. She is angry because Mr. Garfield proposed to me, and I refused."

My relief expanded profoundly. "You refused him? Thank God for that." I let out a heartfelt sigh. "You might have made my wife unhappy, dear Gabriella, but you have pleased *me* enormously."

I thought to make her smile, but she did not. Her sorrow remained, with a touch of … fear?

Gabriella pleated nervous folds in her shawl. "Please let me finish. When Lady Breckenridge demanded to know why I was so foolish as to refuse a fine young man like Mr. Garfield, I had to tell her. She would not listen until I explained." Gabriella closed her eyes, and tears slid from beneath her lashes. "I am sorry, Father. I am already spoken for."

CHAPTER 27

I went very still. Gabriella opened her eyes, and her expression broke my heart.

"Spoken for," I repeated, my voice quiet. "By whom? Mr. Marsden?" He was another of Gabriella's suitors, a much more deferential young man than Garfield. I wasn't pleased with him either, but I could put up with him.

"No," Gabriella said quickly. "None of them. It is a young man in France. He is in Lyon now."

I rose abruptly. "Lyon?" This was a matter of an entirely different calibre. "Your uncle never mentioned this. Or your … The major." I still could not bring myself to call Major Auberge Gabriella's father. He might have raised her, but she was mine.

"Papa and Uncle Quentin know nothing of this," Gabriella said. "We have kept it secret."

"What about your mother?"

Gabriella shook her head. "No one knows."

I paced, the rows of Dante and Petrarch, Copernicus and Huygens frowning down at me.

"Bloody hell, no wonder you were so resistant to Donata's

schemes. How far has it gone? Are you actually married? Have you …?"

I trailed off, unable to say it. I shuddered to think of my daughter in any man's arms, shied forcibly from it.

Gabriella gave me a puzzled look, as though to say *Have I what?*

The innocence of her bewilderment relieved me. "You are not married, then?" I asked.

"No, no." The shy words eased her tears. "We decided to tell no one until after the Season was over and I was back in France. I believe my mama and papa will be more amenable if I have proved I could not find a wealthy husband in London. Emile is not well off yet, but he will inherit a little money in a few years."

I remembered a conversation I'd had with Major Auberge when he and Carlotta had brought Gabriella to London. Carlotta had come to complete our divorce, and Major Auberge explained that they'd brought Gabriella with them because a young man had been sniffing around her at home.

"Is this the same gentleman?" I asked, "that the major disapproved of before?"

Gabriella nodded. "Emile has always been kind to me. We have been friends for a very long time."

"He has proposed to you?"

"Not formally. He will wait and approach Papa when I return. Emile is in Lyon working for his family—we hope to wed next summer." The look she turned to me was guilt-stricken and contrite, but also determined. I'd caught sight of that stubbornness on my own face.

I opened my mouth to curse some more, but shut it abruptly and sat next to her.

"Do you love him?" I made myself ask.

"Yes."

I had left my walking stick leaning against the window seat when I'd leapt up to pace, and now I fixed my eyes on its goose-head handle. The stick had been a gift from Donata when I'd lost the previous one.

Asking Gabriella if she were certain would be pointless. If my daughter had not let the lavish comfort of Donata's house, the extravagance of the balls and soirees, and the obvious interest of her highborn suitors turn her head, then she was indeed loyal to Emile.

"Why did you say nothing to me?" I asked. "Why go through with the Season?"

More quiet tears. "I didn't have the heart to disappoint you."

Dear God. She'd not confessed that she didn't want to anger Donata, or upset her parents, or annoy Lady Aline. She hadn't wanted to disappoint *me*.

My heart burned. "I suppose if young Garfield hadn't pressed his suit, you'd have remained quiet?"

Gabriella nodded. "I did not believe any of the gentlemen would truly propose. I am not one of them, as much as Lady Breckenridge tries to make me be."

But they were healthy young men, and Gabriella was the exotic flower in their midst. Of course they'd been smitten.

"Disappointed, I am not," I said firmly. "Truth to tell, I hoped you'd turn down all the young jackanapes. I hoped they wouldn't have the gall to propose without consulting me. Garfield deserves to be turned away—the cheek of him. But I wish you had confided in me. It would have made things easier."

"It was wrong of me, I know. But I did not quite know what to do."

Gabriella meant she'd decided on her course and was resolute that no one would dissuade her. She'd inherited her strong will from me. At the same time, she was a gentle soul who did not wish to hurt anyone. A troubling combination.

"I do not approve of the gentlemen Donata picked out for you," I said. "But I can't wholeheartedly approve of Emile either, a young man who encourages you to make a secret promise to him. I want to meet him."

Gabriella brightened. "Would you? I would like that. I believe you would get on well."

"That remains to be seen," I said severely. "Please tell me you will do nothing unwise—no elopement, no running off to become his lover, no true engagement until we meet him and decide whether he is good enough for you."

"Of course not." Gabriella's eyes glowed with hope. "We planned to approach my papa when I returned home. I am not so rash as to elope."

I had been plenty rash enough to elope, which was why Gabriella's mother now lived in France with another man. "And Emile had better not be already married with two children, and stringing you along."

Gabriella's smile blossomed. "Oh, no. I have known Emile since we were children. He tells me everything."

I would reserve judgment. I had once caused the arrest of a man who had been married to several different women at the same time. The gentleman had seen no harm in it and protested his guiltlessness to the end.

I let out a long breath. "Well you have neatly stymied us all, haven't you?" I asked. "Thus proving you are indeed my daughter. You made Donata angry enough to storm out of the house, when she knows I do not want her rushing about by herself."

"Mr. Brewster followed her," Gabriella said. "I saw him. He is very protective."

He was. I thought about how Brewster had beaten down the violent Finch without hesitation as he sprang to protect his wife. That thought knocked into another, and another.

"I will speak to Donata," I said, as I had when I'd first entered, though the conversation would be very different now. "But you must write to the major, tonight, and explain things to him."

Gabriella paled. "I know I should, but I fear for Emile."

"You mean the major might charge to Lyon and slam him against a wall?" I felt a moment's camaraderie with the man who'd stolen my wife. "Well he might, and I would not blame him. But if Emile is worthy of you, he will weather it."

Picturing Major Auberge explaining to Emile how he felt about him wooing Gabriella gave me some satisfaction. I'd hated Auberge for a long time, but I knew he loved Gabriella as I did.

"Thank you, Father," Gabriella said. She still looked guilt-stricken and sorrowful, but more hopeful. The determination, however, hadn't wavered.

"Do not thank me until I meet Emile," I said sternly, then relented. "But thank *you* for not making me have to put up with Mr. Garfield's attempt at wit over my supper table. I can be grateful for one thing today, at least."

~

THE SERVANTS PEERED FEARFULLY AT US WHEN WE EMERGED FROM the library, but when I embraced my daughter before she went upstairs to write to the major, they relaxed and went about their business. I had the feeling that if I'd raged at her, they'd have stormed up the stairs to cast me from the house. They adored Gabriella.

Donata had not returned by the time I took my evening meal. Barnstable confirmed that Brewster had indeed accompanied her out, and I knew he'd look after her, though I was not in the least content.

I tried to reason that Stanton was in Lincolnshire chasing my ghost, and Robert St. John was recovering from his accident with his brother, Winston hovering over him. According to Bartholomew's spies among the servants, Donata's cousin

Edwin had returned to Oxfordshire. For the moment, we did not have to worry about Donata's bloody cousins.

I ate a repast alone, as Gabriella did not wish to leave her chamber, and received a hand-delivered reply to my note to Mr. Molodzinski.

I was pleased to read your letter, Captain, he wrote, *and know you remembered an old friend. I am surprised to hear you ask about Mr. Josiah Leeds, who is indeed a neighbor of mine, but I never speak to him, as he keeps very much to himself.*

However, as you know, I always have my ear to the ground, and I have heard over the years a bit about Mr. Leeds. Not enough to condemn him, you understand, but rumors here and there.

My own clerk, who is a font of gossip, says that at one point, it was believed Mr. Leeds had embezzled a large quantity of money from the bank where he is employed.

Mr. Leeds protested his innocence, and even threatened to bring suit against the bank for slander. He readily let those investigating go through all his books and to his house to tear up the floorboards looking for the stolen money.

Nothing was ever proved, and his employers soothed his temper and kept him on. From what my clerk said, Mr. Leeds was an exemplary worker and his colleagues had been amazed at the accusation.

All the same, a large sum disappeared about six years ago and was never recovered. Not in gold, mind, which would have been a feat to carry out, but in banknotes.

But as no large piles of notes were found in Mr. Leeds's rooms or anywhere near the places he frequented, and no discrepancies were found in his books, it was concluded he had nothing to do with it. The matter was put aside, and Mr. Leeds was never accused of such again.

You asked only for information, Captain, and not my opinion, but in my experience, there is a difference between an innocent man and a very careful one. And because the bank currently has a restriction on the payment of gold for banknotes, whenever that restriction is

released, having a large pile of notes at one's disposal will result in
quite a payout. I envy the man who has such a resource.

   I wish you good health, my friend, and the next time you are in
Lombard Street, please look me up, no matter what time of day or
night, and I will stand you a large glass of port.

   Ever your servant,
   Benjamin Molodzinski

~

BY THE TIME I HAD FINISHED MY MEAL—THE LETTER ALMOST, BUT
not quite, intriguing me enough to erase my appetite—Donata
returned.

   I spied Brewster, whom I wished most expressly to speak to,
sitting with the coachman as the landau moved toward
the mews.

   Donata divested herself of her hooded cloak in the central
hall as footmen swarmed around her, then she walked straight
up the stairs as I walked down them. We met on the landing.

   "She told me," I said in a low voice.

   Donata held up her hand. "I do not wish to speak of it,
Gabriel. Not now. Now I must ready myself for the engagements I have already accepted. I will put it about that Gabriella
is ill, and I hope Mr. Garfield has the sense to keep his
mouth shut."

   So saying, she continued upward, Jacinthe and another maid
in attendance, and her chamber door slammed.

   I watched the door a moment, fearing she'd storm out and
confront Gabriella as soon as my back was turned, but the panel
remained closed.

   Donata was not a cruel woman, for all her tart speeches, and
I trusted that she'd leave Gabriella be.

   I went downstairs to be handed another missive by Barnstable—Sir Montague had also answered my letter. I broke the

seal and quickly read through it. He confirmed that Mr. Leeds's employers had once suspected him of embezzlement, but nothing had been proved.

Also, Sir Montague too had been interested in the house where Finch died, and the answer he gave me excited me. I folded the letter and tucked it into my pocket.

I hastened to the mews and cornered Brewster.

"I'll be off home," he said pointedly. "Me colleagues will take over protecting your lady wife when she goes out again. Unless you plan to race about town some more yourself tonight."

"I will accompany you," I said. "I have had some ideas."

"Here we go," Brewster muttered.

He said nothing more, only joined me in a hackney that took us to St. Giles. I told him about what Mr. Molodzinski and Sir Montague had revealed to me about Mr. Leeds as we went.

Because darkness was falling, the driver did not want to wait after he'd let us down at the church, and I told him to go on.

"Why did you drag Finch to *that* particular house?" I asked Brewster as we walked along, a lantern throwing spangles of candlelight across our path. "Where you left him while you went for the money to make him go away?"

Brewster looked blank and took a moment to think. "Were his idea," he said. "I don't mean he told me to carry him off there, but when he first turned up, raging at Em to hand him a hundred pounds, if you please, he wanted her to bring it to the house at the end of Priory Court. I knew the place—thought maybe he'd hired it to stash things in. He obviously weren't living in it. So when I knocked him down, I decided, might as well take him there. That way I'd know where he'd be when I returned. I didn't fancy leaving him in our flat, alone with Em."

"Very wise," I said. "You unlocked it with a key."

"Stolen from his pocket. Didn't want him going nowhere until I came back."

"But someone killed him in the meantime. How did they get in?"

I saw Brewster's glare, even in the dark. "How do ye think I'd know about that? Maybe Finch had another key. Maybe the killer had one. Maybe he picked the lock. Hobson admitted he did that."

"And picked it closed again," I went on. "Which must have taken some effort, but likely he didn't want anyone finding the body before he could put some time and distance between himself and it. Did you know who owned the house?"

"Haven't the faintest bloody idea. What other damn fool questions do ye want to ask me?"

"If you'd ever seen Mr. Leeds before today."

Brewster looked puzzled. "Wheezing bloke from the Bank of England? No. I never go to no bank. I told you. What's happened to make you this daft tonight?"

"Just thinking," I assured him.

We walked for a time in silence, St. Giles coming alive around us, its inhabitants making ready to prey on the weak in the dark.

"By the bye," I asked presently. "Where *do* you stash your pay?"

Brewster huffed a laugh. "*Truly* daft. Nowhere I'm going to tell you, guv. Especially not on the street."

"That is my point," I said. "You don't keep it at your house, or in a bank, or with a man of business."

"'Course not. I want to be able to lay hands on it when I like but keep all others away. Including you."

I took no offense. "It occurred to me that a man who wishes to hide the fact that he has money would keep it far from where he lived. Somewhere unconnected with him."

"Yes," Brewster said cautiously.

"Like a house in St. Giles everyone avoids."

"Now you've lost me."

"Let us walk there, shall we?"

Brewster gave one of his resigned sighs, but he led me down the lanes to Priory Court, where Finch had died. Neither of us had a key, as I'd given it to Quimby, but Brewster deftly picked the lock.

Finch's body was long gone, but the smell of death lingered in the house. The front room was nothing but a large foyer without furniture. It had a door on the wall opposite the entrance, which led into a plain chamber that was likewise empty.

Brewster lit the lantern he'd left in the front room, and I lifted it and flashed it around. "How does one ascend to the rest of the house?"

There were no stairs here or outside, yet the house rose three stories, with windows all the way to the roof, like medieval gate towers I'd seen in walled towns in France and Spain.

Brewster, finally looking interested, took the lantern back from me. The paneled walls of the rear chamber had once been painted white, though the paint had long since blistered and cracked.

"Here," Brewster said, pulling at one of the panels.

I helped him pry it loose and found it hid a door that, when opened, revealed a stair.

"Why close it off?" Brewster asked, staring upward in suspicion. "What does he have up there?"

"If I am correct, banknotes," I said. "Shall we?"

Brewster sent me a warning look before he ascended ahead of me. I decided to hang back and let him scout—the stairs could be rotten and not take our combined weight.

"Come up," Brewster grunted after a few minutes. "Seems solid enough."

I climbed the stairs, finding them hard beneath my boots.

The house above the ground floor appeared to be in good

repair. The single room the stair emerged into was also paneled, but in polished, unpainted wood, and the corners held only a light film of dust.

Another door, this one in plain sight, led to a second stair, which emerged into yet another single room that took up the entire floor. The ceiling was low, fitting under the eaves.

I had intended to examine this room quite closely— knocking on the ceiling, pulling at the panels, tapping my walking stick on every floorboard. But I saw it wouldn't be necessary. In the corner where two walls and the ceiling came together, the plaster had been pulled away to reveal a small hole. Brewster and I used my walking stick and fists to widen the gap.

The hole led to a cavity, quite a large one, between the beams holding up the peaked roof and the joists of the ceiling.

Brewster boosted me, and I flashed the lantern inside.

Nothing was there. But I saw a depression on the joists that might have been made by a heavy box, one that had rubbed the beams of the roof a bit smooth where the lid would have touched it.

"Damnation," I growled. "He's moved it. Or Finch did."

"You mean Mr. Leeds's cache of what he stole from the bank."

"Certainly." I dropped to the floor from where Brewster had been holding me, catching myself on my stronger leg.

"This is what I think—Mr. Leeds is in a good position to embezzle from the bank, and Mr. Molodzinski is certain he did. Leeds's own records might be pristine, but what is to stop him doctoring other records, moving a bit here and a bit there to another account, perhaps even inventing a person to own such an account? He could have ceased withdrawing notes by the time anyone at the bank caught on that the account was false— or perhaps he had several different accounts and closed each one after withdrawing only a little.

"By the time the bank finally suspected him of embezzlement, he'd already moved the notes to his hiding place, far from his rooms. Sir Montague confirmed that long ago, Mr. Leeds's father owned this house, and Leeds inherited it on his death."

"You're painting him to be very clever," Brewster said. "I thought Mr. Leeds were a bit thick, meself."

"On stage, it takes an intelligent actor—or actress—to play the part of the imbecile," I said. "So Miss Simmons tells me. I am speculating of course, but there was certainly a heavy box here."

"Fair point," Brewster said.

I gazed around the barren room as I continued. "Finch, who regularly visited his daughter nearby, and Blackmore, who was often with him, observe Leeds's comings and goings, conclude the man can't be up to anything good, find out about his embezzlement, and start to blackmail him. They could demand plenty of money to keep his secret. Even though Leeds had managed to get free of the accusations when he was suspected, a person marching in and vowing he had seen Leeds with all the money and that he knew exactly where the banknotes were is a different matter."

"Who'd believe a villain like Finch?" Brewster asked.

"Finch could always coerce another to make the report for him. He had a hold over many people."

"He did that," Brewster said darkly. "But why not simply knock Leeds on the head and take the lot?"

"Finch was a blackmailer, a fraudster, and a bully, not a robber and murderer. While kill Leeds when he can be a continuous source of funds? And remember, the banknotes can't be cashed at the moment for their value in gold, but the notes can be held until such time as they're honored again. Might as well leave them stashed for now, and have Leeds pay him and Blackmore to keep silent."

Brewster nodded. "I take your meaning."

"When Finch was arrested, it wasn't because he was robbing Leeds of tuppence and a handkerchief. I'd wager Finch and

Blackmore were demanding more money from Leeds, using their fists as reinforcement. Leeds sees a patroller and cries out for him. His great fortune that, instead of turning tail and running, as one of the Watch might, the patroller was Timothy Spendlove, delighted he could finally arrest Finch for an obvious crime. Spendlove could only hold on to one of them—both Finch and Blackmore were big men and trained pugilists—so Blackmore got away."

"Finch never gave him up." Brewster sounded admiring. "Blackmore's name was never mentioned at the trial."

"Probably to Leeds's relief. Blackmore might have revealed more in the dock than Leeds wished him to. I am guessing Finch kept silent, not only to protect his friend, but so that Blackmore would have the chance to later get more money out of Leeds. Finch might have been already planning his escape from Van Diemen's Land, paying with the large amount of money Blackmore could have ready for him. The only flaw was that before Finch could reach home, Blackmore died."

"Sounds reasonable, guv." Brewster lifted the lantern. "But where's the box of banknotes then? And the money Blackmore was saving up for Finch's passage?"

"That I do not know. Likely when Finch died, Leeds moved the box. Blackmore's money I'm certain is long gone, possibly another reason Charlotte told us Finch was so upset."

"So all you can show Mr. Quimby or Mr. Pomeroy is this empty space."

"Yes," I said, deflating. "But I have another idea."

Brewster groaned. "Leave it alone. Ye can't prove a swindler's a swindler. They cover their tracks too well."

"I won't leave it until you are completely cleared, Brewster."

"Are ye sure I didn't do it?"

Something in his voice made me stop. Brewster held the lantern high, and its starry light speckled his face. His countenance was still, as was his body.

"I am certain," I said with conviction. "You'd have told me."

"I don't have the honor you do, Captain," he said quietly.

We stood looking at each other for a long time. "Yes, you do," I said, and went past him and down the stairs.

When I reached the ground floor, I walked outside into chill darkness, right into a fist that caught me on the side of the head and sent me reeling.

CHAPTER 28

I heard Brewster's shout. My ears ringing, I ducked, narrowly missing another punch, and raised my arm and walking stick. But the next blow never fell.

Brewster was behind the culprit, arms locked around him in a wrestling hold, raising him high.

"Captain!" came a breathless voice.

I retrieved the lantern, which had landed squarely on its base when Brewster had dropped it, the candle still flickering inside. I raised it to reveal the young face of Mr. Oliver.

I exhaled. "You can let him go, Brewster."

"Don't think so, guv."

Oliver had ceased struggling and looked small in Brewster's grip. But I'd seen that Oliver had much strength, even if he didn't have bulk.

"What are you doing here, Mr. Oliver?" I asked.

"Saw the light." Oliver gestured with his chin to the window of the top story. "Up there. Bit odd, I thought. So I came to have a butcher's."

"Courageous of you," I said. "We might have been villains of the first water."

"That's why I struck before waiting to find out." Oliver grinned. "Fell you first was my plan. Only Mr. Brewster was too quick."

I massaged my jaw. "An unfair hit, Mr. Oliver. But a good one."

"Sorry, Captain."

Brewster slowly and with some reluctance set Oliver on his feet. Oliver swayed but never lost his equilibrium. We stood in companionable silence in the deserted lane, and the tension eased.

"You come down here quite a bit," I said as Oliver rubbed his arms against the cold. "You were here the other day, when I had Blackmore's dog with me."

"'Sright." Oliver looked a bit puzzled. "I live nearby."

"You're not from here, though. I don't know all the accents of London, but yours is not St. Giles."

"South London," Oliver said. "Bermondsey. I moved to these parts when I quit Mr. Shaddock. Cheaper, innit? Shaddock says he'll take me back on," he finished to Brewster.

"Ah," I said. I glanced about. "It's interesting. This lane goes nowhere. Except to a house with a box of banknotes stashed under its eaves."

Oliver's face went bright red.

"What did you do with it?" I asked casually. "The box? After Mr. Finch was dead?"

Oliver stared at me in shock. Then he let out a yell.

Fists whirled at me and I stepped hastily back, but again Brewster was there to seize the smaller man. Oliver began to fight in earnest, with fierce kicks and punches.

I came forward to help, but Oliver twisted, bringing his boot up toward Brewster's groin. Brewster deflected the blow with the ease of long practice, but lost his hold on the lad.

Instead of running, Oliver came straight at me.

I raised my fists and walking stick again. In Oliver's eyes I saw not a young man who'd been given the opportunity to make some money and a name fighting in the ring, but a canny lad of the slums, who was as ruthless as Finch had ever been.

His hand went to his coat pocket before his fist lashed out. I blocked, but he held a knife between his fingers which slammed into my arm. Pain blossomed before I managed to turn from the blade.

Brewster grabbed at him. Oliver twisted like a fish and pummeled Brewster several times in the face. Brewster, as hardened as he was, had to give way, allowing Oliver to return to battering me.

I defended myself as I could, but Oliver, young and superbly trained, slashed at me again and again.

Then Brewster's giant fist caught Oliver on the side of the head. He followed that by kicking Oliver's legs out from under him.

Oliver flung out his arms to break his fall, and his knife flew wide. It clattered to the cobbles, and I picked it up.

Brewster grabbed Oliver by the collar and slammed him face-first into the street. I heard a crack, but Oliver screamed, so he was not yet dead.

I saw in Brewster the grim strength of a man who'd learned to throw aside rules long ago. He hit Oliver squarely between the shoulder blades, until the young man screamed again.

"Enough," Oliver croaked. "I'm down."

Brewster planted his large foot in Oliver's back. "I'll decide when you're down, lad."

The knife I'd retrieved had a plain hilt, wrapped in leather, like the one Hobson claimed had been sticking out of Finch. Perhaps Oliver kept several about his person. A good point to remember.

I marched over and stepped on one of Oliver's hands. "Did you kill Finch?"

"No. I swear to you. It weren't me. He was dead, with a little pasty bloke standing over him."

A little pasty bloke—a good description of Josiah Leeds.

"Who had a box of banknotes. Where is it, Mr. Oliver?"

Oliver started to shake his head, but Brewster put his weight on him.

"Gave it … to … Shaddock," Oliver gasped out.

I sent Brewster a nod to haul Oliver up. Brewster did so, twisting the lad's arm behind his back and keeping a firm hold on his neck. Oliver's face was red with the fight and now tinged gray with pain. I quickly stepped in and checked Oliver's coat and boots for hidden knives but found none.

"It weren't me," Oliver said again.

That might be true. But I'd seen murder in Oliver's eyes when he'd come at me with the blade. I had the knife now, tucked into my pocket.

My thoughts circled rapidly. Mr. Leeds was terrified of Finch. Perhaps he'd agreed to meet Finch in this house, which Sir Montague had confirmed he owned, to try to pay him off again, or maybe he'd rushed to make sure his money was safe when he'd heard Finch had returned. He'd found Finch down and seen a quick way out of his problems.

"Tell me exactly what happened," I said to Oliver.

Oliver wet his lips. "I was passing the lane and glimpsed a little fellow what didn't belong in St. Giles. Dressed like a City gent—wouldn't keep that suit long, I thought. I was going to see what he was up to, maybe get him out of here safely if he needed it."

"For a coin," Brewster said.

"Yeah, maybe." Oliver looked shamefaced. "Then I hear him shout. I came running, found Mr. Finch dead on the ground outside the door. Little bloke standing over him, knife sticking out of Finchie's chest. Bloke saw me and couldn't run away fast enough."

"He'd have to go past you to get out of the lane," I pointed out. "Why did you let him?"

"I was that surprised, and he raced by." Oliver stopped. "Truth to tell, it didn't matter, did it? Finchie were dead and couldn't terrify anyone no more. I dragged Finch back inside the house and locked the door with the key that was in the keyhole."

"You didn't chase the man, because he'd left his box behind," I stated.

Oliver shook his head. "I didn't notice right away. I saw it inside when I dragged Finchie in. I opened it—and couldn't believe my eyes. Stacks of notes from the Bank of England. I never seen that much money in me life."

"You said you happened to see the City gent as you passed. Did you observe him go into the lane? Did you follow him?"

"No." Oliver's eyes flickered. "He was just there."

He was lying, I suspected, but why he would about this point, I did not know.

"And you are certain that a key was already in the door?"

"Aye," Oliver said, looking puzzled.

"On the inside or outside?"

He had to think. "Inside. I took it out and used it to lock the door when I went."

"And where is the key now?"

"In the river."

I did not think so, but it was a minor detail.

"What about Oro?" I asked. "The dog you know as Demon?"

Oliver nodded. "He was there. Howling, like. But he'd gone by the time I shut up Finch."

Or else he'd not wanted to bother with him. My sympathy for Oliver dipped.

"What you want to do, guv?" Brewster asked me. "Hunt up your Runners? Maybe be off to the City?"

Oliver sent me a pleading gaze. Pomeroy would drag Oliver

to the lockup for the night, and I had the feeling Mr. Leeds would try to push the murder onto Oliver. Whom would a magistrate believe? A respectable-looking employee of the Bank of England? Or a pugilist from the backstreets?

I knew Oliver was hiding something, and I longed to know what.

"Not yet," I said. "I believe that first, we should retrieve the box."

Oliver did not look happy, but Brewster gave him no choice. He produced a length of thin metal chain—no idea where he'd found it—and wrapped it competently around Oliver's wrists behind his back.

He dragged Oliver out of St. Giles and to a hackney, me following slowly, and instructed the startled driver to take us to Wapping.

~

I PONDERED THINGS AS WE WENT. OLIVER SAT ACROSS FROM ME, looking shaken and ill, held in place by Brewster.

If Oliver hadn't lied about simply spying Mr. Leeds at the end of the lane, perhaps Leeds had already been there. I would tell Mr. Quimby to ask him, of course, but I wondered if Leeds had been in the house, fetching his box from the rafters, when Brewster dragged in Finch.

Brewster had quickly dumped Finch on the floor and left again, locking up with the keys he'd taken from Finch's pocket. Brewster would have had no reason to look through the rest of the house—he'd gone off to retrieve his money to pay Finch to leave the country again.

Mr. Leeds would certainly have had a key to his own house. I pictured Leeds descending the stairs, closing up the panel to hide them. He'd enter the front room to find Finch down and groaning. Seeing a chance to flee, he opened the door with his key …

And here the picture grew dim. Did Finch rise, follow Leeds out, and attack him? And Leeds struck out? When Oliver ran down the lane and discovered the crime, did Leeds panic and run, leaving key and box behind?

Or did Oliver fight Finch as he'd fought me, swinging with his knife? Perhaps he'd killed Finch and demanded the box of money from Leeds as payment—or else Leeds simply saw his chance and ran.

Either explanation could fit, or neither.

I had to wonder why Leeds would abandon the cache of banknotes he'd so cleverly built up—that action spoke of leaving Oliver the box to buy his freedom.

The man Hobson had seen carrying the dead Finch into the house was likely Oliver, not Brewster. The two men did not look alike, but from a distance, Hobson might have mistaken them. Though Oliver did not have all of Brewster's bulk, both men moved like trained fighters.

Hobson had waited until everyone was well gone before he'd had the courage to look inside and find Finch dead. I'd guess he'd stolen the knife, which was how he knew so well what it looked like. Oliver had a similar knife, but I'd been correct in my surmise that many men did.

"Why not report the crime?" I asked Oliver. "If you didn't kill Finch and figured the other man did, why not run to Bow Street?"

"Because he wanted to get away with the money," Brewster said in disgust. "Must have been worrisome for you when Mr. White decided you'd fight in St. Giles so soon after, and we were asking questions about Finchie's murder."

"Or perhaps it was deliberate," I suggested. "So you could see whether that house held more money. I suspect you still have the key. Was that why you returned the day you saw us there with Mr. Blackmore's dog?"

Oliver didn't answer, only shrank back into his seat.

"Why'd ye give the box to Shaddock?" Brewster asked him.

Tears entered Oliver's voice. "A peace offering. I had the box in my rooms—I was going to split it with Mr. White, but he run off on me that day I fought you. We were supposed to meet after with the takings, but he didn't turn up." He looked confused, betrayed. "After you spoke so warmly of Shaddock, I decided to give it to him, ask him to look after me again."

"Never trust a bookmaker," Brewster said with conviction. "To think, Finchie turned out to have more honor than any of you. Even looked after his friend's dog."

"Who certainly didn't like you," I said mildly to Oliver. "I was right, Brewster. Oro did witness this murder, after all."

~

It was very late when we reached the small, neat house in Wapping. Mrs. Shaddock opened the door to me in bewilderment, then her eyes rounded when Brewster dragged a frightened Oliver out of the hackney.

"He's in bed," she started to argue, then closed her mouth and silently admitted us.

We went through, not to the garden room, which was dark and cold, but to a warm kitchen. Bright copper pots gleamed on the mantel and hung from the ceiling, and stools surrounded a work table that was scrubbed clean.

Mr. Shaddock, wrapped in a woolen shawl, sipped from a mug as he sat by the fire.

"It's that captain," his wife said in a loud voice. "And Tommy."

"Eh?" Shaddock raised his head and peered at me with

rheumy eyes. "Captain Lacey? What you want this time of night?" He lifted the mug. "Tell Mrs. S to pour you some. Nothing like a good beef tea—and a bit of whiskey—to chase away the cold."

"Mr. S., Tommy's brought—"

"I'm sorry, Mr. Shaddock."

At the sound of Oliver's voice, the mug shattered on the slate floor. Shaddock struggled to stand, his shawl slipping to join the spilled beef tea.

Brewster said nothing. The two gazed at each other, the large man who'd been a fighter and his mentor, shrunken and aged.

"He owed me, Tommy," Shaddock said in a hoarse whisper, fingers plucking at his coat as though he tried to draw the absent shawl across his shoulders. "He owed me for years of bleeding me dry, ruining me."

"Ye were always weak-willed," Brewster stated. "I saw that, long before ye started throwing fights for men like Finch."

Some of Shaddock's strength seeped back into him. "Young Oliver did right to bring the money to me. He's a good lad, and I should never have run him off. But I'd heard Finchie was coming back, ye see. I didn't want him to get his clutches on Oliver, like he had with me."

"I could have protected ya," Oliver said.

Shaddock gave him a sad look. "No, you couldn't. Not against a man like Finch."

"It don't matter," Oliver said, impassioned. "He's dead and gone. All that money is yours by right."

"The money belongs to the Bank of England," I said, voice hardening. "It wasn't Finch's at all. A banker's clerk stole it, and Finch was blackmailing him because of it."

Shaddock's mouth hung open. His wife stepped behind him and gently laid the shawl she'd retrieved across his shoulders.

"What did you do, boy?" Shaddock demanded. "Ye want to bring the magistrates to *my* door? I don't need the bloody money. Take it, Captain. The fact that Finch can't touch me anymore is enough."

Oliver struggled in Brewster's massive grip. "Ye'd give it up? And leave me with nothing? After all I've done for ye?"

"I didn't train ye to be a bloody robber and a cheat." Shaddock drew himself up, and I glimpsed the powerful man he'd once been. "It's not why we fight. We have honor. Even if we forget that from time to time." He sagged into the circle of his wife's arm. "Take it and go. Leave an old man to die in peace."

Brewster kept a firm hold on Oliver, who drooped. I saw sorrow in Brewster's eyes, and shame. Perhaps not for Shaddock's present broken state, but because he'd deserted the man all those years ago.

"Where is the box?" I asked into the silence.

Shaddock and his wife both swiveled eyes to the garden room and its large windows that looked out into darkness.

I breathed a resigned sigh. "Someone please fetch me a spade."

～

THE BOX WAS BURIED IN THE NEAT ROWS OF EARTH AT WHICH THE birds had industriously pecked. The container was made of polished wood and not very large, perhaps three by two on its sides, and a foot deep.

Inside were banknotes, crisp and neatly stacked, wrapped in oiled cloth. Their denominations were large, which was why the box could be small. Whatever man cashed in the notes once the bank's restrictions were lifted would make a fortune.

I had to dig up the thing myself. Brewster was busy keeping Oliver subdued, and Mr. Shaddock was too feeble. Mrs. Shaddock helped me, and I suspected it was she who'd buried the box in the first place.

"Thank you," she said softly as I balanced myself with my cane and tucked the box under my arm. "Blood money, this is."

I agreed. "I'll tell Brewster to visit again."

"It don't matter." She shook her head. "We make our choices, and we have to live with the consequences."

At her haunted look, I halted. Mrs. Shaddock glanced away from me, but not before I'd seen guilt and self-loathing in her eyes.

I thought about Oliver's hesitancy when I'd asked him whether he'd followed Mr. Leeds into the lane, and a new and more horrible possibility entered my mind.

"Mr. Oliver saw *you*, did he not?" I asked. "That day Finch died?"

Mrs. Shaddock stood still while rain dripped around us.

I went on. "It is another reason he brought you and your husband the money," I said quietly. "To tell you he'd keep your secret safe."

She looked up at me, tears joining the rain on her face.

"I was so afraid Finch would come here and hurt my poor old lad," she said. "So I went looking for him. I knew his sister lived with Tommy in St. Giles. I didn't go with murder in my heart, Captain. I just wanted to warn him off. Or pay him—I'm not sure what I meant to do."

Unhappiness filled me. She was confessing to a murder. I needed to stop her, or find the nearest magistrate, or take her across the river to Sir Montague and Quimby.

Instead, I regarded her with compassion. "Did he threaten you? Try to hurt you?"

"I saw Tommy carrying him along," she said in a low voice, "and I followed. When Tommy put him into that house and went, I saw my chance. No one was in the lane but an old dog. I walked to the door, but before I could reach it, Finch comes staggering out. He sees me, starts bellowing at me—I don't even know what he was saying. Filthy language, about Shaddock and how we owed him. He had a knife and raised it at me. But he was slow, hurt, and Mr. S. has taught me a thing or two."

"You fought him." A smaller hand had marked Shaddock's chest, a woman's we'd considered. "He was trying to kill you."

Mrs. Shaddock regarded me a long time and at last gave me a slow nod. "He were. The knife came at me, and I took it away from him. I couldn't have if he weren't already so hurt. He kept coming. The knife went right up into his chest, and he collapsed. Didn't even bleed much. He fell, and the dog started to howl. I thought someone would come, so I ran."

Sobs shook her, but I noted the careful way she'd told me all I needed to know. She'd rehearsed this speech in her head, probably from the moment she'd fled. I'd fed her the correct cues—as was my intention—and she'd responded.

I didn't mean to. He was attacking me, and I fought for my life.

I fitted in the rest of the pieces. Leeds had still been recovering his box upstairs, or hiding there, waiting for Finch to leave. Mrs. Shaddock arrived as Finch recovered himself and wandered outside, unlocking the door with the key Leeds had left when he'd let himself in, or perhaps Finch had a second one —Brewster must not have noticed it in his hurry. Possibly Finch meant to return to Charlotte's and rest before continuing his quest for money to pay Steadman.

Finch had encountered Mrs. Shaddock in the lane, and in a rage, went at her, as she'd said. The fight had resulted in his death. Mrs. Shaddock had fled. Mr. Leeds had cautiously descended with his box and found Finch dead.

His joy was short-lived as Oliver, likely coming to investigate why he'd seen Mrs. Shaddock dash from the lane, discovered him. Leeds, terrified he'd be accused and arrested of murder, ran. Perhaps he'd not had time to pick up his box, or feared to be found with it, or perhaps he had another stash somewhere else. He'd succeeded in embezzling from the bank once, why not twice?

Oliver, suspecting that Mrs. Shaddock had indeed killed Finch, decided it best to say nothing. He stole the box, and then when White deserted him, carried it to the Shaddocks as both a peace offering and a sign that they could trust him.

"Will you give your story to a magistrate?" I asked in a gentle voice. "Defending oneself is a different thing from murder."

Another tiny nod. "Aye. But please, Captain, don't tell him. This would kill him."

I glanced into the lighted house where Shaddock slumped by the fire, already defeated. I ran my hand across my face.

"Finch was an escaped convict," I said. "And a violent man. If he hadn't died, he'd have continued blackmailing and hurting others."

Never mind that he was fond of his daughter and loyal to his closest friend. His solicitude for them and Oro meant he was a complex person, not a good one.

Mrs. Shaddock studied me, her expression fixed. "What you saying, Captain?"

Throughout this investigation, I'd been driven by one thing —to make sure Brewster wasn't executed for this crime. Now I was confronted with the decision of saving him by sending a woman who wanted only to defend her husband from a frightening villain to the magistrate in his place.

We make our choices, and we have to live with the consequences.

I'd made many choices in my life and paid the full price for them. Finch had as well.

"Finch made a lot of enemies," I said slowly. "I imagine any number of them were dismayed to see him return. Plus, he owed much money to the captain on whose ship he sailed home, and he was having difficulty rounding it up. Also, he knew the secrets of an aristocrat who can't afford more scandal, an aristocrat who has killed before. There were many people in St. Giles that day. One of them must have thrust a knife into him.

Someone quite skilled, I imagine, to hit him so precisely. The magistrates will find many culprits to question."

Mrs. Shaddock's eyes were round. Whether Shaddock had taught her precisely where to strike, or it had been a lucky blow, I was not the one to say.

Mrs. Shaddock swallowed. "Thank you, Captain."

"Stay home with him, Mrs. Shaddock," I finished. "Do not rush about London trying to defend him. He needs you here."

She nodded, her lips parted, her cap and hair wet with rain. "I will. I promise."

I saw relief in her eyes, but no lessoning of guilt. She'd hold that for the rest of her life. One does not lightly take the life of another, not even on the battlefield.

I bade her good night, hefted the box of ill-gotten gains, and departed.

∾

POMEROY COULD NOT HAVE BEEN MORE DELIGHTED WITH OUR gift of a box full of Bank of England notes that made his blue eyes widen until they were ringed with white.

"Love a duck," he breathed. "That's what I call a fair day's work."

"If you can lay your hands on one Mr. Leeds, the owner of this cache," I said, "you'll find the man who has been embezzling from the Bank of England."

"Will I now?" Pomeroy's smile beamed. "And will I also find the murderer of Jack Finch?"

"Mr. Leeds is not the culprit for that," I said. "Though Finch was blackmailing him. Mr. Leeds is a thief who got in over his head. I believe you'll find the killer by pursuing the henchmen of Captain Steadman or the Earl of Mercer." Brewster did not murder him." My last words were firm.

Pomeroy gave me a steady look. "So you've told me."

"I know this," I said. "I will give you my word of honor, Sergeant. , and you know what my honor is to me."

"I do," Pomeroy said, watching me closely. "And I know you never give your word if you do not mean it."

"Precisely."

He studied me a few moments more before he pursed his lips and nodded. "Right you are, Captain. Mr. Brewster is an innocent man. Of this crime, anyway."

I realized it was possible Leeds had seen Mrs. Shaddock shove the knife into Finch. But I would make certain his words were worth nothing, a liar who'd long gotten away with stealing from his own employer. It was unlikely a magistrate would believe him if he tried to incriminate a woman who lived far from the place, in any case, and perhaps Leeds wouldn't want to admit being anywhere near the dead Finch. Leeds didn't know Mrs. Shaddock, and her description—a stout female with gray hair—could fit any number of women.

"And if you can find a bookmaker named Mr. White," I went on, "I am certain many of his victims will be happy to prosecute him for swindling. He was also involved in the pugilist matches Lord Mercer got up for his guests using convicts from the hulks."

"Oho, Captain. So many possible convictions you're handing me tonight. I'll collect my winnings and take me girl to the seaside."

"Mr. Quimby ought to share in those winnings," I said sternly.

"Oh, aye," Pomeroy answered. "Fair is fair. But Mr. Quimby is enjoying himself arresting Captain Steadman for returning transported criminals, and is talking to Sir Montague about a your Lord Mercer. You've made a few Runners quite happy, sir. Tell your lady wife to reward you well."

"I'm afraid no one knows where Mr. White is," I said.

"No matter," Pomeroy answered, unconcerned. "I'll put out a hue and cry. We'll nab him."

He and I shared one more look. He no doubt knew why I'd brought this to him and not to Quimby. Mr. Quimby seemed a man with scruples. I could trust Pomeroy to close the case and bring no more suspicion on Brewster.

"Good evening to you, Captain," he said.

Pomeroy had known me a very long time. "Good evening, Sergeant," I answered.

And that was that.

Spendlove entered as I went out. He gazed at me with his cool blue eyes and I at him. I gave him a nod and tip of my hat, and departed.

~

I THOUGHT IT ONLY FAIR TO TELL BREWSTER THE TRUTH. HE insisted on accompanying me home—his task to keep me safe, he said. Catching villains was only a happenstance.

In the hackney, alone, I told him. "I asked Pomeroy to leave you alone, and he will. But if the crime goes unsolved, you could still be fitted for it. Mr. Quimby will likely not cease." I faced him squarely. "What do you want me to do?"

Brewster regarded me in his stoic way. "Guv, I'm the first suspected in many a crime. Any who work for His Nibs is. He sees to it that we're let be. 'Sides, Quimby is a fair bloke. He knows I didn't do it. Now, if you're asking if I should give up Shaddock's wife, I say no. They're getting on in age, and Finchie were a bad 'un, don't know matter what. She saved her husband and many another from Finch's terrorizing ways. If Captain Steadman and this earl get their comeuppance, Finchie will have his justice for Blackmore. And you've taken in the dog, and given Em a niece to look after."

A long speech for Brewster. He finished, closed his mouth, and peered out the window.

"I set out to spare you," I said. "Have I succeeded, or failed? This is the sort of question that will gnaw at me."

Brewster turned to me, eyes glittering. "Now, what you on about? You done more for me, guv, than any man alive ever has, except maybe His Nibs. Ye didn't shove me off on a magistrate first thing and have done. Ye could have stayed in your soft house with your wife and daughter and left me dangling. But ye didn't. You're a good bloke, for all I say you're hard. Which you are. Now, if you want me to get all teary for ye, you'll be unlucky. That's an end to it."

He turned firmly to the window after that. I sat back into the stiff cushions and made myself remain silent.

We descended in South Audley street, rather awkwardly. But before he left me on my doorstep, Brewster turned to me, his expression serious. "Thank you, guv."

He paused as though he wanted to say more, then he gave a little salute, turned, and disappeared into the night.

Bartholomew, who'd opened the door, stared aghast at the blood on my coat and waited impatiently for me to come inside.

"Mr. Lacey is here, sir," he said. "He's in the drawing room, with her ladyship."

Marcus? What the devil?

My wounds suddenly hurt less as coldness spread through me. I charged into the ground floor drawing room to find Donata pacing in agitation.

"Gabriel, thank heavens." She gave me a startled once-over, but like Bartholomew was too distracted to ask questions. "Mr. Lacey has just come to tell me that Stanton has retreated from Lincolnshire. He raced straight to the Breckenridge house in Hampshire, and there he squats, like a toad, demanding I give him custody of Peter at once, or he'll have me arrested for kidnapping."

CHAPTER 29

*H*agen had the coach ready to take us to Hampshire before I could inquire for it.

Brewster, who'd not reached the end of the street before Bartholomew had passed him on the way to the mews, declared he'd come with us. He sent one of our stable lads down the road to Mr. Denis, letting him know what was happening.

In a very short time, Donata, Marcus, and I, with Brewster riding with the coachman, were rumbling through London on the way to Hampshire. Gabriella and Anne had been sent to Lady Aline's with Denis's men to watch over them.

I was tense and angry, Donata silent in her worry. Marcus left the two of us alone, so it was a quiet journey. None of us slept.

It was fifty-five miles to the Breckenridge estate north of Winchester. Hagen changed the horses several times along the way, Donata paying to hire the best Hagen could find.

We reached Branbury Castle, the centuries-old home of the viscounts Breckenridge, at eight the next morning, a fine spring day. The countryside should have been soothing, with flowers budding on the sides of the road, fields spreading under the open sky, sheep wandering the pastures, spring lambs behind them.

We rode through the village nearest the manor, a cluster of cottages with thatched roofs around a green and a church with a stumpy spire set off on its own.

Branbury Castle, which had ceased to be a castle long ago, was now a tall Palladian house of golden brick with a wide portico at its front entrance. The long windows on every side of the house were designed to give all rooms a view of the surrounding park and garden. I'd admired the place when we'd visited briefly last summer, musing that the architect had made the gardens a part of the inner decor.

At the moment, all doors and windows were closed tightly, shutting out the spring air.

Donata alighted from the coach, ready to storm inside. I was too slow to stop her, but Brewster put his bulk between her and the door.

"Best not, your ladyship," he said. "Let us go in first."

"He will not keep me out of my own house," Donata snapped. "He is trespassing."

"He might be trespassing with a pistol," Brewster said, not moving. "Easy to remove you as a threat if he shoots you through the heart."

Donata glared at him. Brewster's intervention had allowed me to reach her, Marcus just behind of me.

"Very well, I take your point," Donata said sourly. "Perhaps one of you gentlemen should go 'round to the back to make sure the rat doesn't run from his burrow."

She had ceased referring to Stanton as a person. He was a rat, a toad, a snake ...

"I'll go," Marcus said, and strode away.

I stepped in front of Donata and started to lift the door knocker, but Donata stopped me.

"Do not bother. They know we're here, and the servants

ought to open the door for me—ought to have done so when the carriage was approaching. I never bother with keys, and I'll not knock as though I have to request admittance."

Brewster looked up at the many rows of windows. "Might stand here a while then."

"Then we do," Donata said in a hard voice.

It was perhaps two minutes. We heard the sound of bolts drawing back, and then the door creaked open and the castle's stately majordomo peered out.

Atherton had more haughtiness in him than any crown prince, definitely more than Britain's own. His silver hair was cropped close, his suit as fine as anything Grenville would wear.

"Your ladyship," he said, bowing with a coolness that belied the situation. "Mr. St. John has arrived. He is in the dining room."

"Thank you, Atherton. If the chef is here and not visiting his father, perhaps he could scare up some breakfast? It has been a long journey."

"Of course, your ladyship."

Atherton waited until Donata and I had entered the large square hall, dominated by a wide staircase of polished walnut, before he withdrew to the backstairs.

I tried to move ahead of Donata and prevent her from entering the dining room at all, and Brewster pushed past us both. He flung open the door and charged inside, sidestepping so that any frontal attack might be thwarted.

Stanton waited on one side of the long table, but he did not hold a pistol. No weapons were in sight, though I did not trust him not to have one tucked into his coat.

A second man was just rising from a chair, a sheaf of papers on the table before him. The dining table was a long affair of golden wood, its chairs of the delicate Hepplewhite style. The furnishings went well with the lofty ceiling and the wide French windows that let in the light to make the wood glow.

The second man wore a serviceable suit of a blue tailcoat and dark trousers, his cravat simply tied. I had no idea who he was.

"Good morning, Stanton," Donata said in a ringing voice. "Please get out of my son's house."

"Mrs. Lacey," Stanton said, emphasizing the *Mrs*. The lack of *Lady* anything—Lady Breckenridge as her widowed name or Lady Donata, her courtesy title as the daughter of an earl—was his feeble attempt at discrediting her.

"This is a bailiff," Stanton went on, indicating the man in the blue coat. "He is here to deliver these writs that banish you from the house and to arrest you unless you reveal where Peter St. John, the rightful heir, has been hidden by you and your new husband."

"I know who he is," Donata said tartly with a glance at the man. "Breckenridge used Mr. Pimlott all the time."

Pimlott, a small but solidly built gentleman with a square face and supercilious air, did not look worried.

"*Can* you produce his lordship, my lady?" Pimlott asked her. Behind him, Brewster began to quietly unlock the French windows. Pimlott glanced at him, but turned to Donata for her answer. Stanton ignored Brewster completely.

"Of course I can," Donata said haughtily. "But not for Stanton."

"Mr. St. John has made a case for the adoption of young Lord Breckenridge," Pimlott went on. "And a case for you and your husband absconding with his young lordship and endangering him."

Donata began, "As though I'd harm my own son—"

Her words cut off as I charged around the table and caught handfuls of the front of Stanton's coat. I was exhausted, worried, and angry, had been beaten by a young, energetic, and very good pugilist, and stabbed by him to boot, and I was in no mood to listen to Stanton bleat.

"I told you what would happen if you dared threaten my wife again," I said in a voice full of ice.

Stanton's eyes gleamed even as I shook him. "Yes, you would challenge me. But dueling is illegal. A hanging offense if you kill me."

"You will hardly be in the position to be concerned. You tried to kill Robert St. John by damaging his cabriolet, didn't you? Attempted murder will not go down well with the magistrates."

"I have no idea what you are talking about," Stanton said loudly, though the corners of his mouth whitened. "You have no proof of that, Lacey, whereas I have proof that Peter has been abducted."

"I *will* have proof," I snarled, but I knew I had none. Though Brewster had inquired at Robert St. John's stables, no one had seen anyone tamper with Robert's vehicle.

"I advise you to let him go, Captain," Pimlott said calmly.

"You little worm," Donata said to Pimlott. "You throw in your lot with whomever you believe will win. When I am finished with you, you will have to flee to Canada before anyone will employ you again."

One of the French doors opened, and Marcus stepped quietly inside. Stanton caught sight of him in the mirror over the sideboard and stared, eyes bulging. I made them bulge a bit more by jerking him up onto his toes.

"I see how you deceived me," Stanton spluttered. "Good Lord, it's a doppelgänger."

"He is *my* cousin," I said. Who had once tried to kill me, but I did not mention that. Cousins were dangerous things.

"Someone is coming," Marcus said quietly.

A moment later a black coach rolled to a stop, not at the front door, but beside the dining-room windows. A liveried groom leapt down and opened the coach's plain but polished door.

Out stepped Lucius Grenville, and behind him, James Denis.

Stanton looked confused as he hung in my grasp. The bailiff watched without expression as Brewster opened the door so that first Grenville, and then Denis could step inside.

Several brutish-looking men, who'd ridden on the outside of the coach, followed Denis. They arranged themselves before the windows, one moving to the open dining-room door.

"Good morning, Grenville," Donata said, as though she were receiving expected callers. "Mr. Denis. Atherton is rounding up some breakfast for us. Will you partake?"

"Would love to, my lady," Grenville said. "It is a tiring ride, even in the best of conveyances."

Denis said nothing. He studied the tableau before him and made a motion to me with his gloved hand.

I released Stanton, but I didn't do it gently. I simply opened my fingers and let him fall. He stumbled and clutched a chair, coughing.

"I am surprised to see you both," Donata went on. "Quite a long way from London to look us up."

Denis frowned at her continued pretense. "Mr. St. John," he said in his cool voice, "it may interest you to know that you are being sought by the Runners for arrest. Robert St. John has accused you of attempting to kill him."

Stanton put his fingers to his twisted cravat and tried to laugh. "You ought to have arrived five minutes earlier, sir, whoever you are. I have told the bailiff that there is no evidence to bring against me."

Denis regarded him calmly. "There is evidence. The man who cut the linchpin on Mr. St. John's cabriolet at your request has confessed. He is wanted for numerous crimes, and has been given the option of transportation rather than hanging if he will testify against you. Which he will do."

"The testimony of a known thief and horse nobbler?" Stanton spat. "What sort of witness is that?"

"How do you know he nobbles horses?" I asked. "I don't believe Mr. Denis mentioned that."

Stanton shook his head. "It does not matter. You will not get me to trial."

Grenville broke in. "I would not be too certain, Mr. St. John. *I* saw the accident, observed the cut linchpin. Even if you do manage to convince the magistrates not to try you, I can always ruin you." He took a step closer to Stanton and looked him up and down. "A word from me in the right ears, and you will be anathema. No one will receive you. No one will support you adopting the young viscount. No one will want anything to do with you. For any reason."

St. John started to speak, then wavered.

In his own way, Grenville was a powerful man. In a world where influence was everything, a man who had lost his reputation could be certain of nothing. Every door would be closed to him. Likewise, Grenville could ensure that the entire *ton* rallied around Donata.

"Mr. St. John." Denis's cold voice cut through the silence. "You will leave this house now. The coach outside will take you to Southampton. From there you will board a ship for the Continent. Your passage has been booked, the ship's captain expecting you. You will not return. Or, you may wait here for the Runners, who will convey you to London to stand trial."

Stanton stared at him, mouth opening and closing. He took in Grenville, whose face was granite hard and almost as frightening as Denis's.

Donata looked on, as regal as an empress. Brewster, Marcus, and Denis's men were between Stanton and the windows and door, penning him into the room. And I likely appeared equally as formidable, with my bleak expression and mussed and bloody clothes.

"Damn you," Stanton said to me in a fierce whisper. "*Damn* you."

"None of that," Grenville said. "You've threatened a friend of mine, and even worse, her son. For that, you will never be forgiven."

Stanton turned to Pimlott. "*Do* something."

Pimlott shook his head. "Sounds like you've been given a good choice," he said. "Good day, Mr. St. John."

Worm, Donata had called him. She'd had his character well painted.

Pimlott started to gather up the papers, but I slapped my hand on top of them. "Leave them."

Pimlott pretended to consider, then he shrugged and stepped away. He gave Donata a brief bow, then exited through a window, Brewster moving aside for him.

"Damn you!" Stanton roared, then his legs buckled.

"Do cease making such a noise," Grenville admonished him. "Good Lord, I believe the man has fainted."

CHAPTER 30

*T*he Breckenridge chef proved to be in residence and was pleased, so Atherton said, to concoct breakfast for us. We were told to rest ourselves, and a meal would be sent in.

While few of the staff were there, they rose to the occasion. As at the South Audley Street house, Donata had hired most of the servants, and they'd been loyal to her, not the boorish Breckenridge.

The coach, with half of Denis's men and Marcus, had taken Stanton to Southampton where he would board the ship Denis had prepared. Stanton had made his choice.

Denis, to my surprise, decided he would remain and breakfast with us.

An hour later we sat at one end of the large dining table, I washed and combed, in a suit I'd left here last year, Donata in a morning frock I'd helped her into, Grenville and Denis looking none the worse for wear.

Brewster was invited to partake with us, but he declined, declaring he'd feel better eating in the kitchen. "Would use the wrong fork or sommut, guv."

The breakfast was a feast of omelets, bacon, toast, fruit, and a sweet of early berries with clotted cream and sugar. With this came coffee, rich and thick—the beverage of the gods.

"We'll go from here to Dorset," Donata said. "And fetch Peter. That is, after I have heard that Stanton is most definitely out of the country."

She glanced at Denis, who had eaten quietly and now sipped coffee.

"My men will send word," he told her. "He will depart." I thought he would finish there, as cryptic as ever, but Denis continued, "He has run up much debt, and hoped ties to the viscount would reassure his creditors."

"Indeed," Grenville said, sitting back and cradling his porcelain cup in slim fingers. "I found out quite a lot about Stanton from my man of business. It seems he borrowed a great deal of money to improve his properties, and then more to bring suit against the pair of you. He ran through such large sums that legitimate businessmen refused to give him more, and so he turned to more unscrupulous men. I'd say these lads were not as patient with his reluctance to repay them. I believe his decision to flee the country was not too harrowing for him."

"You see?" Donata said with force. "He is a snake."

"Decidedly reptilian," Grenville agreed.

"I thank you, sir, for all you've done for my son," Donata said to Denis. She smiled at him, genuinely grateful.

Denis did things for his own ends, not the kindness of his heart, but he gave her a nod. "My pleasure, my lady. I owe your husband much."

"Yes, you do," Donata, ever blunt, replied. "But it was good of you, all the same. I do not know what sort of case Stanton was preparing in order to take Peter, and a magistrate might have agreed with him. Males do tend to stick together."

"They do, my dear friend," Grenville said. "But sometimes we are on the side of the ladies."

"Who have far more sense than you do." Donata pointed the ends of her fork at him before she returned it to her berries and cream. "Usually, that is," she went on, and looked contrite. "This morning, I find myself in the position of having to apologize to my husband for being too eager to fit his daughter into my mold."

I glanced at her in astonishment. That my wife would admit her chagrin told me she truly thought she had blundered. That she would admit it in front of others told me she believed she had to make amends.

Of course, Donata baring her soul meant I had to come to her defense. "You wanted the best for her," I told her. "A husband who would be good to her, settlements in her favor so she will never be destitute."

"Indeed. Marriage is not always bliss, but it does not have to ruin one completely." Donata sighed. "We must learn everything we can about this Emile person Gabriella believes she is in love with. *You* can do that." She gave Denis a pointed look. "So can you, Grenville. I know you have many acquaintances in France."

"Of course," Grenville said. "Donata told me about Gabriella's choice when I saw her at Lady Featherstone's at-home, Lacey. I pried it out of her when I asked why she was so morose. Never fear, I will discover all I can about this lad."

Denis nodded without saying a word. I was a bit surprised my general of a wife did not demand a report delivered to her by Monday next, but she went back to savoring the last of the sweet cream.

"We will rally 'round," Grenville said. "Make certain Gabriella isn't running off with a blackguard. Major Auberge seems a sensible man, begging your pardon, Lacey, and will hardly let her make an unhappy match."

"He is," I said. "I must concede. And I must concede he made Carlotta happy over the years. Gabriella has seen a good example of what an agreeable marriage can be."

"And you have showed her as well." Donata reached across the table to lay her hand on mine.

"Ah," I said, keeping my voice light. "You admit it?"

"Of course I do. I am no simpleton, and I do understand the difference. Gabriella believes she knows what she wishes, but it is our task to guide her so she does not blunder. Are we agreed, gentlemen? I would not like to push in on your former wife, Gabriel—heaven knows—but perhaps a journey to France is in order, when Gabriella returns there this summer."

I gave her a mock amazed look. "You do not wish to immediately banish her?"

"Good heavens, no. Lady Aline and I have made far too many plans for the Season to withdraw now. That would look very odd. No, we will continue. Gabriella enjoys the outings, and they are good for her. We will simply avoid situations where young men can propose."

"I still think it was bloody cheek of Garfield to propose to her without speaking to me first," I said in irritation.

"You are old-fashioned, Gabriel," Donata said, her calm restored. "Young men and women agree between themselves first these days, and *then* approach the father. It gives them a feeling of independence."

I threaded my fingers through hers. "I suppose I am angry because I see too much of me in him. I eloped with my first wife, and we both paid the price. I will advise Mr. Garfield to emulate the fine manners of Grenville, and he will get along much better in the world."

My attempts to be solemn and sermonizing were undercut by Grenville, who began to laugh.

"You do not agree?" I asked him, a bit annoyed.

"I doubt you'd like Garfield, and more especially, Emile, to follow *my* example," Grenville said.

My annoyance turned to puzzlement, which was reflected in

Donata's expression. "Whyever not?" I asked, while Donata said, "What on earth do you mean, Grenville?"

"I mean I should not be held up as exemplary in the matters of correct proposals." Grenville dabbed his lips with his napkin, but his smile would not be wiped away. "When Marianne and I were in Paris, I married the dear girl."

Donata and I froze. Shock flushed through me, followed by wonderment, followed quickly by mirth. I began to laugh.

My wife drew an expansive breath. "Damnation, Grenville, you ..." And she was off, spouting her exact opinion, from vexation to wonder, in pointed and acerbic words. I listened in great enjoyment.

Denis looked out the window as the soft April breeze rippled through the garden, and took a calm sip of coffee.

AUTHOR'S NOTE

*A*s always, I thank you for reading!

First, I want to state that the Captain Lacey series will indeed continue. I have many more ideas for mysteries for Lacey to solve, places for him to visit, and aspects of the Regency world to explore. I try to write at least one of these books a year, no matter how many other series I have going. I'm also trying to write more mysteries in general.

Every book in the series has a historical detail or two upon which the story hangs. For *Murder in St. Giles*, I learned much about pugilism and prisons in the Regency period. What we think of as England's dark and foggy prisons (e.g., Dartmoor), are Victorian, not Regency. Before the abolition of transportation in the 1850s, a convicted felon of a capital crime in Regency England usually had one of two sentences—hanging or transportation. Existing prisons, such as Coldbath Fields and Milbank, as well as the hulks, served as detention centers where the prisoner waited before he or she was transported. Incarceration as a sentence did not occur until after the Regency period, when prisons were refurbished and monotonous forms of punishment, such as the treadwheel, were introduced.

Dartmoor and the hulks had been used for prisoners of war during the Napoleonic wars, but once those prisoners were released, Dartmoor was left to go derelict, and the hulks were used again, as Seaman Jones tells Lacey, "for our own villains." Conditions, as Lacey discovers, were deplorable.

In the Regency period, most convicts could expect to be sent to New South Wales or to Van Diemen's Land (known as Tasmania by mid-century). There they would do manual labor in work gangs or for colonists until their sentence was up. Most of those released from Van Diemen's Land settled themselves in the colonies that were beginning to burgeon in mainland Australia.

The penalty for returning to Britain from transportation before the sentence was over was death.

I also delved into the fascinating world of pugilism. I learned about Daniel Mendoza, who made himself champion in the late eighteenth century with an unusual boxing style of bending slightly and holding his fists to defend his face. Mendoza was a middleweight but took the heavyweight championship. John Jackson, who went on to open the boxing salon in Bond Street, became famous for beating the great Mendoza by seizing Mendoza by his long hair and raining many blows upon him.

Regency-style pugilism was bare-knuckle boxing at its most raw—the "Queensberry rules" and boxing gloves were years in the future. Men of all classes learned the art of pugilism, but one did not cross class—aristocrats fought others in the *haut ton*, and men of Brewster's class fought only those of their own strata.

A genteel match ended when one boxer's knee or hand touched the ground. An unsanctioned street match might end in the death of one of the fighters. Eye gouging, biting, grappling, and pinning were legal. In many ways, Regency-style pugilism more resembles MMA than the modern boxing it became.

I had the great fortune of taking a class with a bare-knuckle fighter who boxes in the Regency pugilist style. I learned much observing and attempting the many moves, and watching my husband spar valiantly, despite nursing a broken knee. But so might a pugilist have done in Lacey's time.

I hope you enjoyed this adventure—I am amazed we have reached book thirteen!

As always I want to thank readers for encouraging me to continue with Captain Lacey and helping make this series of my heart a bestseller.

If wish to sign up for my email blasts, which I send out when new books are on pre-order or releasing, or to let you know when audio books are available, you can do so at eepurl.com/5n7rz . (Privacy policy: I never collect any more information than an email address, and I never sell or give data to any third party. You may unsubscribe or update your information at any time.)

Thank you again!

Best wishes,

Ashley Gardner

ALSO BY ASHLEY GARDNER

Captain Lacey Regency Mystery Series
(writing as Ashley Gardner)
The Hanover Square Affair
A Regimental Murder
The Glass House
The Sudbury School Murders
The Necklace Affair
A Body in Berkeley Square
A Covent Garden Mystery
A Death in Norfolk
A Disappearance in Drury Lane
Murder in Grosvenor Square
The Thames River Murders
The Alexandria Affair
A Mystery at Carlton House
Murder in St. Giles

The Gentleman's Walking Stick
(short stories: in print in
The Necklace Affair and Other Stories)

Kat Holloway "Below Stairs" Victorian Mysteries
(writing as Jennifer Ashley)
A Soupçon of Poison
Death Below Stairs
Scandal Above Stairs

Leonidas the Gladiator Mysteries
(writing as Ashley Gardner)
Blood Debts
(More to come)

Mystery Anthologies
Murder Most Historical
Past Crimes

ABOUT THE AUTHOR

Award-winning and *USA Today* bestselling Ashley Gardner is a pseudonym for *New York Times* bestselling author Jennifer Ashley. Under both names—and a third, Allyson James—Ashley has written more than 100 published novels and novellas in mystery, romance, and fantasy. Her books have won several *RT BookReviews* Reviewers Choice awards (including Best Historical Mystery for *The Sudbury School Murders*), and Romance Writers of America's RITA (given for the best romance novels and novellas of the year). Ashley's books have been translated into many different languages and have earned starred reviews in *Booklist* and *Publisher's Weekly*. When she isn't writing, she indulges her love for history by researching and building miniature houses and furniture from many periods.

More about the Captain Lacey series can be found at the website: www.gardnermysteries.com. Stay up to date on new releases by joining her email alerts here:

http://eepurl.com/5n7rz

73749859R00188

Made in the USA
San Bernardino, CA
09 April 2018